THE WOODCUTTER

THE WOODCUTTER

by Stephanie Ellis

The Woodcutter

Edited by Carrie Allison-Rolling
Proofread and formatted by S.D. Vassallo
Cover illustration and design by Elizabeth Leggett
www.archwayportico.com

First Edition: August 2023

ISBN (paperback): 9781957537580
ISBN (ebook): 9781957537573
Library of Congress Control Number: 2023935161

BRIGIDS GATE PRESS
Bucyrus, Kansas
www.brigidsgatepress.com

Printed in the United States of America

To my parents, Alan and Elsie Brooks
- for everything

Content warnings are provided at the end of the book

CHAPTER ONE

When Alec opened the door, it was like looking in a mirror. Admittedly, his caller appeared a few years younger, was of a more athletic build but the other similarities were too strong to deny. If not twins, they could be brothers. An uncomfortable idea.

Alec's thoughts were interrupted as the rain, which had eased off after a day of relentless onslaught, renewed its efforts to drown the country. Adding insult to injury, the wind changed direction and delivered the deluge straight at him, his porch providing no protection. He hoped whatever his visitor wanted could be dealt with quickly. The stranger stood in silence, ignoring the discomfort of the elements.

"Yes. Can I help you?" prompted Alec, hoping his meaningful look at the heavy clouds would convey enough of a hint to bloody well get on with it.

"Alec? Alec Eades?"

"Yes."

At this affirmative, the stranger stared at him harder, making him feel as if he'd been put under a microscope. He squirmed.

"Yes?" Alec could hear the irritation in his voice, disliked seeming rude, but the man wasn't helping himself, seemed almost to be on the point of turning away.

Whatever he wanted to say, he was in two minds about it.

The rain came down harder. Alec wanted nothing more than to shut the door on his intruder but despite his annoyance, he was curious. Meeting your doppelganger on your doorstep late at night was something which didn't happen very often.

Alec tried again. "And you are?"

The man looked him directly in the eye as if coming to a decision. "Cameron. Cameron Reeves."

The name rang a vague bell, too vague for any recognition. He continued to wait.

"Look, this is bloody awkward and there's no easy way to say this, so I'll go ahead and say it anyway …"

A gust of wind drove another blast of rain at the two men. His visitor was getting a real soaking but did not seem to care.

"Yes," encouraged Alec, trying to place the man's accent. It seemed so familiar.

Miserable eyes looked at him, despair tinged with something else—pity? "I'm … I'm your brother." It came out in a rush. "Half-brother, if you want to be completely accurate."

They continued to stare at each other, uncomfortable, each not knowing what to say. Alec had seen family reunions on TV, always joyful, even when members had only just learned of each other's existence. He had occasionally pondered his own circumstances, wondered if reconnecting with those his mother had separated him from would result in a similar response. He had his answer—a resounding 'no'. Instead, it felt as if disaster was about to strike.

Alec found he wasn't surprised however, had almost expected this information. After all, his mother warned him this might happen one day. His father would try and reclaim him, she had said, and so she had spent most of his childhood hiding him from imaginary kidnappers: grabbing his hand at the approach of a stranger and running off down alleys and side-streets until the illusory danger passed. It made him a nervous child, always jumping at shadows, scared to take a risk. Unable to settle in one place and continually moving until finally she felt there were enough miles between them and his birthplace, his mother's fears had cost him a happy childhood. He'd refused to let her do the same to the rest of his life. There'd been many arguments about it before she died.

"Mark my words," she'd said. "I won't be in my grave five minutes before the past comes crawling out of the woodwork."

It didn't matter he was a grown man—fifty-two, for Christ's sake—more than capable of looking after himself. Nor would she explain. Alec hadn't seen his father since he was five years old and could remember little of the man, or anything of those early years, come to that. What his mum had predicted seemed to be coming true. He was curious.

"You'd better come inside," he said, reluctant to admit the stranger but allowing wind, rain, curiosity—and yes, good old-fashioned common sense—to override his wariness.

Cameron nodded, his relief evident and stepped past Alec.

Alec took the man's—his *brother's*—coat and hung it up, its drips already pooling on the hardwood floor. *Reeves*, the name continued to itch at the back of his mind. He had heard it before, no, *seen* it. But where?

"Through there. I'll grab you a towel …"

"No, no," said Cameron. "I don't have time." His eyes kept moving to the window against which the rain continued to hammer. He wore the look of a hunted man.

And still Alec waited until it almost became a repeat of their doorstep conversation, albeit a somewhat drier version. For a man in a hurry, Cameron seemed to be very slow in coming to the point. It gave Alec a chance to study his visitor a little more closely, note the dark smudges beneath his eyes as if he hadn't slept for a week. A feeling Alec knew well.

A sudden crack and a rumble made them both jump and Cameron paled at the sound.

Alec moved to the window and closed the curtains.

"Better?" he asked. "Can't stand thunder and lightning myself. Always frightens the life out of me. Mum used to say it was the

Devil losing his temper. She never was very good at reassuring me when I was a kid. Actually, she spent most of my childhood telling me stories which terrified me. I used to have so many nightmares."

Still do, he almost added, stopping himself as he realised he was beginning to ramble, unsure why he'd even started talking about this. He rarely talked about his mum to anybody. Not that he had anyone to talk to even if he'd wanted to. *She'd* made sure of that, no woman stuck around once they'd met *her*. He waved a whisky bottle at his guest. Perhaps the drink would loosen the man's tongue, get him to say what he needed to say—speed him up. Alec wasn't a great drinker but he felt tonight, it might help. "Time for a quick one?"

Cameron nodded, taking the glass from him although not drinking. Instead, he stared at its still surface as if seeking something. Minutes passed before he responded. Minutes which felt like an age. "So you might know something then."

His guest's behaviour was becoming unnerving, was beginning to make Alec worry perhaps he wasn't all there.

"I don't understand," said Alec, sitting down opposite him. "Look, I appreciate you've got something to tell me, I mean you wouldn't have come all this way on a night like this for the fun of it, but it's late and I'm tired. Perhaps tomorrow?"

His words had the desired effect, stirred Cameron. "Tomorrow? No, no. I've got tonight. One night only as they say." He gave a hollow laugh and Alec's heart sank.

Whatever was coming would not be good. *Reeves.* With a start, Alec remembered finding a document with the name on it and an old address of theirs. Asking his mum about it had put her in a temper. She had said it was a name she had once used but explained no further beyond saying she never wanted to hear it again. How old had he been? Eight? Nine? Old enough to know to do as he was told—to do otherwise was to ensure he remained in her bad books for days and he'd wanted to keep her happy, keep the worry lines from her face. He realized now that must've been her married name but it hadn't sunk in at the time. *Keep the past at bay* had been his mum's mantra and so he had; everything had been buried and he had never gone digging. He looked at Cameron with fresh eyes, felt a strange certainty that they were indeed brothers. How had the man found him? Who had told *him* that Alec existed? He had so many questions but so, it appeared, did Cameron. And they were not what he expected.

"What do you know about your—our—dad?" asked Cameron. "What'd your mum tell you?"

"Not to go near him. Not in those words exactly but that was always the gist. She said he was the sort of man who'd sell his own child to the Devil. When she left him, she reverted to her maiden name, changed mine as well. Never told me what her married name, my original name was. My birth certificate never showed his name either. She had it changed somehow. Said she didn't want me 'contaminated'. As you can gather, there wasn't a lot of love lost between them. For myself, I can't remember anything, not much anyway." Little things were coming back to him as he recalled her words but he kept those to himself, he wanted to hear what Cameron had to say first.

Cameron nodded. "Your mum was right," he said. "That's why I'm here."

As Alec digested his words, he noticed the man's pallor, his grey-tinged skin, bloodshot eyes. Illness marked him. The idea struck that the visit might be due to some unpleasant hereditary condition he needed to be made aware of. He bit down on his impatience. If this was the case, he needed to be understanding.

"I, we, live in a village called Little Hatchet. It's pretty much in the middle of nowhere, borders an area called The Devil's Axe."

"Yeah," said Alec. "That's as much as Mum would remind me. As I said, I don't have any memory of then. I was five when we left. She asked me to at least wait until she'd died before I ever went poking around in her family. She was always so upset about it; I did as she asked."

"She's dead then? I'm sorry." A shadow passed over Cameron's face, his words, coming as they did from a stranger, seemed genuine.

"A month ago. She'd lost it towards the end, all those stories she used to tell me as a kid, that's all she went on about. Obsessed she was. And there was this bloody stupid story about a bloodthirsty monster called the Woodcutter. Kept banging on about him being the Devil in disguise. If I'm honest, I was glad when she finally passed. Dementia destroys so much of a person." *Why was he telling Cameron—a stranger—all this?*

"And what if it wasn't dementia?"

The question pulled him up short. "What do you mean? What else could it be? The doctor seemed pretty certain."

The consultations had been short, almost dismissive. They had given his mother a label and he had never questioned it. It had allowed him to dismiss her stories, her obsessions, as simply part of her diagnosis. Cameron shook his head. "What if I told you there might be some truth behind those stories?"

Alec stared at Cameron. *Was the man nuts? Evidence that lunacy ran in their family?* "For God's sake. Don't tell me you've come to simply tell me the same stories. You probably mean well—in some bizarre way—but it's late, I'm tired. I think you should go."

Cameron ignored his request. "You're not sleeping well, are you? Dreams, nightmares?"

"Look …"

Cameron waved his hand to cut him off. "I'm the same. Haven't had a good night's sleep for weeks."

"Can you get to the point?" said Alec, taking Cameron's glass from him and standing, a not-so-subtle hint that perhaps it was time to go. The gesture was ignored.

"I need your help. I—we've—got a younger brother. I want you to come back to the village with me. *We* need your help."

Ten minutes ago, Alec had been alone in the world. To all intents and purposes an orphan, regardless his father was alive somewhere. Now he had two brothers. He sat back down, torn between wanting Cameron gone and finding out more.

"Help with what? Look, we've never met before tonight. I know nothing about you and you expect my help. If you've got trouble, you should go to the police." Another thought struck him. "Is he ill? Are you after a donor for something or other?" Alec shifted uneasily in his chair at the thought he might be put on the spot to offer up a part of himself. How was he going to say no without being made to feel guilty? He could not look Cameron in the eye but his 'brother' merely laughed.

"Don't worry, he's not ill or anything like that. The sort of trouble in our family isn't the sort you can go to the authorities—or the doctors—with. They'd laugh at us, say we're mad. Like your mum."

That stung. Alec had his own opinions on his mother's mental state but it didn't mean anyone else could make those statements.

"I don't know what this is, what trouble you're in, but I can't help you." He wanted rid of the man. An even louder clap of thunder boomed over their heads. They both jumped.

Alec rose to his feet. "Please, I think you should leave."

He wanted the man gone. Cameron had brought something unpleasant with him into his house, a sense of futility, of something reaching out to snare him—and he felt as if he'd been caught.

His newly-discovered brother finished his drink and nodded to himself. "Can't blame a man for trying," he said. "I hoped you'd hear me out. After all, the Woodcutter'll come for *you* one day and you won't stand a chance. It was nice to meet you, anyway."

He held out his hand and Alec shook it, felt the rough skin of his hand, worn and calloused as if used to hard work, wielding an axe. Alec pushed the thought away, the storm, his mother's death, the appearance of Cameron, it was sending his mind down a very dark path. The downcast expression on Cameron's face made Alec feel ashamed. He felt bad for his dismissal of Cameron, wanted to make amends. "Perhaps we could meet tomorrow. Have a proper talk, after we've both rested."

"Perhaps," said Cameron. "But I doubt I'll be allowed." And with that he was gone, a dark shadow disappearing into the wind and the rain.

"Is there any way I can contact you? A phone number?" shouted Alec after the retreating figure but Cameron didn't stop, kept walking into the darkness. A sudden burst of thunder made any further attempts to attract Cameron's attention pointless.

Retreating into the warmth of the front room, Alec sank back into the sofa, reaching for the nearby whisky and this time drinking straight from the bottle. As he stretched out and tried to rid himself of the guilt beginning to gnaw at him for his treatment of Cameron, his eye fell on a box tucked under the coffee table. It contained papers and photos belonging to his mum, one of the final things left to go through but which he hadn't been able to bring himself to look at. He'd a feeling it linked to his past and he hadn't been quite ready to look, although he had kept it in plain sight as a reminder he needed to get on with it—at some point. After Cameron's visit, perhaps now was the time. He'd track Cameron down tomorrow, somehow. Alec took another drink from the bottle and hooked his foot around the box, nudging it out into the open, when it was near enough, he reached out and pulled it closer.

Did he really want to look? There was another clap of thunder but it was more distant, the storm moving away, following Cameron, poor sod. Alec rolled over onto his stomach, placing the bottle on the floor beside the box, and pushed the lid off. An old, black-and-white photograph lay on top showing a cottage in the middle of a wood. It sat in a glade, surrounded by huge trees. An ominous protection. Nothing about the image indicated a rural idyll. He turned it over. 'Grandma's cottage' was scribbled on its back. No date. Grandma. Those old stories of his mother's. He shuddered and put the photo to one side. It was too much like the building in his nightmares, the one filled with blood—and the boy.

Another picture. This time a man with his arm around a young woman he recognised as his mum. Her arm rested across her belly. Had this been taken when she was expecting him? He turned it over. 'Me and Doug, 1965'. No. That was two years before he was born.

Did he have another brother, a sister even? When she left, forty-seven years ago, wouldn't she have brought them too? But Cameron didn't mention an older sibling, only a younger one. He'd had an older brother—or sister. Family.

For as long as he could remember it had just been him and his mum. She'd never allowed anyone else, any man, into her life. Said she'd had enough of marriage to last her a lifetime and would keep the surname she'd been born with rather than the name of the man who'd declared his ownership. *Bloody hell, Mum*, he muttered, *why didn't you explain?*

He continued to pull papers and photos out at random, fragments of family trees, showing the intertwining lineage of Reeves and Eades. A picture of a young boy who looked nothing like himself, yet seemed familiar. Was he family? The name Oliver Talbot was scrawled across the bottom, yellowing newspaper clippings accompanied the image. Alec read them with a growing sense of revulsion. He picked up the photo of the cottage again, the clippings which seemed to revel in their gruesome tale of the horrific murder of a young mother and her new-born child within that dwelling. Scanning the lines, he saw that the boy, Oliver, had been a part of those terrible deeds despite his young age. Alec took another drink vaguely aware the bottle was emptying fast. He needed it though. The boy was the child from his nightmares. How could that be?

The victims, Rosie Groves and her son, were killed by a drug-crazed couple who'd believed themselves to be the Woodcutter and Grandma reincarnated. Woodcutter and Grandma, those horrors of local legend, those stories of his mother. Groves? He'd seen that name somewhere. Alec looked again at the family tree, saw the link to the Groves family. The woman was his aunt, his mother's sister. He was beginning to understand why his mum never wanted to talk about it.

Finally, he reached the bottom of the box and an old envelope addressed to his mum, it carried her married name—Mary Reeves. Disappointingly, it was empty. Alec rolled onto his back, felt his eyes grow heavy as he studied the envelope. Why did she keep it? On the back was the sender's name and address: Doug Reeves, Hatchet Bookshop, Little Hatchet. His father. Had she deliberately left it for him, a blessing on any future reunion or was it merely something she'd forgotten? The owner of a bookshop, that was a surprise. How could something so unexciting harbour the monster of his mother's stories?

His focus was slipping and his eyes gradually closed as the empty bottle fell from his grasp to lie amongst the papers and pictures scattered alongside the sofa. The envelope remained clutched to his chest. As he slept, the storm continued to rage.

When he eventually awoke, bright sunlight streamed in around the curtains. He groaned as he pulled himself up; his head pounded and his body ached. He remembered why he hated drinking. He needed a shower and a lot of coffee.

An hour later and he began to feel human as the caffeine revived him, whilst the autumnal sun filtered through the glass of his kitchen window and warmed him up. It almost put him in a good mood, almost, until his mind went back to the envelope and the events of the previous night.

He cast around for the envelope but it had vanished. Lifting cushions and peering under the sofa revealed nothing except crumbs and old crisp packets. Closing his eyes, he tried to picture it. The scrawled address on the front, the scribble on the back. He was disturbed in his efforts by a knock at the door.

When he opened it, it took a while to register his visitor was a serious-looking policeman, his mind still full of the mysterious envelope, the sudden appearance of his unknown brother.

"Sir?"

The officer's voice startled him from his reverie.

"Oh, sorry, sorry. Not quite with it this morning. Late night." He ran his hand through his hair, realised he was not only waffling but probably looked a state despite his shower. He had done nothing wrong but automatically felt guilty, expected handcuffs to appear at any minute.

The officer smiled sympathetically. "I can empathise," he said. "We're in the same boat. Accident down the road from you has kept me up all night. Going door-to-door, checking to see if anyone heard anything."

Alec peered over his shoulder to try and see but there was nothing apart from the empty road leading out of his crescent. He noticed the curtains twitch next door. The old bag was probably putting two and two together and making five as usual.

"You won't be able to see from here. It's further down. Not a pretty sight."

Alec felt his skin crawl, an unwelcome thought growing. "The driver?"

The policeman shook his head. "Sadly, no."

"You know who it is?"

"Yes, but we have to go through formal identification first and let family know. You understand."

"Yes," said Alec, unable to shake off his unease. "Of course."

He thought back to his late-night visitor, the storm, those factors were still clear in his mind. The rest was fuzzy, a whisky-soaked memory. "I don't remember hearing anything. I mean, I had a visitor and after he went, that bloody thunder sounded as though it was right overhead. Drowned everything out."

"A visitor? What time?"

Alec felt the questions become more interrogative, less friendly. *Standard procedure*, he told himself. "About nine," he said. "It was a bit late. Turned up out of the blue. Told me he was my brother. Half-brother. Cameron Reeves. A bloody shock, I can tell you."

He stopped talking when he noticed the man's eyes take on a more focussed look. The policeman peered down at his notebook and then back at Alec.

"What time did he leave?"

"About ten."

"Did he have anything to drink?"

"One small whisky," said Alec. "I didn't know he was driving and he didn't say."

The policeman nodded, scribbled a note, continued. "What sort of mood was he in?"

Alec pictured Cameron's face, his tired, defeated expression when Alec asked him to leave. "He seemed to be a bit down. I had the feeling he wasn't very well."

"What makes you say that?"

"He seemed tired. No, not tired, exhausted. Great black smudges under his eyes and he was very pale."

"Must've been quite a shock to meet him like that."

"It was," said Alec. "My mum left Dad when I was five. Never had anything to do with him after that and Mum didn't like to talk about him."

The policeman wrote something down. "Does your mother know anything about, um, Cameron?"

Alec shook his head. "Not as far as I'm aware. Didn't keep in touch with anyone from then. As you can guess, it wasn't an amicable split. I can't really tell you anymore and Mum died a month ago."

"I'm sorry." The officer tapped his pen against his notepad seemed to be considering his next words. "Well, as you are technically family, I suppose ..."

He paused, deliberated a moment, then sighed. "I can't see any harm in telling you. I'm sorry, but your brother is dead."

By this time Alec knew. As they stood talking on the doorstep, the unease became a cold certainty.

CHAPTER TWO

A nightmare. No, not a nightmare, a memory. Dead eyes stared up at Reverend Edmund Chadwick as an engine ticked over and the night roared above. The storm hadn't left him since then, continued to rage within, disturbed the balance he'd fought so hard to maintain all those years.

His Bible accused him, his faith a closed book offering no guidance or comfort. How had it come to this? To find himself carving the Woodcutter's mark onto a dead man's face? His hand still shook at the memory, the reality of the mutilation he had performed. Reverend Edmund Chadwick had long known his time was drawing to an end. There was to be no quiet retirement for him, his body seeking its own rest regardless of the desires of his soul. Medical opinion sided with flesh and there was nothing to be done.

Instead, Fred Groves filled his ear with a lifetime of suffering and injustice at the loss of his wife and child and demanded Chadwick's complicity in his revenge, forced him to mark Cameron for the Woodcutter. Brand a man and offer the blood and the monster would come. And Cameron was of the blood, the Reeves family links were historically known.

As he thought of the completion of the offering, which could only be made after the funeral, he buried his head in his hands. Superstition continued to rule the village, binding Chadwick to church, and both to the woods. He could not leave. He would never leave. He had failed to keep the Devil at bay. Growing up in the village, his father had done his duty and Edmund had watched, all the time allowing the seed of scepticism to grow so when it was his turn to take to the pulpit, he turned his back on the past.

No longer did he subscribe to that old tradition of walking the parish perimeter to define its boundaries. As a child, he and his friends followed his father, carrying sticks or boughs, and beating the boundary markers as they went. Prayers and blessings for the land, for its inhabitants, for its harvest, were repeated at each marker. In most parts of England, this ritual was carried out during spring when the world was full of light.

The Beating of the Bounds in Little Hatchet differed in two important respects. In this small village, lurking in a remote corner of the country, not far from the Welsh border, a variation of the rites was also carried out on October 31st, Halloween. Their focus this time was not to keep trespassers out or stop land disputes between property owners, here it was to keep GodBeGone Wood, and those who dwelt beneath its canopy, *in*.

This forest, a huge body of oak and ash, beech and yew, curved round the village as if Nature decided to colour in a thick black border across the landscape to define Little Hatchet's presence. The local priest, always a Chadwick, would lead the inhabitants of the settlement around its edges, touching the boundary with the crucifix carried by an altar boy and sprinkling Holy Water as they walked. In this manner, the village was kept safe from the demon lurking in that darkness and the forest could not move forward.

That was then.

The Reverend Edmund Chadwick had long decided the stories surrounding GodBeGone Wood were mere superstition and so the rites stopped, occasionally to be revived as a village re-enactment, a bit of fun, but that was all.

"Old Lewis lost his lambs this spring, crops are failing, estate's in some developer's hands. The place is dying, Edmund. This place has been poisoned," had said Fred. "The bonds protecting the village from the wood and what lives there are too weak. You've let the evil out."

With the death of Cameron, he had begun to feel his parishioner was right, albeit Chadwick was still convinced much of what was happening had its roots very much in the human world.

"Can't you see it? Feel it?" asked Fred, when they had walked the woods the previous day. "Look around you. The forest has grown, needs only a little push to gobble the village up. Something else too, is coming. Haven't you noticed?"

Something else. Ominous words indicating a presence unseen but making itself felt. The woods had begun to talk, the branches whispering, the crows gathering beneath skies which pressed down on him. Changes so subtle he hadn't noticed, until now and already it was too late.

A knock at the door stirred him from his thoughts. The clock chiming the hour as he headed towards the sound. Three a.m., an ungodly hour for an ungodly man. Framed pictures of different generations watched him pass. There was no condemnation in those dead eyes, only understanding. It didn't make him feel any better. He didn't want to walk their path but he had no choice. He took his coat from the peg and opened the door. Fred was waiting for him.

"Thank you," he said. "I didn't think you'd go through with it."

"It's not as if you'd asked me to kill anyone," said Chadwick, slamming the door. "Merely mutilate a corpse."

"You don't waste the bloodline," said Fred, as they walked along the lane. "Not in our family."

"I take it Doug doesn't know Cameron was marked?"

"Not yet," said Fred. "I'll tell him—soon. He'll understand."

"I hope so," said Chadwick. "I don't want him thinking I was responsible for his son's death." Doug blamed him for a lot of things, including the breakdown of his first marriage. When Mary came to him with her fears about the Woodcutter legend and its hold on her family and the village, he'd been unable to lie to her. Told her she needed to leave and make a break with the past, find a healthier environment for their child. Doug refused to leave and so she'd gone, taking young Alec.

"You were following, like I asked. And what happened was merely chance, an accident."

"I still don't understand why I had to follow and not you. You've got more energy for this sort of thing than I have."

Chadwick had felt a twit, driving behind Cameron, trying not to be seen, like a bit part actor in a bad film. That terrible storm hadn't helped either. His purpose that night was simply to make sure Cameron went where he was supposed to. Do as his mother asked, despite his reluctance. *Nothing sinister in that*, said Fred, overriding Chadwick's objections at the time. He was an old man concerned about his nephew's state of mind. That was all. Who better to turn to for help than the Church? Or at least its nominal representative, Edmund Chadwick.

"I wouldn't have been able to mark him. Only the Chadwicks can do that."

Only the Chadwicks. That unspoken little pagan ritual carried out by every incumbent of his name whenever demanded. Note demanded, never asked. A monstrous desecration of the flesh. Chadwick stared at Fred; a horrible thought crawled its way to the front of his mind. "For God's sake man, you didn't … you didn't do anything to his car, did you?"

Fred laughed, a sudden crack of sound echoing across the entrance to the graveyard. Chadwick looked back at the quietly slumbering village, no lights appeared or windows opened to investigate. He envied them their escape into sleep.

"No," said Fred, his eyes hard. "What sort of monster do you take me for?"

One like himself, thought Chadwick. He couldn't throw stones.

"I'd a feeling, a premonition if you like," said Fred. "I told you something was coming, to be on your guard. This is all part of it."

"A premonition you didn't think to tell Cameron?"

Fred shrugged. "I tried but he got hold of the wrong end of the stick. He thought I was mad, wouldn't listen. I was worried he might go off script."

They'd crossed through the lych gate and Chadwick shivered. Wondering if the ghosts waiting there watched the two men, both liars, both sinners. God had fled the woods long ago, when had he abandoned this church? Had he ever been there?

Edmund had walked amongst the dead for so long, it felt as if he too had become a dead man walking. Already, he felt separate to the world around him, a ghost. To cross that line, would no longer be so hard. It was a mere hair's breadth away. Once he dreaded that step, now he welcomed it.

The two men had not discussed meeting at this hour, nor their destination. It was already known. Behind them lay well-tended graves, manicured death. Ahead lay something else entirely. The woods admitted them, the rear guard of wooden crosses watching. Fred paused briefly at the plot holding his wife and the memory of a child, then set his jaw and continued onward. Everything happening was for her, in her name. A debt to be repaid in full by Oliver Talbot, although these days he went by the name of Oliver Hayward.

They continued to walk in silence. Around them, shadows shifted, the creeping breath of night drifting alongside, monitoring their every movement. Chadwick never went further than the boundary without company knowing it was never fully safe for one of his name. *Some* superstitions remained ingrained despite appearances to the contrary. Should they step out of line, the woods had a place for them. Their gallows, the Preacher's Tree had been created as a very public punishment for his family. A reminder. He had no intention of swinging from it yet. Even so, the paths were familiar. Fred had made him walk them often enough of late.

"Don't worry," said Fred. "He's not fully woken yet. But he stirs, oh yes, he stirs."

Chadwick fought down a sigh at this reference to the Woodcutter. He still could not understand the persistency of this folk belief in the village. He could comprehend Fred's, born of trauma so many years ago but not that of the others of their generation. Nor their willingness to go along with Oliver Hayward's hare-brained idea to raise money for the village. Fred's agreement to it all struck him as particularly odd. It filled him with foreboding. Chadwick was too old—and too ill—to try to get to the bottom of the mystery, easier to go along with whatever they said. What the eventual cost would be, he'd no idea. Already it felt as if the price was too high.

"You really think branding Cameron has summoned him?"

"Still the sceptic, eh Reverend?" chuckled Fred. "You might find that a problem in days to come."

The ghost of metal in hand, the split of flesh channelling blood, turning that well-known face into a mask, a corruption. *I didn't kill him*, he told himself, *he was already dead*. Chadwick considered his actions. Immoral? No. Fred deserved something as his days declined and if it meant he had to play a part in acting out an old man's fantasy to gain some closure for past suffering, then he would do so. But yes, his actions disgusted him, he was unclean. There would be a reckoning.

They were deeper in the forest than he'd ever been before. Despite the years he'd lived in the village, he'd stayed away from the black heart of the wood, the corrupt pulse which guided Fred and his family, which his own were supposed to prevent spreading further. The Chadwicks were gatekeepers, maintaining the boundary between the wood, preventing the horror from spilling out. By not performing the boundary rites, Fred said Chadwick opened the gate. He'd been smiling at the time.

"Here," said Fred, stopping at the edge of a glade.

Chadwick stared at the monstrous tree in front of them, its gnarled and twisted body reared up in the middle of the space, heavy boughs reaching out as if to embrace the woods in their entirety.

This was the Old One of legend from which the offerings were hung. He raised his eyes to its boughs, limbs reaching out to those who walked beneath.

"You'll bring Cameron here," said Fred.

"Yes," said Chadwick. "After."

After the man was buried by his father and tears shed by those who knew and loved him. After memories were shared. After he was no more.

Chadwick looked up at the nearest branch, imagined Cameron hanging there. An offering. The offering which Fred believed would call the giant to walk amongst them and rip out the corruption, rid them of Oliver Hayward. And after he'd gone? For he was in no doubt, his life could be measured in mere days. Would there be balance, the justice Fred craved or was there a further, greater reckoning making its way towards them? Such questions would no longer be for him.

Fred settled himself on a fallen trunk at the perimeter. Chadwick joined him, feeling a surprising smoothness in the bark, the depressions curving into an almost comfortable seat. He wondered at who sat here previously and so often, for it was use which shaped it so.

"His seat," said Fred. "His and his apprentice. They would sit here and wait for the offerings to empty themselves. Wait for their blood, their essence to decant into the soil. Alec will sit here one day. He should've stayed. They chose him you know. Ah, but you do know, don't you? Interfered. None of this would've happened if you'd kept out of it but you're helping now. It'll count in your favour when the time comes."

Chadwick's head began to pound. The surroundings were oppressive, Fred's ramblings sickening, the past returning to haunt him overwhelming. He sought out a break in the canopy, looking for anything to relieve the feeling he was being buried alive. As he did, he took in other shapes hanging from Old One's branches.

He swallowed, shocked at the sight of such an abomination. "Oh my God! Fred?"

Fred laughed. "Don't worry yourself, Reverend. I'm not a murderer."

Yet, thought Chadwick, unable to register fully what he was seeing.

"Wanted to decorate a little, remind Hayward or rather, Talbot, of what he did. These," Fred waved his hand at the two bodies dangling, "belong to those bastards who killed my Rosie."

But that was years ago, he thought. "How … how did you find them?"

"Victim's rights," said Fred. "I went to the parole boards, asked them to make sure they would never be released. They told me both died. So I did a bit of digging, you might say."

He'd gone mad! He'd tracked down and dug up old corpses! How could he have done that on his own? The man must be in his eighties.

"Cameron gave me a hand," said Fred, as if reading his thoughts. "Didn't like doing it, mind. Thought I'd flipped, no doubt you do too. Think that's the main reason he went skedaddling off to find Alec after first refusing to be involved with Mary's crazy idea. Poor Cam, never listened, did he? But he'd a good heart. Helped his poor uncle out."

Chadwick thought of everything he, and Cameron it appeared, had done to humour the old man's delusions. Nothing good was going to come of it. All they'd done was fan the flames. *As ye sow, so shall ye reap.* He shivered as an early morning mist slipped through the trees behind them, moved in to carpet the ground. Fred washed his hand through the miasma as if it were water to be scooped up, allowed it to trickle through his fingers. Never had Chadwick felt more isolated, more separate to the world around them.

"There," whispered Fred. "Look."

Chadwick turned to see what Fred was pointing at. The mist, the darkness of the enclosure, the grey light seeping in and out behind them. It distorted his perception but there was something. A figure. The shape of a man. A giant of a man, wreathed in wood.

He blinked and the image disappeared.
"You saw him," said Fred.
"No," lied Chadwick. "I saw nothing."
Fred did not argue.

CHAPTER THREE

It had been a surprise, that cottage in the woods, nature camouflaged it so well. The land surveys hadn't revealed its presence in the reports supplied during the purchasing process. He'd employed foresters, but Oliver had tired of paperwork and never-ending meetings. He had felt the urge to get out, get his hands dirty. Oliver had discovered the building when, whilst hacking through dense bramble, he'd hit stone. The sudden barrier to his progress sent jarring vibrations up his arm and caused him to stumble backwards, grabbing unwarily at the spiky and resistant foliage in a vain attempt to prevent his fall. It took some time to release himself from the sly stabs of barbed wood and sharp-toothed vine as they took their bloody revenge for their unwelcome disturbance.

It had been a surprise because the cottage often featured in both the dreams and nightmares of his childhood.

It had been a surprise because when he'd described it to his parents, they told him the cottage didn't exist, was merely a seven-year-old's overactive imagination.

He could remember his visits to the therapist. A cold, clinical woman who buried the idea of the cottage—and much else—as effectively as Mother Nature had the dwelling in the forest. She'd taken so much of his past away from him he could barely remember anything of the little boy he must've been. When he asked, his parents refused to discuss those missing years, their 'other' history.

"Don't ask," his dad said. "It's not good for your mother's nerves."

"Don't ask," his mum said. "It's not good for your father's heart."

Sometimes he felt their decision to live in a different country to him was their way of avoiding the subject.

Yet the black, black hole of lost memory remained a constant irritation, became something he was desperate to fill. Recent events conspired to bring him here; a business deal, an impulse buy, his parents' deaths, it was as if *now* was the time for discovery. Fate had got involved and was pointing at him and when you'd got the universe handing you a shovel, what else are you going to do except dig?

As Oliver hacked away at the tangled web crawling over the structure, the barrier the counsellor constructed over his blanked-out childhood began to crumble. He was bringing both back into the light. The trees around him, dark and silent, watched intently. He felt their regard, understood there was something else to be discovered there, but that would be for another time.

"It was real," he said, slashing at branches with renewed vigour, long-buried muscle memories guiding his swing. Someone taught him how to hack and cut, chop and saw. Who?

"Real!" he yelled as he pulled at ivy and brambles with growing fury, ignoring the scratches, the welling blood. His audience of crows, perched in the branches above, did not fly off at his noise. Instead, more came to watch. Oliver paid them no heed.

"It was all real," he whispered as he panted for breath, leaning forward, palm flat against the wall to support him. Sweat trickled down his back and his muscles ached, the machete a dead weight in his hand, deepening his sudden weariness. He dropped the implement at his feet and stared at the soiled edge of the discarded blade, noting its curve, its sharpness.

It too belonged here. Not this steel exactly, but one very much like it. In his slowly reemerging remembrance, the blade didn't just cut but would rip and tear, carve and shape. It had been a part of him once, was becoming part of him again. The memory soothed him, quieted his body's protests and he picked up the machete. He'd the strongest feeling they both belonged inside those hidden walls.

Eventually, he found the door; so low he would be forced to bow to enter—to submit. Oliver didn't remember that. Such things don't affect small children, and he'd been small for his age—back then. He ran his fingers over the ancient grain of wood, traced the patterns carved in oak, grotesques peering out from leaf and branch, their smiles wide, hungry. They'd not faded, the door hadn't rotted, the shroud of vegetation protecting it surprisingly well all these years, a continuation of its centuries-old survival.

He took a deep breath and pushed the door open. It gave way easily beneath his hand, swinging wide without protest. A mouth opening to reveal darkness. Oliver regretted not clearing the external area a little more; there were windows, eyes through which he once peered, they remained camouflaged, would have to stay closed a little longer.

He unhooked the torch from his belt and cast its beam ahead of him. Then he stepped inside, bowing as required. He breathed in deeply, inhaled the dry, dusty air, the scent of mould, the undertones of something else which he couldn't quite recall yet which momentarily dizzied him. He walked around the room, concentrating on his breathing, in and out, deep, long and controlled. It steadied his heart which had begun to beat that bit faster. He took his time scanning the room, the light's beam taking in the long workbench, the range, the rocking chair, the small stool at its side—his stool. The bed, a little behind. He'd slept there sometimes. Further round, almost back to the door, to the wall and those tools of the trade he'd been supposed to learn. They hung there still, though rusted and blunt. Briefly, he wondered why it'd been left as it was, not destroyed. Hadn't they howled for its destruction?

"It's been waiting," he answered himself. "Waiting for me. Waiting for the Woodcutter. Waiting for Grandma. They protected it."

Oliver took another deep breath, this time experiencing an even more overwhelming dizziness as competing memories vied for his attention, like neglected children clamouring to be noticed. He eased himself into the rocking chair.

"You won't mind if I rest here a while—will you, Grandma?"

The silence was his answer, her approval. He began to rock himself back and forth.

The motion, steady and hypnotic, calmed his agitated mind and allowed his weary body to relax into a deep, deep, sleep. The torch on his lap continued to shine its light into the gloom, fixing on an image on the back of the door, but eventually the battery fizzled out and the flashlight too, closed its eyes.

Nothing moved around him. The chair's creaks ceased and the rustling of leaves died away. Nothing scuttled across the ancient floorboards or through the rafters. It was as if a cocoon had been wrapped around the dwelling and its occupant, protecting it whilst it underwent its necessary metamorphosis.

At one point a stray breeze invaded the cottage, a tentative breach through a gap in the door left slightly ajar. Its uninvited assault did little beyond stirring up resting spores, letting them drift and float freely around Oliver. Still he breathed steadily and even when he inhaled his microscopic companions, coughed or sneezed, he continued to sleep, unaware of their corrupting infiltration.

The forest left him alone, its inhabitants continuing their nocturnal routine as they had done since the wood first came into being. They were a little more aware however, that something was about to change, that the return had begun.

And still he slept. If Oliver's business friends could've seen him, they would've been surprised. The man often bragged of needing only four hours sleep a night, but in the cottage, he dozed as the sun went down and did not see it when it rose again. His eyes remained closed as the day pushed towards noon.

It was his phone vibrating which eventually roused him, caused him to stare around groggily in some confusion. Oliver groaned loudly as he tried to move, felt the ache in his muscles from the previous day's exertions, the awkwardness of the chair. A glance at his watch told him how much time had passed. He waited for the old panic to return. The fear of a broken schedule, a missed meeting, of being out of control. It did not come. Despite his aches and pains, his mind felt calm and rested, almost content. It was true what they said about country air being good for you. The cottage was good for him. It felt like home. He *was* home.

Then and there, he decided it would be his bolt-hole. Only he would work on it, would stay here. It would remain private, his secret. He would send the foresters away. He had no further need of them either here or further down the edge of the forest where they'd created the clearing he'd required for geological testing. As to the other workers operating in the vicinity, he would ensure this area was out of bounds. Here he could be invisible. It was a liberating feeling.

Reluctantly, he rose and made his way out of the cottage, every step exacerbating every ache. Only after he'd walked back along the track to the forest entrance and eased himself into his Range Rover, did he remember he'd left both machete and torch behind. It didn't matter, he would go back soon.

His car bumped over the gravelled track along the edge of the fields which took him to the lane. From there it was straight across and up the drive to his house. The old family home which no one in the family ever talked about. When Oliver purchased the property as part of a larger business deal its address threw up no reminders, nor had the photographs or surveyor's reports. The professional internment of his memories, paid for by his parents, had been complete. Ironically, it was their deaths which brought him back. His inheritance had funded his latest project and with no siblings there was no one to remind or advise him. There was an aunt. Estranged from his parents for some long, lost reason. When he had a moment, perhaps he might contact her, dig a little deeper.

It was curious the hold this land was already exerting over him, yet it felt almost a relief, an antidote against the stresses and strains of the non-stop business world he inhabited. His board advised him to ease up, find a distraction, as had his doctor. He grinned as he got out of the car and looked back at the huge dense form of GodBeGone Wood. He would go back, and soon.

The phone was ringing as he stepped through the doorway. He ignored it, let it switch to answerphone.

"Oliver? Oliver? Where the hell have you been?"

Her voice faded away as he drifted up the stairs. He wanted to hold on to his state of calm for as long as possible and Liz, although beautiful, and more importantly, useful, would shatter that. There would be plenty of time for her machinations, after a long hot soak.

An hour later, clean and freshly clothed, Oliver had cooked himself a meal and poured a glass of wine. It was a very Sunday afternoon thing to do but this was not normal for Oliver. He didn't 'do' Sundays, treated them as every other day of the week. Alongside his plate were a couple of old journals and some very ancient pamphlets in clear plastic sleeves. They looked the sort to disintegrate should they so much as be touched. These were buried at the bottom of an old safe-deposit box, emptied on the death of his father. There'd been other things, stocks, bonds, share certificates, jewellery … and these. He hadn't had time to look at them, hadn't realised he'd brought them with him, scooping them up unconsciously with the pile of files on his desk demanding his attention.

As he ate, he gazed at the illustration on the pamphlet. An old woodcut from the seventeenth century, probably worth something, probably should be in a museum. It wasn't as if his dad was ever a collector or anything—beyond money and other people's misery, including Oliver's.

The image was the same. The same face as that carved on the cottage door. The man—a giant—towered over the trees and inhabitants of a nearby village. Huge and muscular, he hefted an axe with one hand and grasped a wriggling boy with the finger and thumb of the other. When Oliver first saw it, he'd assumed it was some retelling of the old *Jack and the Beanstalk* fairy tale. The giant wasn't smiling. He looked angry.

Oliver pushed his plate way, picked up the pamphlet and journal —and his wine—and made his way to the window seat in the lounge. As he looked from the illustration to the wood below and saw the chimney smoke hinting at the village on the other side, it struck him this picture could have been drawn from this vantage point. The blotchy ink and old-fashioned writing was hard to read but with the aid of a magnifying glass, he managed to decipher it. GodBeGone Wood. It *was* this place. It even labelled the village of Little Hatchet. Against the giant was simply one word, 'Woodcutter'. And he had a devil's tail. *If only they knew.*

As the giant held the struggling boy, a priest raised a crucifix towards him. It didn't seem as if he was having any success as other figures could be seen running away from the giant—apart from one woman, weeping and wailing nearby. Probably the boy's mother. He thought of the folk festival, the re-enactment the village was so keen to help him put on. They were already casting themselves in the roles needed for that performance. The lead role however, had yet to be filled. When he'd asked, Fred's nephew Vinnie said it was all in hand. A pity Cam wouldn't get to see it. And nobody seemed to remember who he was—or pretended not to know. The village needed his investment too much to allow unwelcome memories to get in the way of progress.

This was the Woodcutter they'd talked about. An untold story to the rest of the country. Originality and horror would be a perfect mix for their little drama. Even better, some appeared to believe in it still.

Oliver moved the magnifier to the giant's face. Initially he'd looked bearded, hair rampant along cheekbones and jaw. The 'hair' actually turned out to be lines, traceries of vine, carvings. Carving. A distant memory hovered briefly and then vanished before he could grasp it. He sipped at his wine and continued to look down at the wood, tried to superimpose the illustration over the landscape, imagine the screams of the villagers, the protestations of the priest. The despair of the mother. An old fairy tale? Perhaps. Perhaps not. When you dug deep you would often find strange things buried and forgotten … and true.

Oliver poured himself another glass and opened the journal. The phone rang and again Liz's voice echoed in the hall. Again, he ignored it. She would be easy to pacify. He would invite her over for the weekend. In a few weeks. Once he'd got the cottage straight. He laughed and drained his glass. Opened the book and began to read.

When he'd finished, he realised he'd read, or rather heard the story before. Here in this house. He closed his eyes and tried to remember. How old? Six? Seven? Seven. His memory stirred but was still fuzzy.

Seven. Sat on a stool swinging his legs, the smell of cooking, the heat of the oven. The kitchen. Seven years old and sat in the kitchen. A woman was rolling out pastry. A door opened and a man had come in. Looked like a farmer. He'd brought eggs—and death. Dead glassy eyes peered out from bright-coloured feathers. Pheasant for dinner. The woman made him a drink, told him to stay a while. He remembered their smiles at each other.

"I think I will, Rosie," he'd said.

Rosie, that was the cook's name. Whatever happened to her? He pushed the query aside, concentrated on the man. Fred, he remembered. Another jolt. Another push back. Fred had started to tell a story. The very same one as in the journal. The one about Grandma and the Woodcutter and the cottage in the woods.

His parents joined them and listened. Declared it a gruesome old fairy tale but interesting nonetheless. As Fred took his leave—and his payment—he'd turned to them and said "T'ain't no fairy tale. These things happened. You find her cottage and you'll see."

They'd laughed after he'd gone, teasing Rosie about her superstitious husband. "I suggest you be the one to read the bedtime stories in your house when the little one arrives." More laughter.

He remembered Rosie. Her cooking. Her hugs even when her belly was huge. She would let him feel the baby kick. The rest was a blank.

Oliver wanted to know more. The gap in his life was eating away at him in a way it never had before. He put the journal down and went over to the sofa. A wall of boxes was arranged in front of it. His parents' files and books. Perhaps there was something in there. A diary. A journal. The boxes had arrived a day ago. His parents lived abroad and he'd left it to the family lawyer to settle the property in Switzerland, put everything into storage until he'd time to deal with it. Until he discovered their link to this estate and the itch developed. Only then did he ask for any papers to be sent to him.

Those early memories told him they were a close family once. Something happened however and it all changed. Their surname. Therapists. Boarding school. Distance. The rest of his childhood became one of arms-length relationships with the distance expanding into a literal continent as he moved to adulthood.

He ripped open the top box and began to plough through several containers. It was in the eighth box he found a clue. A clothbound book, covered in butterflies and tied with ribbon. The name Maria Talbot looped across the surface. Talbot, not Hayward. The year 1966 printed below. His mother's diary for the year he was born. He dug deeper, found more, a dozen or so. He flicked through them. He wanted the year he sat with Rosie in the kitchen, when her belly was huge. He'd turned seven in 1973 but there was no journal for that year or 1974. He was certain one of these two was the year he wanted.

Frustrated, Oliver tore through the other boxes but could find nothing. He picked up the phone and dialled his lawyer. Swearing as a recorded message played. He quickly relayed his request for someone to search storage for the missing documents and then turned his attention back to 1972. At least he could get a glimpse of what life had been like, get some answers. He stretched out on the sofa and began to read.

CHAPTER FOUR

He'd been told he needn't attend the inquest, his written statement sufficient for the coroner's purposes, but Alec decided to go anyway. He was curious as to the need to hold one in the first place. Hadn't the accident simply been an unfortunate combination of factors: driving conditions, tiredness, drink? He also had to admit to himself he hoped to see his father, or at least some representative of Cameron's family. The pull of blood which lay dormant whilst his mother was alive had come rushing to the fore. A handful of people sat near him in the public area. He recognised none of them. One or two had notebooks marking them out as journalists. The remainder, with weather-beaten faces and worn clothing, struck him as odd. Out of place in a city setting. From the countryside then? Family? He tried to take a closer look. Cameron's—his—father, would surely be among them.

"Can you describe his face?"

The question filtered through Alec's consciousness, turned his attention back to the man on the stand. A young constable, although not the one who knocked on his door that night.

"His head was back against the headrest. His eyes and mouth were … they were wide open. He appeared to have some sort of facial tattoo. A pattern like leaves and vines traced onto his cheeks. When I looked closer, I saw it wasn't ink. It had been drawn in blood. Shallow cuts made in his skin to create the lines, form the patterns."

Alec started. He'd seen no such markings on Cameron, although the policeman had made a point of asking about his brother's face when he made his formal statement. The officer gave no indication anything strange had been found.

The summing up went surprisingly quickly despite this strange feature of Cameron's death. The coroner stated the facts of the night and then gave his verdict. Cameron suffered a massive heart attack, unusual for his age, but even so, the main culprit. Death by natural causes. The facial tattoo, whilst strange and unexplained, had no bearing on his death and was therefore outside the scope of the court. He understood the family didn't want any investigation into that aspect of his death. They just wanted to bury him. The inquest was over. It told Alec nothing, apart from the fact his brother must've been seriously disturbed to have done that to himself, if indeed he had.

As everyone filed out of court, Alec sensed he was being watched. He turned and saw the farmers, as he thought of them, huddled in a group in the car park. All were fixed on him, none of them smiled. It was unnerving. The thought flashed through his mind they blamed him in some way for Cameron's death. Then one peeled away, walked towards him.

An older man, about seventy, his clothes somewhat smarter than the others, his face less ruddy. A man who worked indoors. Alec waited. The man was close enough to make out his features. The same brown eyes as his and Cameron's, the same thick, dark hair, the same jaw. Not much had changed since that early photo. So much the same. For the first time, Alec wondered what his mother thought when she looked at her son, had it coloured her feelings towards him in any way? If it had, she'd certainly never let it show. It was strange looking at him, knowing they'd shared the first five years of his life and yet he had no memory.

"Alec?" That same accent, the faint rural burr.

"Yes."

The man's hands were shoved into his jacket pocket. He shifted awkwardly. It was almost a repeat of his meeting with Cameron. Alec felt a strange ambivalence towards him. He was surprised to discover he'd no strong feelings towards the man. None of the hate his mother tried to instil. None of the overwhelming curiosity he'd had as a child. No emotional bond. Nothing. That in itself surprised him.

"A sad business," said the man.

"Yes." Alec continued to wait. He had no idea what to say.

"Cameron was my son." A matter-of-fact statement delivered whilst looking Alec straight in the eye.

Alec sensed the man wanted something from him, but for the life of him he couldn't think what. Apart from the respectful recognition of another person's loss, what else could he say for someone who held no emotional connection for him? *A father comes for his sons*, whispered his mother.

There was nothing else to say except the usual, the not enough, *I'm sorry*.

Still their relationship went unmentioned. Each knew who the other was. Doug Reeves, father. Alec Eades, son.

"His funeral's next week. I was thinking you might like to come?"

Like? A strange word but appropriate. He felt obliged to attend, his feeling of guilt at sending Cameron away that night resurfacing.

"Right," said Alec, taking a note with the details from him. "I'll be there."

"Good, good," said Doug Reeves, still studying him, much as Cameron had done. "Right, well. I'll see you soon." He gave him a quick nod and then turned and walked away.

With their awkward conversation concluded, Alec slid into his car and watched in his rear-view mirror as Doug rejoined the group. He did not leave until they all clambered into their minibus and drove away.

A week later and he found himself driving to Little Hatchet, trying hard to keep his mother's nightmare stories, her hatred of her ex-husband at bay. He had decided to come with an open mind. Memories and emotion could cloud so much. Little Hatchet, buried in the Axe Valley, and surrounded by GodBeGone Wood, was as much of a backwater as he'd expected. One narrow winding lane in, the same one out, brought you to this dead-end of a village. He doubted it got many visitors. Even the voice on his sat-nav sounded unsure when he punched in the address.

He was at the crossroads which would take him down into the village. From his position, almost on the brow of a hill, his view was blocked and he could see nothing of the settlement. Instead, he was faced with a never-ending throng of trees. GodBeGone Woods. They were waiting for him. Waiting? Where had that thought come from? He shook himself. Focussed instead on the road ahead, a gaping black hole, a bottomless pit. Like his missing past.

"Get a bloody grip, man," he muttered. The stories his mother told him of the woods had left their mark on him, that was all it was.

He'd turned the sat-nav off, annoyed at its continual commands to keep going. He wasn't quite sure he could. A nagging little voice telling him he would regret this became an insistent clamour. No. He owed Cameron something, didn't he? The courtesy of a goodbye, a silent apology. Alec was unable to shake his feeling of guilt at the man's death. If only he'd let him stay, if only they'd talked long into the night, if only he'd offered to put him up. If only. The saddest of regrets. This was why he was here in the end. To stop the words haunting him. Resolve strengthened, he looked both ways and pulled out. The sound of a horn forced him to slam on the brakes as a monstrous Range Rover roared across his vision. The windows were tinted, preventing him from getting a view of the driver.

Christ, that was close. Yet the road was clear when he'd looked. Perhaps it was a sign he should turn back. No. He shook himself.

He would go and pay his respects to his late brother, solve the mystery of his family, then go home and carry on with the rest of his life.

Taking a deep breath, he eased his car across the road and into the lane which would take him down into Little Hatchet. Almost immediately the temperature dropped. The sun, warming him through the window, vanished, blocked out by towering hedgerows. The upper branches reached over from both sides to form a canopy, creating a tunnel, a mouth which wanted to swallow him up. The local council appeared to be somewhat negligent in the upkeep of this particular highway.

He switched on his lights, lifting the gloom, alerting any on-comers to his presence. The lane was a tight squeeze and there was little room for manoeuvre. So far, he'd seen no passing spaces. He dreaded to think what would happen should someone like that moron in the Range Rover appear.

The lane continued to gulp him down and he found himself going slower and slower, the incline and lack of visibility increasing his anxiety. And then the road flattened and the massed guard of hedgerow vanished, the tunnel disgorging him into the village of Little Hatchet. The lane widened out and there was a small lay-by near the first houses. He pulled in and took a moment to ease his hands from the wheel, take some deep breaths to slow his racing heart. He was shocked at how tense that short drive made him feel. Short. The map showed it to be a mile long, yet as he'd driven its length, it seemed never-ending, the minutes masquerading as hours.

A nearby road sign told him he'd travelled down Pit Lane. An apt description. The village curved round in front of him. The shape of its neighbouring woods providing a thick black border to the settlement. A funereal ribbon. Tracing it with his eyes, he followed it round and saw it encircled the village almost completely. It stamped its ownership, its possession on the houses and people within its embrace. Alec shuddered. This view alone would have been enough to make him leave the place. His mother's flight began to make some sense.

The roads within the village itself allowed a clear view of its layout and he could see the inn where he'd booked a room, a little way down to the left. He started up the engine and drove to the pub's car park which sat next to a bookshop. His dad's place. He hadn't expected to be confronted by this feature of his visit so soon. He wasn't ready yet. He turned into the car park and slid to a halt next to the one other vehicle. Despite the uncertainty of what lay ahead, he was relieved the journey was finally over. A few hours remained until the funeral; he could relax a while.

Hoisting his bag from the boot, he crunched across the gravel to the pub's front door. Whilst he waited to be admitted, he took in the village. Nothing moved. Nobody appeared to be around. Yet he couldn't shake the feeling he was being watched—from all sides. It was certainly a village to induce a sense of paranoia. Luckily, he wasn't kept waiting too long and a bear of a man opened the door. He was not what he'd pictured when speaking to Len on the phone. Mine host looked more than capable of dealing with any trouble. Despite the threat of his build, his expression was warm and welcoming and Alec felt immediately at ease.

"Come in, come in," said Len. "Good journey?"

"Yeah," said Alec, "although I almost didn't make it. Some jerk in a Range Rover cut me up on the hill."

Len pulled a face. "Big black job, tinted windows?"

"Yeah."

"That would be Oliver Hayward. One of those city types who buy up all the land and then treats it like his private playground."

"Sounds like you don't have much time for him," said Alec, signing the register.

"On the contrary," said Len. "We've got time for him, all the time in the world in fact."

The man's smile wasn't pleasant and it sent a shiver down Alec's spine. Something told him the locals had plans for Oliver.

"You've got a few hours before the funeral," said Len. "I can rustle you up something to eat if you're hungry. Fiona's almost done getting the food ready for the wake so it'll be no problem …"

"I don't want to put your wife out," interrupted Alec.

Len laughed but it was a hollow sound. "Oh, she's not my wife. Fiona's from the village. Offered to help out."

Shit. Way to go and put your foot in it. "I'm sorry," said Alec. "I made the assumption—from your website, it said …"

Len dismissed him with a wave of the hand. "Don't worry," he said. "I've not updated the bloody thing. The missus bolted a little while ago."

Alec got the impression the man's feelings were pretty raw on the subject. Understandable.

"Come on, I'll show you to your room," said Len. "I'll give you a knock when the food's ready. Bacon butty do you?"

Alec smiled. The man had hit on his weakness. "Perfect."

Left alone in his room, he took stock. This was very much olde worlde country. The pub was advertised as having been a hostelry of sorts from at least the sixteenth century, if not before. Despite the cosy, but modern, furnishings, he could almost feel the history seep out of its walls. The floor was uneven and the ceiling timbered; the leaded window practically at floor height, and the walls curved slightly. He felt a bit unbalanced by the effect. As he unpacked his suit and hung it up, he pondered the possibility of the place being haunted. Most places of this age had a tendency to claim at least one ghost, if not more.

There was a knock at the door. "Grub up," called Len.

"Good timing," said Alec, as his stomach growled.

Hunger sated and changed to black suit and tie, Alec stood uncomfortably in the main bar. As it was hosting the wake, it was shut for business but there was plenty of coming and going—with not a few curious looks thrown in his direction. Looks he returned as he sought out any he recognised. He drew a blank. Those first five years of his life had left him with no recall.

At present, his father was talking over the final details with Len. They were laughing and joking which seemed somewhat out of place, then again people handled grief differently. Perhaps this was their way, bizarre as it was.

When Doug Reeves entered the pub, he'd given Alec a smile and asked him to wait whilst he spoke to Len. That had been a while ago and he was beginning to feel forgotten, although how could you forget a long-lost son stood in the same room?

He watched the hands of the clock move towards midday. The funeral was at one. An hour to go.

He walked over to a bench by the window and sat down. Outside, he could see small clusters of people begin to form. All dressed for a funeral. The whole village appeared to be turning out.

"Sorry to keep you waiting," said Doug, making Alec jump.

He put two pints down on the table. "I'd always hoped we'd meet again, that you would come back to the village. Not under these circumstances, however. Anyway," he said, picking up his pint, "here's to Cameron, God rest his soul, and to the prodigal."

Doug was holding his glass towards Alec so he had to share the toast but he disliked the note of satisfaction in the man's voice.

"To Cameron," said Alec.

They sipped their beer in silence for a moment. Then Doug smiled, a genuine smile this time.

"You know you look a lot like I did at your age," he said. "I always wondered who you'd take after. Doubt your mum could've liked that much."

"She never said," replied Alec, ignoring the dig. "Until I saw a photo of you the night Cameron ... well until that night, I'd never seen what you looked like. Or rather, I couldn't remember."

Doug took a few more sips.

"Did she ... did she ever say why she'd left—anything at all?

"Not really," said Alec. "She said the village was evil, the people evil. Spent a lot of time telling me horrible old fairy stories and legends about the place. She wanted to make sure I never came back. And I promised I wouldn't."

"And yet here you are."

"Here I am. Mainly because of Cameron you understand, but I figured it couldn't do much harm to finally meet you again. Make up my own mind."

"You wanted to see if any of those stories were true," said Doug, calmly. "Understandable."

"Yeah," said Alec, "and I wanted to find out what drove her away."

"Drove? Nothing *drove* her away. She ran." The friendliness disappeared.

"Then what was she running from?"

They were glaring at each other. Apparently, Alec had declared whose side he was on in those few words. He was his mother's son. He could feel the anger ripple off Doug but his father was spared answering as the door slammed open and a young man entered. He looked about mid-twenties. He looked like Cameron, like Doug, like himself.

"Dad, we'd better go," said the man. "Chadwick's waiting for us." He shot Alec a curious look.

"*Reverend* Chadwick," said Doug. "Have some respect."

The sarcasm in his voice betrayed a certain hostility, causing Alec to wonder at the dynamics within the village, at what lay beneath its seemingly quaint surface.

Doug rose to his feet, yet made no attempt to introduce Alec to the man he was convinced was his half-brother. The one Cameron wanted him to rescue, although there was nothing about him indicating any such need.

"We'll talk after the service," said Doug and headed out with his son.

A hand on his shoulder prevented him from following. Len shook his head. "We'll go over in a bit. I said I'd look after you."

"Look after me?"

Len laughed. "You're a stranger in a tiny, close-knit community. Plus, you're the prodigal son. *Everyone* will want to talk to you. It can be a bit overwhelming. I'll keep the vultures away from you."

Alec nodded his thanks but the little voice which tried to get him to turn back, whispered perhaps it was to stop *him* from talking, from answering questions. "I assume you knew Cameron well," said Alec. "I mean living next door, drinking in here."

"Oh, I knew him alright," said Len. "A good man. Kept his dad's business afloat by setting up online trade—did my website as well—even recently got a job with that Oliver Hayward. Not that he needed it. Doug said there was more than enough work with the bookshop to keep him busy. Cameron didn't listen, said he wanted something different. Wouldn't listen to me either. Told him it doesn't do to work for outsiders round here. It only ever brings trouble."

"What about his brother?"

"Vinnie? Oh, young Vincent's alright. Needs to be hauled back into line on occasion ... bit of a reputation for the ladies," he added in response to Alec's raised eyebrows.

"When Cameron visited me, he seemed a bit worried about him," said Alec.

"Oh?" Len's tone was casual, almost too casual, but his eyes were hawk-like. "What did he say?"

"Nothing really." Alec didn't want to say anymore, that mentioning the need to rescue—to save Vinnie—would not be a good idea. He looked out the window. "I think we should go," he said. "Everyone seems to be heading towards the church."

Len nodded. "Come on then. Time to meet the village."

Alec was more-or-less frogmarched to the church. Len greeting everyone they passed, preventing anyone from speaking to Alec, although none made any secret of their curiosity. Up to Doug and Vinnie and another man, introduced as Vinnie's Uncle Fred. Expressing his condolences. Sitting behind them in the ancient church as Reverend Chadwick delivered the service. There was no one else on the family pew except Doug, Vinnie and Fred. Alec wondered where Cameron's mother was. Perhaps the funeral was more than she could face.

He could understand that. Children should not die before their parents.

Cameron's coffin lay ahead of them. Alec's nearness allowing him to see it in detail. There were no flowers, instead an interwoven wreath of branches and ivy sat atop. Nor was the wood of the casket smooth, carved as it was with swooping coils and patterns. With a start, he realised it was like the tattoo described on Cameron's face at the inquest, ivy and vines, leaves and branches, creeping along the panels.

Alec paid little attention to Chadwick's words, he'd no time for religious platitudes and he continued to ponder over the coffin. A riddle he put aside as he took in the stained-glass window behind the altar. It carried no image of a crucifixion, no benevolent disciple administering to his flock. In place of the expected illustration stood one dominating figure, a giant, a giant with an axe— an axe whose blade appeared about to scythe through the people cowering beneath him. This was the Woodcutter. It shocked him to see the giant's face painted with a tattoo of foliage. Like Cameron's. Another puzzle. Behind them all, hovered a host of trees and Alec knew this was the forest of GodBeGone Woods. The picture instilled no hope or comfort, only fear and despair. He made a mental note to look up the history of the church.

Eventually, the service reached its conclusion and they followed the coffin out to its burial ground. The villagers peeled away at that point. Only Doug and Vinnie were following the coffin being pushed along on its gurney. "Alec," called Doug. "Come with us."

Alec didn't move.

"Go on," nudged Len. "You're family. That's what he's telling the village. Means they'll leave you alone."

Telling the village? An odd turn of phrase. It didn't stop them watching him leave Len's side and join Doug. He could feel their eyes boring into his back, a feeling that didn't dissipate until they'd turned the corner of the church, where the graveyard sat between the woods and the building.

Chadwick walked ahead of the coffin, the narrow path leading them down to the back of the graveyard. Alec was surprised to see no physical boundary to its exterior, the low stone wall vanishing, allowing the path to enter unimpeded into the trees.

CHAPTER FIVE

"You can go," said Chadwick, dismissing the men who pushed the gurney.

They turned and left without a word, leaving the five with the coffin. It was an unsettling feeling, being a stranger—although amongst family, standing on a boundary between the hallowed and the hidden. Alec shivered in his light jacket as the wind picked up.

"The family plot is ahead," said Doug. "It's a bit secluded but it means our dead are disturbed no more than necessary."

An odd phrase. What was considered round here to be 'necessary' in dealing with the dead?

"Trespassers will be prosecuted and all that crap," said Vinnie. "Don't want to get caught out here without permission."

Beyond family visiting the graveside or the modern blight of vandals, Alec could think of no other reason to come anywhere near the area. It certainly didn't feel welcoming, almost seemed to be the church's dirty little secret, tucked away out of sight.

"Vinnie," warned Doug. "Keep a civil tongue in your head. Remember where you are."

"As if I could forget," said Vinnie. The two men glared at each other, their hostility not tempered by the sadness of the occasion.

Fred remained quiet, apparently lost in thought.

"Ahem." The vicar's polite cough drew their attention back to him, prevented any further outburst. "I know this is an emotional time but we do have a task to complete. It's time to put Cameron to rest. Gentlemen?"

Alec looked at the ground. Although there was a track, it was uneven and meandering. It would be difficult to push the gurney along it.

"We have to carry him the rest of the way," said Doug, answering Alec's unspoken question.

Doug and Fred took up their positions at the front of the coffin, Doug on the left, Fred on the right. Vinnie moved into place behind his dad, leaving Alec to follow his uncle. He wished they'd warned him this was going to happen but at least he knew what to do. He'd carried his mum's coffin not so long ago.

"Ready?" asked Doug. "On three—one, two, three."

They hoisted the coffin onto their shoulders. Alec almost buckled under the weight. It was more than he'd expected.

"Don't worry," said Vinnie, noticing the tremor. "It's not far. And who knows? A few weeks of Hatchet air and you'll be able to handle a coffin like a pro."

Vinnie was joking—surely?

"Vinnie." Doug's reproof was sharp.

They started to walk. The wind picked up further but did not disturb the trees through which they walked, whilst the discarded foliage of dead leaves and withered plants, refused to be whipped up or moved around. It was an unnatural stillness.

Their route, dry and carpeted with needles felt soft and springy beneath his soles, making progress easy. Most of the time, Alec kept his eyes fixed on the ground. He had horrible visions of tripping over a tree root or stumbling over a hidden rut and dropping his burden. He dreaded the horror, the embarrassment. They continued on their way, the ridge of the casket digging into him, its panels pressed against his cheek so he felt the tracery of the carving on its side. It tickled at him, as if the vines sought to free themselves from the wood and find a home in his flesh. He edged his face away.

The trees weren't too thick at this point, allowed some light to filter through and guide them but there was little in the way of undergrowth in this part. Nothing for tiny creatures to scurry through, to hide and make the noises of the countryside. Silence reigned as even the wind's whisperings receded, broken only by Chadwick's dirge, *"Yea, though I walk through the valley of the shadow of death …"*

Alec considered those words. The shadow of death had certainly kept him company in recent times, become a near constant companion. Hopefully, life would re-assert itself when this was all over, allow him to have a bit of fun. As Chadwick said his 'amen', the small group found themselves in a glade. The trees held themselves back at a distance, grass had been allowed to grow and it felt almost pleasant. Until his eyes touched on the rows of wooden crosses, one of which stood watch over a gaping hole. They wove their way around the existing graves towards it. Straps lay ready and with little effort, the coffin was lowered into the ground.

"Here you go, lads," said Chadwick, handing Vinnie and Alec the shovels leaning against the grave marker.

"No last words?" asked Alec, somewhat surprised as Chadwick, Fred and Doug moved away and were soon deep in conversation on the far side of the clearing.

"Not yet. When this is done, he'll come back. Mutter a few things, you might find them a bit … odd. They're tradition and if there's one thing they're big on round here it's tradition."

"Sounds like *you're* not that keen," said Alec, dropping soil onto the casket.

"I want out," said Vinnie, grunting as he shovelled in a pile of dirt. "So did Cameron. Could even say he managed it."

For the first time, Alec sensed a genuine sadness at their dead brother's passing.

"I've probably come across as a bit of a heartless bastard to you but it's this place," said Vinnie, jerking his head back towards the church and village, "and people like them." This time he nodded at the three. "You have to keep your true feelings hidden otherwise you end up as cannon fodder. Cameron was always looking out for me, covering up if I slipped up. I didn't make it easy for him."

Alec remembered the look on Cameron's face when he'd mentioned the younger brother, the mixture of fear and anxiety—and Alec had ignored it.

"He was worried about you," said Alec. "You were the main reason he visited me." He realised as soon as he said it, he'd probably inflicted a heap of guilt on Vinnie, he felt bad.

His brother's eyebrows shot up. "Really? What did he say?"

"Not much, I'm afraid I wasn't very welcoming—although I did tell him to come back the next day. You've no idea how guilty I've been feeling about all this."

Vinnie shovelled the soil faster. Was he angry at Alec for his treatment of Cameron? Trying to deal with his own anger and guilt? There certainly seemed to be plenty of that simmering beneath the surface.

"Let's get this done," said Vinnie. "Maybe we could talk later, properly. Away from Dad's watchful eye."

"I'll buy you a drink," said Alec. "I think you could probably do with one after everything."

"I'll hold you to it," said Vinnie, standing straight and wiping his brow. "Regardless of the shit Dad's sure to come out with, there's no harm us getting to know each other a bit."

"And if you're serious about leaving," said Alec. "I can at least help, my way of apologising to Cameron." He glanced across the three other men. They'd stopped talking and were watching them. Vinnie tamped down the surface with the back of his shovel and waited for the others to rejoin them at the graveside.

Doug, Vinnie, Fred and Alec lined up alongside the grave. Chadwick faced them on the opposite side and began to speak. It was no prayer Alec ever heard before. "Today we return the lost, make them found. We give to the woods, the timber of man, let him rot in Nature's womb. Let the axe fall wherever it may."

Short, dismissive, thrown away like rubbish. Yet there felt to be a purpose here, something special about this particular family with its own hidden plot in the graveyard.

Reverend Chadwick pondered the mound at his feet for a moment, frowning almost nervously as his gaze lifted and took in the darkness of the body of the wood beyond.

"I'll leave you to make your own farewells," he said, and left the three alone, walking swiftly back to the church.

"The man can't stand being out here," muttered Doug. "He's afraid he's next for the chop."

"Sacked? Why, what's he done?"

The bark of Doug's laugh made Alec jump. "He'll never get the sack. His tenure runs in the family, handed down from generation to generation. Been that way for centuries."

"More's the pity," said Vinnie. "At least he's the last."

"And then what happens?" asked Doug.

Vinnie shrugged. "Nothing, nothing happens. And you and the rest of the village will learn that none of that stuff," he nodded towards the woods, "is real."

Doug looked as though he was about to respond but he appeared to remember Alec and stopped. Mystery piled upon mystery.

"I still don't understand why your—our—family's here."

"Because it's the only place we're allowed to be buried," said Doug. "A compromise made by the church I suppose you could say. Don't want us on their grounds proper but don't want us out of their sight either. It's where we all come, where you'll come if the woods ask for you."

Alec looked around him and the woods looked back. He could feel the threat in the air, invisible but there. Gradually, the feeling faded.

"Remember that feeling," said Doug, as if aware of what Alec had experienced. "It'll keep you safe."

Alec thought about the way the trees enveloped the village, encroached on the boundaries, laid siege to the church. "Why has it never been cut back?" He waved his arm to indicate the jungle.

Doug grimaced. "Oh, it gets cut alright."

He found that hard to believe. "Who does it then?" asked Alec.

"The Woodcutter, who else?" And with that Doug walked away from them. The silent Fred at his side.

"You had to ask, didn't you," said Vinnie. "You'll get him talking about nothing else. Bloody superstitious claptrap."

"Sounds like my mum before she died. Started spouting a load of nonsense about him and Grandma."

"It's local legend," said Vinnie. "I've never believed any of it but the older folk do. They're stuck in a time warp round here. The village is dying and they won't lift a finger to help it. Unlike Oliver Hayward. He's got loads of ideas, was telling Cameron some of them. Even been bunging a few quid here and there from what others have told me. There's more than a few folk on his side. You'll have to meet him."

"Almost did," laughed Alec and told him about his close shave.

"Yeah, well, he's not as bad as some make out. They're scared of change. Come on, we'd better get back."

Their return journey was quicker and Alec experienced an overwhelming relief at being out under a clear sky. The pub was full, it was the same everywhere, wherever free food or drink was on offer. They cleaned themselves up and then joined the throng. As if by magic, Len appeared at his shoulder.

"Doug would like you *both* to join him," he said, directing them to a separate small room.

Doug and Chadwick were sat at a table, four plates of food laid out and waiting. They were expected. Surprising how two men who appeared to be so at odds over something were to be continually found in each other's company.

"I was sorry to hear about your mother," said Chadwick. "She was a lovely woman, showed so much promise."

Alec almost choked, forced himself to swallow.

The impression his mother had given was of one disliked by the locals, by everyone. The minister talking about his mum was the last thing he expected.

"Thank you," said Alec. "Although promise feels an odd word to choose."

Chadwick ignored him and turned to Vinnie. "*Your* mother will need some extra care. She'll be relying on you."

It was a horrible ploy; one anyone could see through. It would do the trick though, tie Vinnie that little bit tighter to home. Mothers and sons. A bond to be manipulated indeed. He saw Vinnie's jaw twitch but the young man remained admirably silent. He wondered at the life people led in this backwater hole. To him as a city dweller, it felt alien to every experience he'd ever had.

His mother never took him on trips into the countryside, blamed her aversion on invisible allergies. His only experience provided by one or two school trips when at primary school. By his teens the excitement of gaining the freedom to wander his urban environment pushed any thought of green fields from his mind. Darkened streets and their hidden dangers were safer, so his mum said, than anything out in the country. He'd laughed at that.

"I'll leave you to it, then," said Chadwick picking up his plate, moving away into the bosom of his congregation. "I'm sure you'll have a lot to catch up on." Then to Alec. "I hope to see you stay a while, perhaps when you do go, you might be persuaded to take young Vincent here with you. Get him out into the world. Get away. There's a sickness here."

"Chadwick," snapped Doug. "I've warned you."

The minister shrugged, smiled at Alec and then turned his attention on his parishioners. Alec watched him circulate, everyone politely listening, all seeming to sigh with relief once he'd gone. There was something amiss here.

"So," said Doug. "Here we are. A father and his sons." There was a bitterness in his emphasis.

Alec could understand a little. The man might have gained one long-lost son, but he had lost another. He must've spent years imagining some sort of reunion between them but not one like this.

"Yeah," said Vinnie. "Cameron certainly managed to bring us together didn't he? Can't believe you and Fred. Neither of you have shed a tear, not one fucking tear. Cam was right. You're all nuts and it's him and me—and even Alec most likely—who'll have to pay. All so you can indulge in that bloody stupid fantasy of yours. Bet you didn't realise Cam saw through you, realised what you were both up to."

More family secrets. It seemed both Alec's mum and his dad hid much from their children. He'd have to get Vinnie to explain when they met up alone. At the moment it was like a jigsaw, a few pieces appearing, none fitting. It left him at a loss.

"The men in this family don't cry," said Doug. "Especially when they are privileged enough to be given in offering."

"But you haven't realised, have you, Dad?" asked Vinnie. "Cam has actually chucked the proverbial spanner in the works, hasn't he? Got people asking questions about us. You think it's all done and dusted but people are curious. A tattoo carved in blood? They smell a mystery, they'll come hunting. You'll have to keep your little *traditions* hidden. How's your invisible Woodcutter going to like that? Your devil in the woods. What will they say when they discover grown men have imaginary friends?"

"I don't understand," said Alec.

"Bet you wondered why Cameron had those images on his face. Why the coffin was carved like that. Backwater bullshit, delusion."

"Vinnie. That's enough."

"Yes, Dad," said Vinnie. "It is enough. Time it all stopped."

"Vinnie, I suggest you go home," said Doug. "You've clearly had too much to drink."

Alec noticed his brother hadn't even finished his first pint.

"And you're spouting nonsense. Go home."

Vinnie slammed his drink down and stormed out, pushing his way through the crowd, ignoring the protests.

"Ignore him, he's upset," said Doug. "He and Cameron were close. And as you know, it was a heart attack, pure and simple. The face thing? I don't know and I don't think we'll ever know. I'm not even sure I want to know. I mean Cameron's not going to come back, it's not going to change anything. And don't worry too much about this Woodcutter tale, it's a family custom. Nothing to worry about."

Alec nodded and took another drink. He wasn't worried but he was curious, particularly by his evident lies, understood now was not the time to ask. He had other pressing questions.

"So, you're back, I'm assuming you have questions for me?"

Alec stared at him. "I … um … didn't think this would be the right time to talk to you about Mum."

"Len'll keep everyone away."

Alec thought for a minute and pulled out the photo showing his parents when she was expecting that earlier baby. Doug, took the photo from him, a genuine smile this time playing across his face, his features softening as he gazed at the picture. "We were so happy then. If only …"

If only. Ominous words.

"The baby?" Alec prompted.

"A boy," said Doug. "Charlie. He was a year old when he went."

"What did he die of?" asked Alec.

"Die? He didn't die. He disappeared, vanished. Mary, your mum, went to pieces. I don't think she was ever right after that. I mean we tried to hold it together, I thought things were improving when we found out she was expecting you."

This was all a revelation. He really thought his brother died and why had there been clippings about that murder but not her own son's disappearance? He found an element of sympathy growing towards his father.

"He'll suck you in, deceive you," said his mum. "He's the Devil, him and your Uncle Fred."

He could see nothing of this in the man in front of him. That element of strangeness crafted by his mother's prejudices was fading and instead he saw an ageing man, someone who'd lost two sons, experienced tragedy.

His mother's delusions born of her own suffering tainted his childhood and cost him his father. Yes, there appeared to be some oddity about the village but he allowed himself to relax. He decided not to tell Doug about the stories his mum told him. It wouldn't help them get to know each other properly. Yet he allowed the little warning voice to caution him. Vinnie clearly had his own stories to tell him and he owed it to him to listen. But he would listen to his father as well.

"I'm sorry I didn't come back sooner," he blurted out, surprising himself as he did so with the realisation he meant it.

"Here." Doug pulled his wallet out, rifled through for a photo which he handed over.

It was a little boy, standing on his own but looking as though he was about to fall over. Blonde hair but those same dark eyes, his father's, his own.

"Charlie'd only just started to walk by himself. He always looked so pleased when he stood on his own. It was hard … I'd better get home. Look, I've enjoyed talking to you despite the day. Come by tomorrow. We can talk some more if you want."

"I'd like that," said Alec, again meaning it.

He watched the man leave, the pub emptied and Len stuck his head through the door.

"Glad to see you getting on so well. It killed him you know when your mum left. He lost two sons in as many years. Not many men could survive that. I'm going to clear up and go upstairs but feel free to help yourself to anything, make yourself at home. No charge."

"Thanks," said Alec. "I think I might be crashing out soon. You can tell you're getting old when you need your afternoon nap!"

"Tell me about it," said Len, laughing.

Alec finished his drink. It felt as if things would not be as bad as he'd thought.

CHAPTER SIX

"I really don't know why you bought this place," said Liz Riverdale, television personality of at least Z-list status, although she behaved as if she was the alpha and not the omega.

She stood at the window, gazing out on the wide panorama offered by the position of his mansion on the hill. In the summer, the rolling landscape of Axe Vale displayed the picture postcard idyll of rural England. With winter round the corner, the grey skies and bare fields formed a bleak landscape, oppressive and depressing. A feeling exacerbated by the hulking, brooding GodBeGone Wood which formed an almost complete boundary marker along the edge of the valley. At this time of the year, its dark mass demanded the eye should see it, the mind register its presence. It was a discrete, and natural, screen for his activities. The villagers on the other side in Little Hatchet were completely unaware of his doings, or rather his eventual intentions.

Of course, he made sure to drink in the local pub, listening to the inevitable gossip with quiet amusement, noticing the sidelong looks which kept him permanently under observation. He didn't mind, in fact he revelled in the attention. Soon, his actions would get that bit louder, that bit more noticeable.

It was time to build his smoke-screen and he needed Liz to do it.

"It's a goldmine, darling. I told you," he murmured, nuzzling her neck, slipping his arms around her waist. "It might not look much, but there's gold in them there hills."

"And you, my love," she said, turning to kiss him, "have the Midas touch I suppose?"

"Never failed yet," he said.

"Always a first time."

He pulled back. Annoyed. Somehow, she always managed to spoil the moment. He needed her though. Her celebrity status, however miniscule, was something to be used and would help see his scheme through. It was time to bring her in on it.

"Come on," he said, taking her hand, trying to appear playful.

She submitted but he could see a calculating look in her eyes. They were both sharks.

"We're only going to my office," he said. "I want to show you what I've got in mind."

She grinned as she misread the situation, grabbed the wine bottle on their way out. Her face fell once inside. Land plans were tacked up around the room. Statistical reports were scattered on the desk. She didn't notice the illustrations hanging in a corner of the office, the door throwing its shadow over them.

"Oh, God, Oliver. Boring! All work and no play ..."

"Plenty of time to play," he said, pulling a report from his desk drawer and passing it to her.

With a sigh, she sat down on the small leather sofa by the window, reluctantly put the wine bottle on the nearby coffee table and began to read. Oliver meanwhile, settled himself behind his desk and watched her, noticing how her interest deepened as she read on, occasionally flipping back to reread something, waited for her to get to the last page.

Eventually she raised her eyes to his.

"These figures are accurate?"

"Checked and rechecked," he said.

"But there are a lot of environmental groups against this sort of thing. You won't be able to hide what you're doing much longer. In fact, I'm surprised you've managed it so far.

They'll be drawn here like a plague of locusts once word gets out."

"And that's where you come in, my love," he said. "I have an idea which I must admit might seem a bit … elaborate, over the top even, but it appeals to me, would be a bit of fun."

"I could think of something a bit more fun," said Liz, rising from her chair, settling herself on his lap.

He laughed but removed her arms from around his neck, pushed her regretfully back to her feet. "Later," he said. "First we are going for a walk. But you might want to change into something more suitable."

"You mean you don't like me in this?" she asked, twirling in front of him, her figure-hugging mini-dress revealing long bare legs.

"Of course I do," he said. "But as my mum used to say, *you'll catch your death of cold.*"

"Better do what your mother says, then, hadn't I?"

He watched her go. Never mix business with pleasure was the old adage, but in this instance, it seemed to be working perfectly.

Ten minutes later she reappeared in jeans, walking boots and waxed Barbour jacket. She still looked good, he noted. As he closed the office door behind them, he cast a glance at the images on the wall and grinned. Monsters about to be brought to life.

"What's the rifle for?" she asked, as he stopped to unlock a cabinet and take out the weapon.

"You never know," he said. The key to Liz was to pique her curiosity. He also picked up a small backpack. Like any good Scout, he was always prepared.

"I thought we were going for a walk," she said as they climbed into his Range Rover.

"We are, but this'll save us a bit of a trek," he said, swinging the car out of the drive and straight across the road into the field opposite.

The vehicle bumped and jolted a little as it bounced over the land. Not as bad as when he'd first driven down, he'd created a wide gravel track to make it easier—but nothing more permanent yet. Concrete would be more noticeable, get the tongues wagging. Once everyone was distracted, he could really put things in place, build the required infrastructure. Liz remained quiet but he knew he'd aroused her curiosity.

Eventually they reached the boundary of GodBeGone Wood, the single-rail gate blocking access. He could drive in but he wanted them to walk in. It would build up the atmosphere as he told the tale. He knew it would appeal to Liz, the drama, the theatrics, the publicity possibilities. It would guarantee a boost to her own career.

"These trees are huge," said Liz gazing up and around. "How old is this wood?"

"It's ancient," he said. "Hundreds and hundreds of years old."

"And you own it?"

"Yes," he said without hesitation. A little bit of bribery, a touch of blackmail, allowed his land boundaries to be expanded to include the land. The Land Registry Office had never been able to discover who the original owners were—which surprised him because as his memory began to play back, he'd been certain the wood came with the house and so belonged to his parents. Instead the LRO discovered the not insignificant patch of land had never appeared on its maps or records, in fact declared it didn't exist. This made it easier for Oliver, there was nobody to come chasing after him and he'd removed an anomaly from the land records. Every acre was noted and accounted for. They should really be thanking him.

"It's a bit creepy," she said, staring down the track ahead of them.

"What makes you say that?" he asked. He shared her feelings but wanted to know her exact responses, it was necessary for the success of his venture.

Liz paused before replying, contemplating her surroundings.

"The birds," she said. "Look."

Above them, the foliage was dense, black, barely letting in any light but if you concentrated long enough there would be a slight movement. The boughs were packed with crows and ravens, beady black eyes staring down at them.

When he'd first gone in and noticed them, he'd visualised the Hitchcock film, *The Birds*, expected them to fly down and attack him, rip him to shreds. They remained still and silent, and that in a way was even more unnerving. When he'd sent in the lumberjacks to fell the trees to make the track, he'd expected some sort of corvidian protest but again, they merely watched. The men themselves were spooked and demanded assurances about their safety so he'd accompanied them, armed with a rifle ready to shoot. His gun had remained unfired and gradually everyone relaxed, not completely, but enough to get the job done.

Once they'd got to the cottage, he'd let them go, worked on his own creating a narrower path to the centre of the woods. Those days passed in a trance-like state and he couldn't quite comprehend how he'd achieved it, preferred not to think about it.

"Why don't they move?" she asked.

He shrugged. "Probably because no one ever comes in here. They're not afraid."

Liz stared at the birds for some time until Oliver nudged her forward. He didn't tell her how he too stared at them only to find, when the spell eventually broke, he'd been stood there for hours.

"The air," she added, as they moved on. "It feels different, thick, sort of musty, decaying." Her nose wrinkled in distaste.

"There's a very dense canopy here," he said. "Nobody's ever done any coppicing. It's all grown up over itself, stopped the air from circulating. This track has helped matters, it's like an airway."

"And if you stepped off the track?"

"You would find it harder to breath," he admitted. "I'd advise you not to."

"Like Little Red Riding Hood," she grinned.

Oliver smiled. She was picking up on the vibes, like he knew she would.

"All we need is the Big Bad Wolf." She looked at him. "Oliver, you're not going to tell me …"

"Let's keep walking," he said. "Don't worry, you're perfectly safe." He adjusted the rifle strap over his shoulder.

"I'm glad you brought that," she said.

They continued to walk along the grassy track, occasionally snapping a twig beneath their feet. It did little to break the silence.

"It's dark, like being in a cave," said Liz. She was still analysing their surroundings as they moved. Her journalistic mind taking it all in, probably wondering where it would all end, what on earth it would have to do with *her*.

"I don't hear any animals. There's usually something moving around, mice, rats, squirrels, foxes, *something*," she continued.

"They're here," he said. "But you're right, you never hear them or see them. Just traces, tracks, droppings."

"They're hiding from us. Although if they knew you as well as I do, they'd realise that's the best action they could take."

Both laughed. Oliver's ruthlessness when it came to business was becoming legendary. Neither was under any illusion about the other.

"How much further?"

"Almost half way," he said. "We'll stop there."

"Something interesting?"

"Very."

A few minutes later the track opened into a clearing. Not huge, just wide enough for the cottage in its midst and what once could have been a small garden.

Liz's mouth dropped open. "Wow. Little Red Riding Hood! I was right, Grandma's cottage. Can we go in?"

"Follow me."

He led the way up the garden path, almost knocked on the heavy oak door before realising no one was home, and then pushed it open. It made no noise. He'd not intended to share it with anyone but Liz needed to see it, this once.

"Oh … my … God."

Oliver hadn't touched anything since he'd first discovered it, apart from ensuring neither walls nor roof were in imminent danger of collapse, which surprisingly they weren't.

"It's a time capsule," she breathed. "So, who lived here?"

"You've already guessed," he said. "Grandma, or at least an old woman—many say a witch—who was known by that name."

Dust still coated the interior, except for the rocking chair and the area in front of it—as if someone had been sitting there. He had, however, cleared the foliage around the outside to allow the windows to admit what little light there was and to let the occupant look deeper into the forest, to the track that would take them on the second part of their journey.

"All the furniture's made of wood, yet nothing's rotted," she said. "Are you sure this isn't a setup?" She eyed him suspiciously.

"No, no," he said, spreading his arms apart to emphasise his innocence. "This is exactly as I found it. *Nobody* has been here but you and me."

"Correction. Not everything's made of wood." Liz turned her attention to the darkest corner of the room, which also held the most interesting objects.

Here were instruments of death and pain. Evil-toothed man-traps, sharp-bladed axes and smaller hatchets, flensing blades and sinister knives. There was not a spot of rust on them.

"That's impossible," she said. "Someone must've cleaned them"

"No. I promise," said Oliver. "And I've got pictures and film to prove it. Recorded everything from the moment I started working in the woods."

"Why?"

"Because what I was discovering was incredible. Impossible in a way. This cottage was last lived in, according to local records over two hundred years ago ..."

He was bending the truth, skipping the horrific facts of more recent times, guiding her back to the folk history of the past.

By the time she discovered his little subterfuge, it would be too late.

"Well, someone's been here more recently," said Liz, looking around her.

"I thought that, dug into everything. Old archives, parish records, villagers. No one, and I repeat no one, came here. They didn't dare. My recordings are a sort of proof if you like. They would also make good source material for any, um, documentary. You can look at them when we get back. As to the condition of everything here, have you noticed how dry, almost empty the air is? I think *that's* why everything is so well preserved."

"Hmm, I'm not sure about the air quality in here. It smells a bit … *odd*. I'd say you really need to ventilate the place. You never know *what* you might be breathing in. Hundreds of years, you say? Could be plague spores or what's that other thing, *ergot*? The stuff that makes you see things?"

Oliver laughed. "I think I can put your mind at rest there," he said. "I've been spending quite some time here and I have seen nothing. No monsters, *nothing*." He didn't mention the Woodcutter or Grandma.

Liz moved to the one door, her line of thought pushing her outside. "I still feel as though I can't breathe," she said. "Come on. Where's the next part of the walk take us?"

"That is something even more bizarre. Just … just keep an open mind."

She nodded thoughtfully. "Okay, but I think I'd like to get this done and over with as quickly as possible. I really don't want to be in here when it gets dark."

He understood her feelings. There was a definite change in the mood of the wood at night. When he stood at its edge, he could feel its coldness, its malevolence, reach out to him.

"Couldn't you have made *this* track any wider?" asked Liz as they started down the arched corridor.

"I tried," he said, "but the wood wouldn't let me."

"The way you've been talking, you make it sound as though the wood is alive, I mean I know it's *alive*, but I mean like a thinking being, something with its own mind."

"You're getting the idea," he said, and pulled a torch from his pocket.

"We'll need that?!"

"You could try without it," he said, flicking it off and stepping into the darkness.

"No, no," said Liz, grabbing the torch from his hand and switching it on.

There was just room for them to walk through the corridor of undergrowth side-by-side although they had to continually brush dangling tendrils of ivy from their faces. Oliver was thankful she couldn't see yet, or hadn't noticed, what was buried in the wall of foliage on either side.

"I'm glad I'm not claustrophobic," said Liz. "I can hardly breathe as it is. I take back everything I said about your place being boring. Although I think I'd take boring over this any day …"

The tunnel came to an end and opened not into a glade but a cavern, a cathedral. Unlike the rest of the wood, this area seemed created to a specific design. The tree trunks lining the perimeter formed a dense palisade, like an old fort, built to keep something out—or something in. A wide path ran around the inside of this barrier and across from this an arrangement of five large vats spaced at regular intervals around the trunk of a monstrous tree which stood at the centre. Its girth was enormous, spoke of an age beyond anything Oliver could comprehend.

He watched Liz take that beast in, follow the line of its body up and up and up into darkness until she was dizzy from looking and, in that darkness, he knew what she saw. The shapes hanging, shrouded and amorphous, each directly above a vat below. There was also a smell, familiar and meaty, metallic. This place wasn't life, it was death.

"Shit, Oliver. What is this place?"

He shone the torch up to highlight one of the objects. The shroud had nearly disintegrated, barely held on to its contents, pieces of bone, a skull with a screaming mouth.

He heard a crunch and a low cry, swung his torch round.

Liz was backing away and fallen against one of the vats. She looked terrified, ready to run.

"Come on," he said, quickly helping her up, slipping his arm around her. "I think that's enough. I'll tell you the story about all this when we get back. I don't think here would be the right place."

"No," agreed Liz. "I feel as if we're being watched, listened to."

They walked quickly back along the tracks, not noticing how their pace wasn't much short of a jog, they were almost running. When they finally exited the wood, both exhaled loudly, both had been holding their breath. Their emotions however were completely different. Whereas Liz had been filled with panic, he'd felt nothing but excitement at the thought of this particular project coming to life.

"I want to get back, have a hot hot shower and one long stiff drink," said Liz. "I don't want to talk about anything or discuss this in any way whatsoever until after that." Then as an afterthought, "Have you called the police?"

Oliver remained silent.

"You haven't! Have you? For fuck's sake, Oliver. Those are *bodies* hanging there."

"Old bodies," he countered. "They've been there a while ..."

"How do you *know*?"

"It's obvious isn't it." He glanced at her, noticed the incredulity in her eyes. "Look, if it makes you feel any better, I've only left them hanging there until some forensic friends of mine get back to this country and can look at them. I wanted to get a rough idea of what I'm dealing with before I formally notify the police, cut the bodies down."

"You are not supposed to keep the discovery of a body, even an old body, from the police," said Liz.

"It's a matter of what? A few months. And I want the village to have its bit of fun before then. If we get the police in, it'll mess up everything. It'll mess up my plans for *you*."

"Me?"

"You haven't been very successful lately, have you?"

"I have my show …"

"You have five minutes on the daily local news. An occasional slot on an obscure regional channel. I *know* you want more than that and I can give it you."

"Really?"

He heard the doubt in her voice but saw the hope in her eyes. "Look, I'm sorry I shook you up. I suppose I could've warned you, prepared you a little but I didn't think you'd believe me. I needed you to see. It all feeds into everything else. Let's get back and I'll explain everything." Or almost everything.

He turned the ignition key and the engine roared to life. It was a comforting sound, the noise of a civilised world. He turned the vehicle round and headed back to the mansion.

Behind them, thousands of small beady eyes watched them go.

CHAPTER SEVEN

A wooden cross in this remote corner of St. Simon's graveyard is a statement, a sign. It is the highest honour which can be bestowed on any who have been lain to rest in its grounds—almost the highest honour. There is one other.

Reverend Chadwick waited. Dusk would soon fall and it would be time to get to work. He could start whilst there was plenty of light, friends and neighbours around. None of them would be shocked to see him digging up the body, might even come and lend a hand for this part of the proceedings.

He didn't call on them, Fred would be all the company he needed. On cue, Cameron's uncle shuffled down the path towards him, sat down on the memorial bench carrying his wife's name.

"Almost time," said Fred.

"Yes. And the last time—for me, at any rate."

"Are you frightened?"

"What of? This?" he waved his hand at Cameron's grave. "Dying? You can say it you know."

Fred didn't need to answer. Both were facing their own ends, already seen how their last lines would be written. Illness and old age? No, that was not to be for them. Like Cameron, they were to be given to the woods. As they had always known. Their fear remained, for the how, not the fact of it, whilst their shared path gave them some strength.

"It's been a long time since the last one," said Fred, looking across to the tiny grave beside Rosie's.

Chadwick followed his eyes. Little Charlie. The family knew he had been chosen by the woods, was meant to grow amongst the trees, care for them … and Grandma. But he had been taken. He'd disappeared as Doug had told Alec but had been found. A death kept from his newly-returned son to hide his own guilt in the lynching of an innocent man. The minister remembered the anger of the woods, the trees talking nonstop, their whispers sliding into houses and church until Charlie was finally discovered, up at Oliver's estate. The boy, Oliver, staring at them as they pulled Charlie's remains from his playhouse at the bottom of the garden. That had been one of the most unnerving things about that day. Not the body, but the boy. The blank look in his eyes.

"Strange his parents knew nothing," said Chadwick. He'd been there, with the search party, seen the boy, old bloodied clothes of his discarded beside the body. A bucket and spade nearby. The most innocent of childhood toys except he'd started to dig a hole in the ground. A child of five killing a toddler? No, their minds refused to accept that. Another puzzle this, the refusal to accept the obvious whilst believing in intangible, unproven forces in the woods. On that day, they'd taken the easier path and they were reaping the harvest.

"Knew nothing? Of course they did," said Fred. "My Rosie told me. When the village turned on that young lad—what was his name—Simon, Simple Simon, they were quite relieved. It meant they could bury their guilt. Carry on as if nothing happened, their son's act a minor aberration. You protect your own."

Chadwick shifted his gaze to the wood and the path he had to take. He'd been walking it all his life without realising it. There wasn't far to go. His journey was almost over. The village had brought Simon to his father, the incumbent at the time, thrown the confused and injured man at his feet as the wood groaned around them. There'd been no burial and day of rest. He'd stood with the crowd and watched as his father picked up the end of the rope which formed a noose around his neck and dragged his body into the trees. His father had almost vanished when he stopped and called the young Edmund to follow in his footsteps. The young man had gone on that occasion, but ever after they diverged.

"Poor Simon," said Fred. "They named him for the saint, thought it would give him some protection."

"Ignorance and anger are a powerful poison," sighed Chadwick.

"Now you understand," said Fred, as the light dipped lower, their world turning grey.

"Yes," said Chadwick. "And I wish I didn't."

Fred was quiet for a moment, then resumed. "You know I was one of those who went after Simon?"

Oh yes, he remembered. Fred, a younger man, face filled with fury at the murder of his nephew, howling with the others at Simon, clutching one of Charlie's toys in bewilderment. Simon's mother screaming Charlie had given it to him when they last played together. *"Mary! For God's sake, Mary! Don't you remember? Mary!"*

Mary hadn't answered, too shell-shocked with grief to respond, an answer in itself for the mob who turned on Simon. Fred had been one of them, alongside Doug and so many others who vented their fury on the young man's defenceless flesh. And Edmund's father had done nothing. Watched and waited until he was summoned.

"In the end," said Fred. "You could say it was our fault; the village, me, Doug, for what happened to my Rosie, the baby, led to Mary leaving, taking Alec. I've often thought on that. If they'd taken Oliver away from the village back then, he wouldn't have taken my wife to them. Alec would've stayed and become who he was meant to be."

Chadwick stood, lifting his shovel as he did so. He would go through with their demands. He'd given up fighting their superstitions and warped traditions. It didn't matter so much death and misery had simply been caused by human hands. Easier to wash your guilt away by blaming the unseen Devil, rather than the one looking back at you in the mirror.

Closed minds and closed communities had to have their outlet.

He started to dig. Fred watching. The casket was buried in a shallow grave and soon exposed to view. A small mercy for which he was grateful. Then Fred came over and opened the casket, muttered a few words Chadwick could not make out. As they lifted the body, Chadwick felt someone watching. From the corner of his eye, he could see Doug and Vinnie.

They said nothing, remained in the shadows. Were there to say their farewells and bear witness.

Rigor had passed and it was easy to manipulate Cameron into the wheelbarrow. Not the most dignified of transports but they were both too old to carry his weight and the path too uneven for a gurney. Nor could they ask for help from this point. Their roles defined long ago.

"Ready?" asked Fred, as Chadwick stretched and then took hold of the barrow.

"Yes," he muttered. "Let's get this done. Bring it to an end."

He followed Fred down the path and into the trees, the leading man lighting the way with a torch. Although out of sight, he could still feel the eyes of Doug and Vinnie boring into them. Their mouths silently voicing the same mantra as Fred as they went, the words of the Summoning.

Deep beneath his feet, he sensed a stirring, would once have put that down to Oliver's fracking experiment, revealed to him in confidence so he'd been unable to share the information with anyone. It was as if his reasoned barriers against the stories of the woods were crumbling. This was the ground of the Woodcutter, His Church, hidden from the sight of Chadwick's silent God. A darkness despoiling their heaven on earth.

It was hard to fight it. Easier when shielded by the thick stone of his own church, the comfort of its solid protection. Out here, amongst shadows, beneath ancient wooden bodies centuries old, arms embracing each other to hide what walked in their midst, it was so much more difficult. And there was one shadow, taking form, becoming clear, clearer. Oh God, a giant towering over them, the outline of a jagged wreath at his neck, the axe in his hand. The blade always about to fall. The demon had risen and was walking again. He'd been able to pretend for so long the monster was fantasy, mere legend. The Woodcutter had shown himself and Chadwick could no longer deny him. He racked his brain for the devil's true name, drew a blank. The Woodcutter and Grandma, a child's story, not the horror they truly were. If he could remember their names, perhaps there might be a way to fight back. Stop what he helped put in motion.

"No," he muttered, "no, no." A whisper ignored by Fred who continued to chant, ignored by the Woodcutter who led them on, on to his altar, to Old One.

Chadwick could see the dangling noose, the rope already prepared for their offering so he merely had to hoist the corpse up to swing above the earth, dance for the Woodcutter.

Chadwick kept his eyes on Cameron, fought to suppress his shaking hands as he wrapped the noose around the young man's neck, moved to the side of the ancient tree and started to pull. Chadwick took the man's full weight on himself. This was the burden of his family's role, to know, in flesh, the price they must pay.

As he strained on the rope, Fred continued to recite the unhallowed words whilst the giant watched. His form becoming slightly more solid with every minute. It would not be long before he walked fully amongst them.

Chadwick had his own prayer as he swung Cameron up to hang from Old One's arms.

"Forgive me," he whispered, over and over. "Forgive me."

CHAPTER EIGHT

It had been two days since the funeral, time spent next door in Doug's bookshop, talking about the village—its legends and history, the business—but very little about his mother or either of his half-brothers. Alec wasn't too concerned. He was surprised with how much he enjoyed being away from the city, felt the stresses and strains of city life vanish. There was a feeling of belonging here he'd never experienced before.

Work had shown compassion and understanding about his brother's death and the discovery of new family. There was no issue about taking holiday time owed to him and so he stayed. The extra time would allow him to discover the answers he needed. Mysteries remained, including Cameron and Vinnie's mum, Carol. He'd yet to meet the woman kept hidden away. He'd also had no time to talk to Vinnie on his own. Whenever they got together, someone else would miraculously appear to prevent a real conversation.

"Dead tonight," said Alec, scanning the bar. Having seen the prices, he understood the reason for the lack of business. In fact, the only time he'd seen it busy was the wake when everything was free courtesy of Doug. No wonder.

"Should've got a few cans from the supermarket, stayed in," said Vinnie. "You ever thought of charging *reasonable* prices, Len?"

"They are," said the landlord. "But the supermarkets can undercut me every which way. You know I can't compete with them. If more people came in, perhaps I'd be able to lower them."

"But they won't," said Alec, "because they can get it cheaper elsewhere. Vicious circle."

Len wiped away non-existent marks on the bar's surface. His face not the usual jovial mine host. "And it's killing my business. You know lads, I can't go on like this anymore. Think it's time to face facts and sell up before I'm completely bankrupted."

Vinnie choked on his drink. "You can't," he said. "I mean, this place is the hub of the village …"

"Is it?" asked Len, sourly. "Look around you. Not exactly buzzing."

Apart from the three of them, the only other occupant was Fred, long retired and practically living in the pub. Vinnie told Alec he couldn't remember a time he *wasn't* in there, propped up in the corner by the open fire. A widower of many, many years, he never talked about his wife—Vinnie's aunt, Alec's mum's sister— and nobody else mentioned her.

"Village is dying," said Fred, turning towards them. "Can't you feel it? Half the houses empty, only filled at weekends or holidays. Post Office about to go. And Chadwick is the last of his line, so there'll be no minister in the church, no church. And *he's* back."

"He? Who?" asked Alec.

"That bastard, Oliver Talbot …"

"Talbot? You mean Hayward. And what do you mean back? I've never seen him before."

"You're too young to remember," he said to Vinnie. "Forty-seven years ago. Surprised he came back, after …" Fred stopped. There was obviously more to say but he was too overwhelmed to continue.

"You're sure?" Len asked Fred.

"Positive," said Fred. "I've seen him, he might've been a child then but I'd recognise him anywhere."

"I thought he looked familiar," said Len. "I couldn't place him."

Alec noticed Fred's hand was shaking as he lifted his glass to his mouth, gulped down its remaining contents in an almost desperate manner.

"What? I've spent a bit of time with him lately," said Vinnie. "He never said anything about living here before."

"He wouldn't," said Fred. "He was only a youngster, probably can't even remember, can't remember what he did …" There was a surprisingly bitter edge to Fred's voice. "But I can. I can *never* forget."

Alec sipped his drink, not sure if he should say anything about his mother's papers. He decided to remain quiet.

"What happened?" asked Vinnie.

Fred stayed silent, his face as he stared at his pint, a mask of anguish.

"Unc?" prompted Vinnie.

The man ignored him, pushing himself to his feet and stumbling past the others at the table. His pint spilled over, the glass crashing to the floor.

"Fred!" called Len behind him but his voice was drowned out by the door slamming behind him.

The three looked at each other.

"Should someone go after him?" asked Alec.

Len shook his head. "Leave him be. Reckon he needs some time on his own. I'll go check on him in the morning. Seeing Oliver again like that must've been a hell of a shock."

"He's seen him before?"

"Yeah," said Len. "Knew him well as a kid. His wife used to cook for the Talbot family. That boy was the one who took his wife into the woods to those murdering bastards. Helped deliver Fred's baby. Helped kill them."

Vinnie's mouth dropped open. "Fucking hell. The poor bastard. Oliver's got a nerve coming back here. He bloody had me fooled. I mean, that was my aunt, my cousin. Shit. When I get my hands on him."

"You'll do nothing," said Len. "I believe Fred and Chadwick have been making certain arrangements."

"You mean summoning some make-believe monster," said Vinnie. "Yeah, I like that. Like that'll *really* tell him."

The landlord looked at Vinnie but ignored his comments. "You and Cameron have spent a lot of time with him. Did he ever say anything about having been here before? I mean he's been in here a few times, but never given any indication."

"No, I mean he's said something, I'm … oh, I don't know." Vinnie stopped. He seemed to be struggling with something. "Me and Cameron were looking at ways of building up business—not just the bookshop, but something for the rest of the village. I mean you only have to look around you to see it's dying. No work for younger people, nothing to breathe life into the place. You can't even commute easily—no buses, trains, roads are crap. People move away and no one replaces them. We've managed to keep the bookshop afloat by building up the web side of the business, the only thing keeping us going at the moment, but we knew we needed more. The village needed more. We thought if we could come up with something to draw people to the village, some sort of event. It might bring a bit of life to the place, put us on the map. And Oliver … crap. I can't believe it."

"Don't think you'll be wanting to get into bed with him," said Len. "I know I don't want him in my pub."

"Yeah," said Vinnie. "Trouble is we'd come up with something, or rather he had. Something which would make the news, get people returning year after year. Oliver said he might pop in this evening. But … you know I don't think he remembers anything; I mean his idea, I mean he'd have to be a monster …"

"Tell us," said Alec.

"He wants to run an event based on the Woodcutter legend."

Alec stared at him. The man must be seriously wrong in the head to even think of this, unless he really didn't remember anything.

"He wants to recreate the Summoning of the Woodcutter and the choosing of the apprentice."

"No way," said Alec.

"You can tell him where to stick his event," said Len, his face grim.

"Yeah," said Vinnie, then he smiled.

Alec looked at him in surprise.

"No. I've an idea, it'll mean a little payback for Fred. I'll explain later but when he comes in, carry on as if we don't know anything."

"Not sure I can do that," said Len.

"Please," said Vinnie. "I promise I'll fill you in but there's no time. I mean he'll be here soon."

He was still smiling, a smile that to Alec meant nothing good.

"I'll try," he said. "Although I don't think it'll be easy."

How could you talk to someone who was a murderer—or been involved in a murder—as if nothing had happened. Was being a child any excuse? Even at seven you would know right from wrong and you would certainly know it was wrong to kill anyone. He recalled Fred's expression, the man's pain. This was going to be a difficult call.

He had no more time to think as the pub door burst open, its accompanying gust of wind making the flames dance in the fire behind them. The three looked at each other, fixed smiles on their faces and turned to the new arrival.

"Oliver!" said Len, rising up to do his duty. "Good to see you. The usual?"

Oliver nodded and joined the group without asking.

"We've been thinking," said Vinnie, to Alec and Len, as if he hadn't told them anything already. "Of using our local history to create something. You get the Wicker Man events these days, Beltane festivals, all sorts of New Age stuff and people love it. They make shed loads of money. We do something like that and we could invest it in the village, in the small businesses, pump a bit of lifeblood into Hatchet."

Oliver merely listened as Vinnie talked, knocked back his whiskey before he joined in. It would not be his last and Len brought the bottle over to make his life easier. Or was it to make their lives easier. Every time it looked as though Vinnie was about to choke on his words, Len would pour the man another drink, Alec's own glass, too, was regularly topped up. Did his face show his disgust?

From what Doug and Alec said, Oliver Hayward was very much a self-made man. There was local talk of an inheritance but that came later in life, *after* he'd made his first fortune. An entrepreneur, he'd a supreme belief in himself and his abilities. He'd not been in the area six months before he'd bought up a number of farms for 'development', stirred things up. Alec watched Oliver as he spoke, struggled to push the crime to the back of his mind. The atmosphere was tense. He wondered if Oliver sensed something off.

"We need a new angle," said Oliver. "That sort of thing has become old hat. The market is saturated with things like that. We need to be different. We've been thinking about a rural festival. I've got some friends who've been involved with the biggest and the best, seen their figures. You get it right, you'll be raking it in. But you do need to be original and that's getting harder these days."

Vinnie leaned forward, taking over the conversation. "We've been thinking of a Halloween event," he said, arms folded on the table as if physically trying to restrain himself.

"It's only a month from today," said Oliver. "We haven't got a lot of lead-in time. We were thinking of something small this year, gauge reaction."

Alec's mind turned to the Woodcutter. His mother's stories had given him nightmares but a few local history pamphlets in the bookshop intrigued him, even as they continued to make him uncomfortable. Knowing Oliver's involvement in a real 'Woodcutter-inspired' murder added to the unease. But in the end, they were ultimately stories, fairy tales—weren't they?

"Makes a sort of sense, I suppose," said Len. "What have you got in mind?" They knew exactly what he had in mind but needed to keep up the pretence.

"Well … the Woodcutter. Grandma." Was there a hesitation, a remembrance in his tone?

"I've read the stories and my mum used to tell me them as a kid as well. They're horrific," said Alec. "How can you turn this into a 'fun' event?"

"We recreate the Woodcutter's Apprentice. Have that bit as a sponsored event. Then there's Grandma. Thought of a parade of sorts. We could have woodcutting competitions, the usual craft stalls, storytelling, beer tents and bonfires."

Fair play to him, thought Alec. He'd made it sound family friendly, a quaint country event. If Alec hadn't been aware of Oliver's past, his murderous link to the Woodcutter, he would've been all for it.

"They're very old stories," said Vinnie, "and we'll have to tweak things a bit to make them more interesting but I believe it's material we can work with."

The look he gave him told Alec he was already playing out whatever plan he had for Oliver in his head. It was making him smile with satisfaction. A smile, Oliver seemed to misread.

"So, tell them the story," said Oliver, pouring himself another drink, this time not waiting for Len.

"It all begins with The Summoning," said Vinnie. "These are the words used to call up a giant, the Woodcutter, from GodBeGone Wood. A place which nobody ever goes into because an ancient barrier, an unseen force, prevents both entry and exit. We are kept out and the Woodcutter is kept in."

"Yeah, well that's a bit of a myth," said Len. "Everybody denies going in there but we've all snuck in from time to time. Even visiting that area behind the church." The family plot.

"Cam … Cameron did a little survey," said Vinnie. "You're right, Len. Most admitted to going in once or twice, usually in response to a dare when younger but they never went in after that. The only regular visitor appears to be our Uncle Fred. Haunts the place apparently."

Alec could understand that although it seemed morbid. To put yourself through such pain for all those years. If it was him, he'd have moved away. He noticed Oliver starting at the mention of Fred's name but recovered himself.

"People don't seem to like the woods," agreed Alec. "I know they creep me out." It exerted a strange influence over him. The view from his bedroom window at the back of the inn, looked out at the forest wall. It butted right up against the garden, the boughs of the trees reaching over, seeking their way towards him. The trees cast a strange, hypnotic spell and he found himself gazing out for an hour at a time without realising it. Was it the same for everyone else? And there was that underlying rhythm, a creaking, rocking, back and forth; a sound he alone heard and felt.

"It's due to the barrier," said Vinnie. "Apparently this barrier was originally created by the old ritual of the Beating of the Bounds on Halloween."

Vinnie paused as Oliver took out a notebook and started jotting things down. No doubt more money-making ideas.

"Beating of the Bounds?"

"A ritual not quite like those carried out in other parts of the country," continued Vinnie.

Oliver smiled. "Something we could stage. Religion versus Paganism. Theatrical. *I* like it."

"Perhaps," said Vinnie. "The result is the Woodcutter stays in the woods and looks after the trees and occasionally sleeps. The village is safe from his, and Grandma's ... demands. But the Woodcutter will always hear if someone speaks the words of The Summoning, even if it is said in a whisper because these are the words that will free him. And if that invisible barrier is weak or non-existent, the words allow him to roam the countryside once more. However, the Beating of the Bounds has not been carried out since Edmund Chadwick took up his tenure, doesn't believe in it all apparently. Fred told me the last time was when Chadwick's father was in the job."

"Doesn't seem very scary, so far," said Alec, acting his part.

Vinnie pulled a journal from his pocket. Flipped it open to a page and put it on the table in front of his two companions. It was a very old book and Alec wondered at this treatment of it, surely it belonged in a museum.

"This book belonged to the ancestors of our old minister Reverend Chadwick. They recorded the story of the Woodcutter. *This*, is the Woodcutter." Vinnie stabbed the image with his finger. This was the monster. Deep scars round down his cheeks, tracing lines as if the rings of a tree. Whorls and knots adorned his forehead and between his two eyes was another eye, a third eye. Deeper, darker, emptier than anything Alec had ever seen before. Like the forest, it pulled at him, held his gaze and refused to let him go. His eyebrows were thorns, some scars open wounds, insects scuttled across the surface, beetles and weevils, woodlice and worms. The whole surface of his face seemed to move.

"Nasty looking bugger," said Alec, unable to take his eyes from the picture despite his obvious distaste.

"We thought the Woodcutter would make a good effigy for a bonfire," said Oliver. "A touch of the Wicker Man perhaps."

"Now for Grandma." He flipped the pages again, showed another faded ink illustration.

"She won't win any beauty competitions," said Len, looking revolted.

"I'll read you the story, exactly as it is written here."

"Once upon a time," laughed Alec.

"*Once upon a time*," said Vinnie, ignoring him, "and centuries ago, when lives were lived according to the seasons and Church, King and Government were remote entities to those who inhabited these parts, Little Hatchet and other settlements in this area went about their daily toil obedient to the only person they feared. Grandma. She was not the harmless little old lady living in a cottage in the middle of the wood waiting for her granddaughter to bring her food in a basket. Well, not completely. Yes, she lived where the fairy tales say and yes something was brought to her in a basket but it was so much *more* than bread and cake.

"Many thought Grandma a witch. The local priest regarded her as the Devil's Mistress, railed against her as Lilith, Hag of the

Night. Yet he whispered his protestations, too scared to confront her, too fearful to denounce her any further in public. Those who had done so before him vanished without trace. His living was a precarious one. They were not strangers however, Grandma would come to the village, buy food and goods from the market, attend church even and chuckle her way through his sermons. Nor did she sit at the back. No, this ancient crone would make her way to the front of the church and sit in the Lord of the Manor's seat. And neither he, nor his wife, nor their children ever said anything. Simply pretended she wasn't there, behaviour which amused her no end.

"Yet some spoke to her. Those with whom she traded would tell her the local gossip, the latest news, mouths opening so easily and spewing out anything and everything they had heard. Even things they promised to keep secret, forgetting they had done so when they said goodbye to Grandma, a fog always descended over these conversations. And she would have her visitors in the woods, mothers seeking cures for the ailments afflicting their families, young girls hoping to discover their future, young men wanting help seeking fortune and fame, others with more—unsavoury— requests. For good or evil, Grandma made no distinction between appeals and fulfilled the wishes made, provided the villagers paid the price. And at only six lives every six years, what could be cheaper?

"Grandma demanded these lives, young or old, healthy or infirm, sound of mind or feeble, it didn't matter, Grandma would name them and the locals offered them up. The Woodcutter was her assistant, knocking on the door on the Night of the Gathering. A giant, a monster, whom none could deny. If Grandma was regarded as a witch, many thought of the Woodcutter as a demon.

"Lurid tales spread about the fate of these girls. That Grandma and the Woodcutter roasted them on spits and ate them, their flesh allowing them to live for centuries more. Others that the girls were for the Woodcutter, concubines to entertain him at night until he wearied of them and chopped off their heads. None of this was the truth and the reality was actually more gruesome. Yes, Grandma was old beyond imagining, beautiful once and privileged, she had made a deal with the Devil to live forever and her young lover, the Woodcutter, desperate to stay with her, had also made this pact.

"But look at the illustrations in the book, look at the Woodcutter's face," Vinnie showed them the face of the giant again, the jagged marks, the scarring and carvings.

"He did not remain young and handsome; Grandma did not remain beautiful. Instead their faces changed as the lives they took grew in number, became a reflection of the evil they wrought. The two were no longer lovers. They became partners in crime, servants of a Devil who sent them into the woods to inhabit a world he'd created alongside the human. These woods are GodBeGone Woods, the forest which has been the backdrop to all our lives.

"Gradually, they retreated further into its depths, coming out only to gather up the sacrifices and as generations changed, the power once ascribed to the couple faded and when it came to Cromwell's time, the sacrifices stopped completely.

"Some folk from Little Hatchet went into the forest during those turbulent years of the Commonwealth. None of them came out. Another search party went in. And again disappeared. A third tried and by that time, the wood had decided to throw up the defences around its edge which you see around you. It became impenetrable. *Nobody* has ever been able to break into their realm. Some villagers thought they were dead, others they were simply sleeping, waiting for the time when another sacrifice would be made to give Grandma life anew.

"And what was the secret to Grandma's long life? Her cloak. The fairy stories all talk about Little Red Riding Hood but they do not know the truth. Yes, there was a cloak but it was Grandma's. *She* was the figure who walked the paths of the wood in a cloak of red with a wolf trotting at her heels and the Woodcutter as her companion.

"One of those early priests recorded the tale of the cloak *as told by Grandma herself* and wrote it in a journal, one long lost but copied out by descendants before that happened. In those very early days, when Grandma attended church, she had engaged the minister after the sermon. She had let the congregation leave and she and the priest were alone. She said she wanted to confess. But apparently, she smiled when she said it, did not seem at all regretful.

In fact, it was recorded that she told the tale with a smile on her lips and delight in her eyes.

She had come not to confess but to torment the priest in his house of God.

"I have seen you admire my cloak," she said. "It is beautiful is it not. Its texture is truly exquisite."

She held out a corner for the priest to touch, which he reluctantly did.

"The colour is remarkable, such a deep, deep red. A pity it fades over time, as does my own energy. Yet it can return to life. Those six you give us provide both the dye and the material."

The priest had already snatched away his hand, his skin crawling at the texture of the fabric, unable to hide the revulsion it engendered.

"Do you wish to know how?" she continued, and without waiting for an answer, proceeded. "My Woodcutter has a sharp blade; he swaddles each person in a sack—or a shroud if you like—and makes a nick through the material and into the flesh. He is very precise about this cut as it allows the blood to run freely but slowly. Blood has to be decanted carefully to get exactly the right consistency for the dye.

"He has a tree, right in the heart of the woods and he hangs the bodies there, each above a vat into which the blood drips. Once the body can give no more, he takes it down and flenses the flesh, treats the hide. Then these are dipped in the vat until the colour is as you see and he brings the material to me to be fashioned into a cloak. Like the one you see in front of you. So the six give me both cloak and life. And by carrying out these duties, so does the Woodcutter receive his reward from our *Master*."

"So you truly are a servant of the Devil," had said the priest.

"But of course," said Grandma. "And so are you. We all are."

She laughed then, a cackle that followed her out of the church and into the woods.

The priest died two days later. He hanged himself on one of the trees at the edge of the forest.

They say the Woodcutter cut him down and took his body into the forest and it was that, that one act of bringing a man of the cloth into the Devil's world which started the tale of the Woodcutter's apprentice."

Vinnie paused to finish his pint and nodded his thanks to Len who refilled it as swiftly as he had Oliver's. The landlord was paying very close attention. No doubt he, like Alec, was trying to work out what Vinnie had in mind for Oliver.

"The Woodcutter. I told you of the priest taken into the woods by the giant. This was not approved of by the *owner* of the woods, this was the Devil's home and no place for a priest. It was viewed as a contamination and so the Woodcutter had to be punished. Whilst his life had always been bound up with Grandma's, his own immortality was something he had to re-earn. He would have to be 'reborn' and to survive, he would need an apprentice. A youth from the village, one he could train and who would eventually become his 'host'. The Woodcutter, you see, was no longer able to continue as he was. Whilst his spirit would live, his body would always die eventually.

"Now Little Hatchet not only had to offer Grandma her victims, it also had to offer up one of its sons to the Woodcutter. But they learned the hard way. When the Woodcutter first strode into the village and demanded one of their youths, the people ignored him. What could he do? They found their answer the next morning in the slaughter of their cattle. The Woodcutter again returned to the village and repeated his demands.

Again, they ignored him, although this time they had brought their livestock into barns and set up a watch over them. The next morning, they found the shape of an axe carved on some of the doors and when those doors were opened they found the axe had done its work in a different way.

"The funerals changed peoples' minds and so they took six of their sons and bound them, alive, like scarecrows in one of the fields by GodBeGone Wood. After that selection, the new priest railed at them for their superstition and instigated the Beating of the Bounds. It seemed to have worked because neither Grandma nor the Woodcutter were ever seen again. Although occasionally there would be reported sightings of a glimpse of something, moving through the woods." Vinnie paused and took another drink.

"This is the hook. The thing which'll make the news. We recreate the offering," said Oliver, taking advantage of Vinnie's break. "Three days and three nights, perhaps kidnap a couple of the 'victims' on the second night, build up the tension for the third. Would they reappear? Who would be taken? And after all that we Beat the Bounds to keep the Woodcutter in for another year. You know I've some actor friends, some contacts in the media. Turn it into a Halloween Special for TV, folk lore of Olde England. People'll lap it up!"

Vinnie wore a wolf's grin, gave Alec a wink. It told him Oliver had walked into his trap.

"If we give it a real Hammer Horror vibe, the punters'll love it," said Oliver. He knocked back his drink. "I'm off, people to ring, things to do."

People to do, more like, thought Alec. The man gave off that sort of vibe.

"Hang on," said Len. "What about the money raised? What's *your* percentage?"

"We agreed I'd take 10% after expenses. Fair?"

Fair? It sounded almost too good to be true. It did not sound like the sort of profit margin a successful businessman would normally go for. There had to be a reason behind it but for the moment, he couldn't think what that might be.

Alec pounced as soon as the door shut behind Oliver. "So? What's your plan?"

"The Woodcutter story helped kill Fred's wife and child and he's bringing it back. But we turn the Woodcutter on *him*."

"How?" asked Len.

"When the Summoning has been performed and the Woodcutter comes, he goes after him as the apprentice. Give him a really good scare and then make it clear he's not wanted round here. And as it'll all be on film the world will know what a bastard he was."

Alec frowned. He wanted Fred to be rid of the man but he wasn't quite sure this was the right way.

"What?" asked Vinnie, noticing his expression.

"I ... I mean, yes to giving him a scare and getting him away from here, away from Fred. But letting everyone else know? I mean he was a child, doesn't he deserve a chance to redeem himself?"

Their silence was his answer.

CHAPTER NINE

"You're in then?" asked Vinnie, as they made their way back to his house.

Alec had agreed to go with him, talk it through, make sure they didn't go too far. He recalled Cameron's last words, his younger brother needed saving. He was beginning to think Cameron meant the man needed saving from himself. It wasn't late when they returned and Doug joined them in the kitchen. Again, the chance to talk in confidence was gone. As Alec took his seat, he glanced up at the ceiling.

"Carol's asleep," said Doug.

The days were passing and he'd yet to see Vinnie's mother, let alone meet her. Vinnie gave his dad a curious look but said nothing. He too had been kept away. Her breakdown must be bad. As Doug made them all coffee, Vinnie explained his plans, how they knew who Oliver really was, the chance to revenge themselves upon him for all the suffering he had caused them.

"I wondered when that would get out," said Doug.

"What?" The surprise in Vinnie's voice was evident.

Not for the first time, Alec wondered at his new family. They seemed to keep so many secrets from each other.

"I knew who it was as soon as I saw him," said Doug. "And then Fred came to me, asked for my help. It would've been sorted if Cam hadn't gone chasing off after you." He looked at Alec. "Don't misunderstand me, I couldn't be happier to see you—although the circumstances obviously leave a lot to be desired."

"What do you mean 'sorted'?" asked Vinnie.

Doug blew the steam from his mug before he answered. "The Woodcutter."

"Oh, come on, Dad," said Vinnie. "He's not real."

His, their, father smiled thinly. "You know nothing and I would seriously advise you to give up this hare-brained scheme of yours before someone else dies."

"Cameron's death was an accident, natural causes, you know that," said Alec.

Doug stayed quiet. Alec waited, allowed his gaze to settle on photos held by a magnet on an old upright fridge-freezer. A yellowing column amongst a mismatch of units and chipped work surfaces. The lino on the floor had also seen better days. Yet the room did not feel to be one of neglect, it felt loved, like the dog-eared, spine-broken book on his bedside table, or his faded T-shirt with its tiny rips threatening to disintegrate completely with every wash.

This was a room which had nurtured—once. Something was missing and again he thought of the absent mother, the woman who stood at the centre of the smiling family in the photo on the fridge door. He could make out little of her features from this distance, enough to be certain of her link to Vinnie, that certain something which bound a mother to her child even when physically, they could appear completely different.

Through the kitchen windows was nothing but the moving blackness of GodBeGone Woods. All the buildings along Church Lane butted up against the trees—the church, the Reeves' house, their bookshop, the pub—on and on around the village edges. There was no escape from its monstrous presence. The windows were closed, but even so, Alec thought he could hear that strange, rhythmic rocking. A woman's voice. He tried to refocus back in the kitchen.

"All those years ago," said Doug, "our family's lives were ripped apart. We lost Charlie and life was difficult. Gradually, she seemed to rally and then we found we were expecting you. We had five happy years until … until the business with Mary. Losing her sister, her nephew, having already lost her own son. It was too much."

The tale was no different to the one they'd heard earlier, apart from slotting the story of Fred and the murder of Rosie into the tale.

"She changed," continued Doug. "Started going for long walks on her own. I caught her coming out of the church on more than one occasion whereas she'd never been much of a churchgoer before. And then she was gone, left me a long rambling letter claiming the Woodcutter would come for her, for *you*, if she stayed. It was that bloody man's fault."

Alec had been around and heard enough to know his dad meant Reverend Chadwick.

"I tracked her down but couldn't persuade her to come back, she even accused me of being in league with him—the Woodcutter, that is. I tried and tried to persuade her but in the end I gave up. It broke my heart, yet what else could I do?" Doug's body sagged as he relived the past, hands held out in despair, eyes misty with old, but never forgotten, grief.

He could have left the village and gone with her, thought Alec but he kept his comments to himself. It was not the time to pass judgement.

"And then I met Carol and had Cam and Vinnie. I was happy."

"You never told me and Cam all of that, Dad," said Vinnie. "And Fred …"

Doug ran a hand over his close-cropped scalp, grey shot through with silver in a dull halo.

"We agreed, us and others in the village of our age, it was best. No sense in allowing those murders to haunt the sleep of the next generation. Me and Fred—we allow ourselves one day of the year to remember the past, talk about Rosie, Charlie, everything else. The last time turned out to be the day before Cameron visited you, Alec," said Doug.

"He overheard us talking about the Woodcutter and Fred was indulging his fantasy a bit about what would be done to Oliver if the giant existed and would seek revenge on our behalf. The question of sacrifice came up and I think for some reason, Cam got it stuck in his head I was going to sacrifice *you,* Vinnie, in return for the Woodcutter's help. He was wrong of course but nothing I could say would change his mind. I blame myself. If he hadn't heard us, maybe he wouldn't have gone to see you, Alec. Might still be alive."

Alec was utterly confused. His father's story was totally different to his mum's. Admittedly she'd told him nothing of the man beyond he was the Devil, yet her feelings had shown him she believed she'd rescued them both from a bad situation.

"Whatever she told you, Alec," said Doug, "I am not a bad man. And whatever Cameron told you, it was wrong. I wouldn't hurt any of you. I didn't realise Cam had been branded until the inquest and Chadwick promised he was dead when he did it, although how a man of the cloth could do *that—*"

It felt as if the temperature had dropped several degrees. Doug got up and went to stand at the window, gazing into the forest. Something else was coming. "We went into the woods, to the cottage. Strange you might think that Fred would ever want to go back there and way back we kept intending to demolish it but something always stopped us. In the end, Fred would even work on the building, maintain it. A sort of memorial to Rosie. Said he felt close to her there. What could I say? It was his choice and if it helped him cope, well, so be it. Then … then we went into the woods and I let Fred summon the Woodcutter."

"But you said that was all nonsense, all fantasy!" exploded Alec. "You can't have it both ways!"

Doug shrugged. "I'll admit now to believing once upon a time. Don't laugh. But when you're brought up in a place as closed and claustrophobic as Little Hatchet, you believe what you're told. You don't question. I didn't for a long time. It was Mary taking you, Alec, that made me realise how pointless it was, make believe. Fred's different. He believes. The woods have become his church. So, yes, I recited the summoning with him as a way to help Fred, let him feel as if he was getting some small revenge. If the legend had taken Rosie, then it was fair the real Woodcutter could take Oliver. Justice. I still didn't believe any of it but Fred seemed happier, declared it was working, although something *more* was needed for a full return. Then everything went wrong with Cam and here we are. Fred and that bloody Chadwick diving into the forest at any chance, you working for that bastard. It's fucked up."

Alec and Vinnie looked at each other.

"So, Vinnie," said Alec. "As everything is coming out into the open, perhaps you'd like to share more of this plan of yours?"

"You know it might actually give us all the closure we need," said Vinnie. "We go through the whole event as he described but on the third night, the night of the choosing according to the story, we get someone to grab him and tie him to a bloody cross. There'll be people filming and Fred will be able to denounce him to the world. We could even convince him the Woodcutter's coming to take him as his apprentice. And the beauty of all this is that Oliver would be paying for the whole bloody thing out of his own pocket. And can you imagine what his investors will think when they discover his background? He'll go bankrupt. He'll become a pariah."

Alec pondered Vinnie's idea, remembered the picture of Oliver as a little boy—why had that picture ever been published in the newspapers, where was his protection then? A little boy led astray. Vinnie's plan was leaving a bad taste in his mouth.

"You know, Vinnie," said Doug. "That's not actually a bad idea. It would allow Fred—and the village—to lance the wound once and for all. Rid it of its poison. Alec?"

Alec looked at them both, could sense the bond being forged between the three of them, whereas there'd been nothing before.

He decided to put his misgivings aside. He had been unable to help Cameron, perhaps he could redeem himself by supporting them in this, admittedly, bizarre charade. If it gained closure for them as a family, finally healed all wounds, then that was all to the good. Plus he would be helping Vinnie, Cameron's last request of him.

"Yes," he said. "You can count me in."

CHAPTER TEN

As Oliver continued to clear away the undergrowth from the cottage, he considered the previous night's visit to the pub. He was pleased at the general reception to his and Vinnie's idea. It was Fate's way of telling him this was meant to be. His visit to Old One had also shown him Reverend Chadwick had kept to his side of the bargain. He disliked the minister, for a man of God, he seemed untrustworthy, appeared to be following some hidden agenda. It was a shame Cameron wasn't around to see it all come to fruition.

The garden was more clearly defined, even begun to yield up its own secrets. Those findings were in a box under Grandma's workbench, the police never found *those*. Nor did he ache so much, even though he continued to spend many an hour working on the area. His body had become used to the regular physical exertion, he even had muscles. Something which Liz very much appreciated.

Liz. His lips curled in a smile as he remembered her response to his plan. He would provide the money for the show and she would present it. All she needed to do was schmooze a few producers on the TV circuit and he had told her to do what she felt she needed to do—he would not be jealous. But with the backing already provided, who would turn it down? *And even if they do, you know a few actors who could pretend to be cameramen, find a convenient doppelganger for that well-known producer.* Oliver laughed out loud. It was always here, at the cottage, his best ideas came to him and the solutions to any possible problem. The cottage had a voice and it spoke to him, told him the end justified the means.

He stood and looked around him. The garden was almost cleared. He'd uncovered the small fencing running around its perimeter, its posts, once moss green, restored to their former ivory glory. The slight curves and indents, the rounded edges of the uprights, added to the pleasing aesthetics of the boundary. There were occasional gaps but Oliver already had his eye on the replacements and would be harvesting them soon.

He placed his hand against the small of his back, felt himself stiffening slightly as muscles solidified in place. He'd done enough for the afternoon. He studied the machete. It no longer felt heavy, become almost an extension of his arm, and he enjoyed the sense of power it gave as its blade sliced through all he attacked. The metal had disappeared between smudges of green and brown, scrapes of black. Flesh and steel needed cleansing.

Oliver entered the cottage and plunged his face in the bucket of water filled from the well. Another recent rediscovery. The shock of cold, clear water sharpened his senses. The oil and rag lying on the workbench would do the same for the machete. Soon he was sat in Grandma's rocking chair, cleaning and rubbing the steel until it shone. Then he brought the other tools, the axes and hatchets, the traps and saws, from the wall and repeated the process on all. The repetitive action, the silence of his surroundings gradually hypnotised him until eventually the rag dropped from his hand and the last axe lay across his lap as he slept.

A gust of wind closed the door and again Oliver was subjected to another microscopic invasion. Motes feeding his memory, blending the past of Grandma with his forgotten childhood, stirring up what had been buried. The cottage was poisonous in so many ways and its venom was still powerful. As he slept, his hand curled unconsciously around the axe handle. It felt right. It felt like home.

A sudden banging on the door jolted him out of his slumber. Oliver groaned as he rose to his feet, feeling the ache in his muscles, unaware of the tool still in his hand. Annoyance ran through him. This was his refuge, where he could work and rest undisturbed, slough off stress.

He walked slowly over to the door, noting a small beam flickering along its bottom edge. Only then did he realise night had once again fallen whilst he'd rested within its four walls. He barely considered how he'd not needed light to make his way across the cottage floor without stumbling over anything.

The banging continued.

"All right, all right, I'm coming," he said, taking hold of the handle and pulling the door open.

In front of him stood a man, he looked almost ancient but Oliver had the feeling he was not as old as he appeared. The lines on his face carved by something other than time. His clothes hung loosely on his body, a body which seemed frail and almost birdlike. Only when Oliver reached for a nearby lamp and lit it, holding it up to his visitor, did he see the hawklike face, the unshaven chin. He could also smell the alcohol on the man's breath. Perhaps the reason he swayed slightly as he stood. Despite his irritation at this unwanted visit, curiosity overcame him.

"Can I help you?" he asked.

"You don't remember me, do you?"

Oliver leaned closer, bending down slightly. The man had shrunk, bowed by years and misery, his spine curving slightly as it did amongst the aged—and those who no longer wanted to look the world in the eye.

The lamplight revealed a sallow face with sharp cheekbones, the cap, removed, showed a mere wisp of hair. The eyes, glittering in the light, betrayed a watery lack of colour, their brown, sludgy and diffuse. Oliver also detected something else, a smell not quite masked by the drink but emotion, an eruption of both fear and loathing in equal measure.

"No, I'm sorry ..."

"Then you need to leave," said the man, "before you do."

"Look ..."

"You have to go. If you remember, it'll all start again. I've started something but I don't think, I don't want ..."

"All what?" Oliver stared at the man whose eyes had dropped to the axe in his hand. He'd forgotten he still held it. His visitor's eyes widened, the scent of fear grew stronger but he stood his ground.

"You have to go," he repeated.

"No, I really think it's you who has to go," said Oliver. "It's late, I'm tired and I haven't a sodding clue what you're on about."

Still the man stayed. They stared at each other for a few more minutes before Oliver finally relented. Hopefully, he'd get rid of him quicker if he heard him out.

Oliver sighed. "Come in, you can say what you have to and *then* go. But first, *who* are you?"

"You really don't remember, do you? I'm Fred, one of your dad's tenant farmers when you used to live here. My wife Rosie was your family's cook."

Oliver stared, his mouth dropping open.

This was nothing like the man he remembered. Still the same rough workman's clothes, even though he seemed to be pensionable age. How old had he been back then? Forty-ish? So, around eighty but he seemed so much more.

Rosie. The warmth of the kitchen, of her smile, came back to him. The desire to see the woman who was more than a mother to him than his own, became overwhelming.

He smiled. "Rosie. I remember Rosie. Of course I do. How could I forget her? She did so much for me. Those wonderful cookies she used to bake when ..." He paused, aware he was beginning to ramble. "So. Rosie. Tell me how she is these days. I'd love to see her."

At his words, Fred's whole demeanour changed. He was still shaking but now he was trembling with anger, his face furious, although his anger was mingled with disbelief. "See her? Are you serious? It was you ... you who ..." the man stumbled over his words, his distress rendering him almost incoherent. For one awful moment, Oliver thought the man was having a stroke.

"Look, come and sit down ..." Oliver gestured towards the chair, Grandma's chair.

Fred's face looked pale, sick in the feeble lamplight. He was moving backwards, away from Oliver, back down the path with its wooden giants towering up behind him. He couldn't let him go, not without some kind of explanation. Oliver edged forward, Fred took another step back. Then another step, stopping at the small gate which swung shut behind him.

Fred had stopped, his hand reaching out to open the gate but hesitating, a look of disgust on his face at what he was about to touch. Yet the man had entered the garden, would have touched the gate then. Or not. It had been propped open earlier, Oliver recalled, allowing him to go in and out as he cleared both sides of the fence. He'd not shut it, even when he had finished, and there'd been no breeze.

"Fred. Come in and sit down. Even if it's only for a minute. You don't look too good."

Fred didn't move.

"For God's sake, Fred. It's not as if you're in any danger!"

His visitor started at his words, paled even more.

Oliver closed in. He softened his voice. "You really should come in and sit a while." One hand grasped Fred's arm, urging him back indoors. The other clenched as if holding an imaginary weapon. They walked side by side, back into the cottage.

Still Fred shrank from the rocking chair and Oliver didn't force him, instead his 'guest' sat on the stool the young Oliver used to occupy when Grandma span her stories and the Woodcutter started him on his apprenticeship.

A deep, pulsing silence settled over them, the lamplight fading slightly, turning to hazy orange, dusky pink, reminiscent of sunrise, or the last glimmerings of its setting. As Oliver continued to gaze quietly at Fred, the room itself distorted and he felt as if he were underwater. Not as a man drowning, no this was as a babe in the womb. He felt the pulse around him deepen, begin to push at him, his memories. The contractions of recall came slowly at first and then faster, faster, forcing themselves out of the darkness of the past, erupting fully-formed into the present.

All they had begun to teach him came back and he found himself looking at Fred with new eyes. His hands felt unnaturally empty, something was missing. Ignoring his guest for the moment, he rose and made his way to the wall on which axes and hatchets, hammers and knives hung. He stared long at the hungry blades, felt the twitch of his muscles as he allowed them to listen to the song each sang, decide what would be the one he should pick.

"Oliver," said Fred, rising from the stool so that when he turned, they were face-to-face, although he also had the feeling he was looking down on the man, become a giant.

"I know ... I know what happened back then wasn't really your fault. That couple who lived here, they were the monsters and they poisoned you, but ... but ... you took my Rosie to them. She treated you, loved you like the son we once thought we could never have and still you offered her up. Why did you come back when you knew it would rip open old wounds, cause so much pain? Or did you hope that all of us who remembered would be dead ..."

Why had he come back? The death of his parents, business, the dark hole of his memory demanding to be filled. It had been all that but there was also something else, a pressure, a pull like a magnet that had brought him back. *It was time, a voice said.* He brought death with him then and he brought death now.

"I had to give them Rosie," said Oliver. "Grandma needed a new cloak. Her old one was fading and so was she. I tried to make Rosie understand."

He could see her, laughing at the antics of the birds in the trees, not at all unfazed by their number, the little dances they'd performed on the ground in front of them, in the canopy above. She'd held his hand, wrapped his small fingers in her own, indulging him in his desire to go further into the wood. She'd never been the superstitious sort, mocked the tales that had been told.

And she'd loved him all the more that day because he'd whispered to her how he wished *she* had been his real mother. Even then he'd somehow understood Rosie, who so loved children would never really have any of her own, regardless of the child growing in her belly. So he'd led her along that rarely used track which had somehow been miraculously cleared, allowing them easy progress towards Grandma's cottage.

"Such a pretty house," Rosie had cried, after getting over the initial shock of discovery. "Well, I never. Who on earth lives here?"

"Why, Grandma, of course," he'd said, holding the small gate open. The scent of roses, in full bloom, perfumed the air.

"Oh, come, Oliver," said Rosie. "Grandma's an old wives' tale."

"No, she's not," he'd insisted. "Come and meet her. I know she'd like to meet *you*. I've told her all about you."

A slightly doubtful look had crossed Rosie's face then but she followed him up the path, as he knew she would, if only to check out the strange, unknown Grandma and report back to his parents, warn them perhaps about the company he kept.

Grandma should be here, thought Oliver. So she could see he remembered, was ready to bring her back. The weight of the axe in his hand felt good.

"Sit down, Fred." The man in front of him glanced down and swallowed, stumbled awkwardly back to his stool.

Oliver retook his place in Grandma's chair, rocking back and forth, stroking the steel on his lap.

"We all had tea together, here. Did you know that? Grandma made scones and cakes for us. Rosie said they were as good as any she'd ever made. They talked for ages about baking, sharing recipes, it was quite boring really." But it had won Rosie's trust so they stayed far longer than she intended.

"That couple. They were lunatics," said Fred, finding his voice. "Don't you remember? Delusional. A lifetime of drugs addled their brains. Turned them into homicidal maniacs. They *thought* they were Grandma and the Woodcutter but it was just … it was just …" Fred trailed off helplessly.

Just the drugs, the papers said, as their pleas of insanity were accepted, their sentences of life in maximum security passed down. They weren't in prison though. Oliver *knew* that. They were nearby, had never left, had simply been waiting for his return, the apprenticeship over.

"My poor Rosie, my poor child," whispered Fred.

"Was a boy!" said Oliver, remembering. "He was perfect!"

"No," groaned Fred. "Don't you dare, spare me that."

And he and the public had been spared this aspect of the trial. Too gruesome for even Rosie's husband and family to hear in detail, they'd stayed away for *that*, although Oliver knew full well they would've been informed. He had to tell him how perfect the babe had been. How he'd lived, breathed, for those few seconds, how Rosie had so briefly, so finally, been allowed to be a mother.

"Grandma gave Rosie one of her herbal teas. Raspberry leaf I think it was. Said it was good for women near their time."

Fred buried his head in his hands, curled in upon himself.

"Rosie drank it and then the contractions began. I remember how scared she looked, worried about how far from help she was, about me. Grandma calmed her, said she'd delivered many a child. And me? Well, I could go and get help. I knew the woods well. I was safe. Rosie calmed at that. She kissed me and I left. I remember Grandma's voice telling her to breathe as I closed the door behind me.

"No, no, no." Fred was rocking himself back and forth and Oliver wondered why the man was staying to hear all this. He could've tried to leave, tried to attack Oliver, both of which would not have been permitted, but something stayed him. Despite all his groans of protest, Fred needed to know. After all this time, he needed to know exactly what had happened. Being a child, the interrogation of Oliver had been limited and the courts bowed to the psychiatrist's opinion he should not be questioned beyond the limited recount he'd given.

"I got help. I found the Woodcutter. He had the blade needed to cut the cord and when we got back it was to find Rosie lying on

Grandma's bed with the baby at her breast. He was feeding quietly and she was smiling. She was so happy.

"Stop, please." Fred's agonised voice cracked across his memory.

"Stop, you say. Of course, if you wish."

Oliver halted the rocking of his chair, leaned forward as Fred raised his face to his. They were so close. He could see the sweat seeping from the pores in his skin, the tears trickling down his cheeks, smell the pain, the fear, the disease, emanating from him. This was why he'd come. Not simply to search for truth, but to suffer what Rosie suffered, to die as she had done. He would soon be dead anyway and as their eyes locked on each other, they both knew that.

"No," he whispered eventually. "Go on. My wife suffered and so should I. I should not be allowed to escape what she could not."

Oliver nodded and resumed. "She called me over to her side and I sat on the bed. The baby opened his eyes and looked at me. So blue, so bright. A skyful of life. And she gave him to me. Showed me how to hold him properly, how to support his head. I could see the cord still connecting them, like a grey snake, coiled and twisted. It meant I had to hold him where I was. I could not walk him around, show him the night. Their moment of separation had not yet come. Rosie pointed out that part of his skull not yet hardened, and I could almost feel the pulse of him through it, see it throb. He felt so fragile. Grandma was smiling too. Said it was time for me to show him the woods. Rosie protested then. The afterbirth had not appeared, the cord needed to be cut.

"Don't worry," said Grandma. "We have the Woodcutter."

And he came forward then. His axe shining as brightly as the babe's eyes. They pulled back the blankets despite Rosie's protests. She looked anxious but Grandma looked after her so well, she wasn't *too* scared. I remember the blood on the sheets, it was still pulsing out of her. Rosie tried to push the sheet down to cover herself but Grandma stopped her, moved her legs further apart so the umbilical cord could be seen clearly and the Woodcutter raised his axe. Only then did she scream as she realised what was to happen. With no clamps in place and the placenta still inside, both mother and child would haemorrhage. I didn't know that then. I looked upon it as freeing them both from an inconvenient physical tie. She tried to move again but Grandma held her firmly. She was so strong, amazing for such an old woman."

"Old! She wasn't that old," spat Fred. "She was only in her forties, although junkies always age badly."

"She was centuries old," said Oliver ignoring him. "And so was the Woodcutter. I took the baby outside like they told me. He didn't cry for long, and I placed him on the ground, near those rose bushes you see as you come in the garden. It was for the wood to decide whether he lived or died. I returned to Rosie and saw the buckets Grandma had started to fill. Rosie was unconscious at that point, possibly dead already but I didn't think so. Grandma said it was time to give her, too, to the forest. You know the rest."

Fred uncurled himself. His tears had stopped. His fear had gone. "Will you take me?"

Oliver nodded and guided him out, picking up a torch to light their way. Not that he needed it. The light was for Fred. They walked in almost companionable silence. The evening was cool but not uncomfortable, the undergrowth alive with the skitterings and rustlings of small creatures. Occasionally, a glint of moonlight slipped through the trees to add to the torch's illumination, turning the pitch darkness into shades of silver in which grey shadows roamed.

They entered the narrow path, leading to their destination. It was the wood's own umbilicus along which the creatures it birthed travelled. Soon they would return to the womb itself. And then it opened out and the two men stood in the glade beneath the towering form of Old One.

"Here?" asked Fred quietly, knowing the answer. "Show me."

The torch beam flicked up, travelled over the gnarled and ancient branches, revealing the distorted orbs Oliver had shown Liz earlier. There was no gasp of shock, only an acknowledgement of someone finding exactly what they expected. Oliver had seen them at work on the tree, watched as Cameron too, was hoisted into place. Blood of family returning to the heart of the wood.

"Not long," said Oliver. "The Woodcutter and Grandma can never die. They're still here, always here, waiting for a host, an apprentice. He's got one and soon, Grandma too, will return."

Fred was shaking his head. "No, I don't believe that. You're a murderer, hiding behind a sick legend and you see a way of making money from a sick mockup. It's linked to that plan of yours I've been hearing about from your girlfriend."

Liz. She was supposed to have kept quiet. The idea that this was a reconstruction rankled. He did not know who the Woodcutter had been in his absence, but this was real. The voice that awoke in him after all these years, was telling him so and that it was his turn. He had finally been chosen.

"They brought the jury here," said Fred. "After everything—back then—was cleared away. To see all this, *here*. Nobody deserves this. My Rosie certainly didn't. And for you to try and make money out of her murder, her—my—pain, beggars belief. It's sick."

"I told you, it was for Grandma."

"For a mind-addled junkie lunatic," spat Fred. "And regardless of then. Why do you insist on believing this now? For fuck's sake, you're an adult. Didn't you have some sort of counselling to put you straight? You sound as warped and twisted as they did back then!"

"And still you don't run," said Oliver. "You want to know what they did to me? Those *professionals*? Hypnotherapy in the end. They couldn't change my view of reality back then so they buried it all. The effect of that's finally gone, worn off and everything's clear again."

He felt an itch crawl down his arm, slithering along to his axe hand. Old One's boughs creaked above him. The rustlings underfoot stilled. This was the time. Fred would be the first of his offerings and soon, Grandma, his beloved Grandma, would return.

"Yes," murmured Fred. "On that we're agreed. Everything's clear this time, isn't it?"

"Yes," said Oliver.

Fred looked up. "I have only one thing to ask," he said.

"Name it."

"That you hang me from the same branch as they did Rosie."

"Of course," said Oliver. "Now turn and face the tree. It is seeking you out already, its branches touch the air around you, feeling your pulse." Oliver continued to talk as Fred turned his back on him, fixed his gaze on the monstrous trunk as he waited for that final blow.

The urge had grown fierce, would not be stilled. It swung his arm up so the blade glinted briefly and then, after a pause, down it rushed. The metal shimmered and dazzled as it cleaved the air, the flesh, the bone. So swift was the action, so clean the cut that Fred made not a sound, merely dropping prostrate at the base of the oak.

Oliver surveyed the body for a moment and then laid down his axe, pulling out the sackcloth shroud rolled up in readiness by the vat closest to him. He worked quickly knowing delay would mean too much blood would be lost to Grandma. Once Fred had been bound, he sought out the rope pulley and hooked up the body, exactly as the Woodcutter had taught him all those years ago.

Carefully, he raised the shroud, swinging it over, as Fred requested, to the branch on which Rosie had hung those few short days before the bodies were discovered. Already a few satisfying drips could be heard in the wooden container.

He looked at the shrouds Liz had seen. They would have to come down, be replaced. They had nothing left to give. Then he would collect others, bleed them, take their cloaks for Grandma. Cameron, Chadwick's gift, could remain a while longer.

The rustlings around him started up again, the world moving on as it always did. He picked up the axe, noticing how the impulse had vanished and wiped its blade on the grass. He would give it a proper clean at the cottage and then he would return to the house. He needed to sleep but he reckoned better there than in the cottage. It wouldn't do to have Liz or others come looking. Yet.

Chapter Eleven

"Can you hack it? Hack it? Geddit?" Groans rumbled along the line. Alec knew he should shut up but the words kept spewing out of his mouth. He couldn't help it, the *sound* of words against the growing darkness reassured him, steadied him with their sense of normality. If he kept hearing it, he knew he wouldn't go mad, although at the same time he knew he was driving his five companions nuts. At least they couldn't strangle him, despite their many threats. The ropes bound them too tightly for that. He still couldn't believe Vinnie had mooted this idea only four weeks ago, and here they were. Out in the cold, tied up looking like scarecrows on bloody Halloween. Oliver had moved with frightening speed. As if he'd planned it all way before Vinnie ever opened his big mouth.

"Knock, knock," he started.

"Shit, Alec. Can't you …"

"Knock, knock," he repeated, ignoring Vinnie, feeling the weight of the blackened sky press down on him. If he kept speaking, he'd keep breathing.

"Who's there?" Callum's slurred voice played its part.

"Wood."

"Wood who?"

Alec remained silent. His punchline vanished as his words, his bloody stupid words, brought him back to their situation. It was the end of their first day, two more still to go and that didn't include the nights. A distant cry cut through him. Some nocturnal animal, that was all. He was an adult, a full-grown man and it shouldn't be fazing him—but it was.

"Cat got your tongue, Alec?" piped up Andy

The runt of the group, he'd been quiet since the villagers had trodden back across the fields to their cosy little homes, their snug little beds. Where he should be, by rights.

"Why the fuck did we agree to this?" he asked plaintively.

"Because we wanted to put things right," snapped Vinnie. "It's for Fred. Remember?"

Alec bit his tongue, tried, really tried. "I …"

"Not one word, not one bloody word," said Vinnie.

The group fell quiet. The novelty of their idea, the buzz of the idea of vengeance had worn off and they were having to deal with the cold reality. Literally. The breeze was mercifully gentle, mild for late October. Alec could smell the freshly-turned soil, the hay from the nearby Dutch barn, the cows in the next field. He wondered briefly why Callum's dad hadn't taken them in, then remembered his state in the pub. The man apparently spent more of his time there than on the farm these days. Whilst they had subsidies to keep the land fallow, it meant a lot of time twiddling thumbs, or downing pints.

Alec's holiday leave had turned into a sabbatical and he'd exchanged his room at the inn for one above the bookshop, the flat having remained empty since Cameron's death. It felt as if the village had sunk its hooks into him and didn't want to let him go. He'd returned home once to pack up his things and then put the house on the rental market. He could at least get some money from the place while he was away. Vinnie had already more than once declared he would be leaving with Alec when the time came. Alec had not said no. Neither said anything to Doug. The event, which had initially been presented as a crazy stunt, a cheesy idea really, to try and breathe some life into the village had taken on a more sinister life of its own. A few knew the hidden aim of the event, most had been kept in the dark.

Folk horror had become big news in recent times. Sparked festivals and gatherings in rural areas across the country, allowed a little of the money sloshing about in towns and cities to trickle out to into the hedgerows and furrows.

Little Hatchet, almost buried in the mouth of GodBeGone Woods, had its own story, a tale more monstrous than many of its rural cousins, and that was the key to this event. The idea of it once being real. They promised chills and thrills at *this* gathering.

Oliver had read out *The Summoning* that morning as the sun rose behind them and the villagers bound their limbs.

When Alec heard the words, his gaze was drawn back to the woods and try as he might, he could not look away. A cold, creeping sensation had taken hold and was with him still. It partly explained his continued non-stop talking. The old rhyme from the journal had been read prior to the Summoning, a nice dramatic touch, even if it increased his strange sense of foreboding:

> *When the worm crawls across the land*
> *And rot eats away at the heart*
> *When decay corrupts the innocent*
> *And families are torn apart*
> *When day is gone and night remains*
> *And no light is seen at all*
> *It is time to call the Woodcutter*
> *And allow his blade to fall*

The audience had lapped it up, spent their money in the beer tent, added their names to the list of sponsors. Oliver Hayward, property developer and self-styled entrepreneur. He had a way of making money. The Midas touch.

And so here they were. The six of them bound to crosses on the Little Hatchet skyline. Six human scarecrows. Waiting for the

Woodcutter. The monster from Fred and Vinnie's resurrected fairy tale.

Three days and three nights they had to last. Would he take one of them, would he take all? When? They'd already agreed two of them would 'disappear' on the second night. An instance which would be conveniently caught on camera by those filming the night's events.

A local journalist had been present, some local teens filming, ready to add to the blogs and vlogs they'd created to publicise the event. Facebook, WhatsApp, Twitter, Instagram. They had social media covered. The youth of the village had already decided this would be their *Blair Witch* moment. Oliver even opened a GoFundMe page, *Save Little Hatchet* and donations had already started to trickle in.

Alec recalled the words of *The Summoning* and shuddered:

Man of the Woods, we offer you
Six of our finest sons
Man of Wood, we offer you
Our children's blood and bones
Man of the Woods, we call on you
As Nature's son of oak
To hew away the rot within
Carve anew our human cloak

Alec found himself staring again at the wood, its presence hypnotising him, its shade a deeper black than the sky above them, forming a void, dense, waiting, hungry. For a moment he felt himself tipping, sliding towards it but the ropes held, although it seemed as if they were cutting into him.

With a start, Alec realised he'd been nodding off, he'd been dreaming. A vague image remained of a tree-lined path and a little boy walking with his father, a cottage ahead and the door open. His memory or just a dream? Soft snores and heavy breathing from the others indicated they had miraculously fallen asleep and remained so. The copious amount of alcohol offered throughout the evening had obviously done the trick. Alec envied them. He didn't want to be this aware of the shadowy world around them. He breathed in, noticing the musty, decaying tang in the air which seemed to become more and more pronounced as the season wore on. A scraping sound reached his ears. Rocking. He shook his head and the noise vanished.

At least Oliver allowed comfort breaks to be factored in, otherwise the next few days could get very messy.

"Do you really think it's just a story?" asked Andy, tied up on his left, the two of them at the end of the row. He'd been quiet for some time and Alec thought he too had been asleep.

The sound of his voice, even if it was Andy, comforted him. It took away his growing sense of isolation.

"Course it is," said Alec. "Old wives' tale. Told to keep the kids in order. You know, like the Sandman'll take your eyes if you don't go to sleep, the Woodcutter'll chop of your head if you don't eat your greens or something ..."

The two chuckled quietly, enjoying the relief of a lighter moment. Until Callum at the other end of the row stirred and started to speak. Only it didn't sound like Callum, his voice deep and scratchy, and at first it seemed as if he was repeating the *The Summoning*.

"*Man of the woods, we offer you*"

"For Christ's sake, Callum, shut it," hissed Alec. "Let the others sleep."

"*Six of our blighted sons,*" he continued.

"He's having a laugh," said Andy. "Changing the words, creepy voice. He's trying to spook us. Like always."

Yeah, thought Alec. He'd got to know this group of young men, Vinnie's friends quite quickly. *Bloody typical and yet ...*

"*Man of Bark, we offer you*
The wood of our children's bones"

"Enough's enough, Callum," said Alec, still hoping not to wake the others. Vinnie with a hangover was not a pleasant experience at close quarters.

"Man of Oak, we call on you
To cleave this gift apart
Man of the Woods, we give to you
Their guilty, blackened hearts."

On Callum's left, Eric stirred. "Wha … what you saying, Callum? Callum?"

But Callum remained quiet. He'd appeared to have fallen asleep again. Alec considered him for a minute. He wasn't the sort to make such things up. More than likely this was one of Oliver's little ideas. Those *touches* he said he would add to the proceedings to aid authenticity.

Nobody else spoke. Alec couldn't tell who was awake or who slept. He could only hear Nature's nocturnal music, the hoot of a distant owl, the rustling of leaves, the sound of small creatures scurrying in the undergrowth. Eventually, even those murmurings faded away and there was nothing except a silence more profound than anything he had ever experienced. It was like a vacuum and it was pulling his gaze back towards GodBeGone Woods which seemed to have expanded, was inching step-by-step towards him, swallowing up the village at its edge, slithering across the fields, up towards the six who were bound there. A river of ink rolling over everything, consuming the world.

A sleeping demon, rolling over and waking up as the offering was made. Hunger pangs of an appetite long-suppressed, rumbling beneath. A creature he'd once known. Walking in the woods, hand-in-hand with his father.

"Wakey, wakey, sleepyheads."

He jerked his head upright. Groaned aloud at the ache in his joints. Oliver and Evan were there, firing up a barbecue. Full English they'd been promised. Every day. Their mothers were keeping away, supportive, whilst still regarding it all as a *'bloody stupid idea'*, as Andy's mum had said.

Alec's mind turned to Fred, wondering where he was. He hadn't been seen in the village for days and his house appeared empty. Reverend Chadwick said he'd probably gone away until the event was over, he disliked the idea so much. That was the message being given out in public, to those not 'in the know'. It worried the rest of them. Fred had worked so hard to bring people round to his side and help him get the closure and justice he craved, it struck them as odd he would disappear like this. They hoped he was hiding in the forest somewhere, would come out soon.

So far, any searches had been brief and perfunctory. The village was too busy for the moment to do anything more. Whilst Doug was worried about his brother-in-law, he also wanted to make sure Oliver's event didn't spiral out of control. His sons had to come first for the time-being.

Alec heard Andy stretch and groan as Evan, Len's occasional barman, released him.

"Shit, I ache."

"Language, boy," admonished Evan.

They had half-an-hour before they were tied up again.

"Time to eat, piss and be merry, for tomorrow we die," joked Callum, looking at his watch.

"Shut it," said Alec. "You kept us awake half the night with that nonsense you were spouting …"

"Nonsense? What nonsense? Last thing I remember was you mentioning the Sandman—and *you* by the way could keep your voice down more—and then I dropped off."

"Can you remember what he said?" asked Evan as they all sipped from the mugs of strong tea doled out by Oliver.

"Some doggerel or other," said Andy, although Alec knew he remembered it as well as himself.

The words etched themselves into him and wouldn't let go. Evan was looking at him expectantly. The smell and sizzle of bacon drifted across. Someone turned on the radio and music danced around them. It was another normal day. He relaxed. Words, that was all. Callum's joke.

Alec looked at Evan and started to recite:

"Man of the woods, we offer you
Six of our blighted sons.
Man of Bark, we offer you
The wood of our children's bones
Man of Oak, we call on you
To cleave this gift apart
Man of the Woods, we give to you
Their guilty, blackened hearts."

When he'd finished, everyone had gone quiet. The radio had stopped and so had the general chatter. Evan was very pale. Alec's stomach sank. That wasn't the effect he'd hoped for.

"And did you *see* anything?" asked the Reverend Chadwick, who had recently arrived and been listening to the conversation. "Anything from the forest?"

"No, nothing," said Alec. "Only the woods, although they seemed so black it was as if the trees were smothering the village."

"That would've been you nodding off, you pillock," said Vinnie.

They all laughed except the minister, who turned to face the woods. "He's waking up," said Chadwick. "He'll be here soon." His tone dampened their spirits further.

Oliver laughed. "Oh, that's good, Chadwick. We'll get that added to the blog to make it creepier, ramp up the views. Good one! That'll put the village on the map."

They all relaxed a little, apart from Chadwick, who refused to join in the banter and kept his gaze fixed firmly on the trees. Eventually, Oliver approached the man and slipped an arm round his shoulders, rather forcefully guiding him towards the beer tent, whispering furiously in his ear. Alec longed to know what that conversation were about, tried to follow but suddenly it was time and Oliver whirled round to face him.

"Half-hour's up," he said.

"Already?"

"Can't be …"

"You need to be in place for the cameras," said Oliver.

"You make that sound like a proper TV …" Vinnie's voice trailed off.

Alec could see Oliver grinning.

"Oh, my fucking God," said Vinnie. "It is. Isn't it? You've gone and got us on the bleedin' telly!"

"Yes, lads. I have. Although, I must ask you to moderate your rather enthusiastic language when they're around. Don't want to be cut from the programme do we?"

Another small group of people could be seen entering the field. Their mothers had been summoned. Alec felt a pang as he thought of his own, noticed Vinnie's was missing—still.

"Come to wash your mouths out," laughed Oliver.

Five minutes later, Alec felt as though his face was on fire. Callum's mum rubbed every bit of exposed skin as hard as she could. A mother's touch, eh? He could do without it.

"Mrs um …," he protested, trying to remember her surname and failing. "I wasn't that dirty to begin with …"

"None of the men of our village is going to appear on national TV with a dirty neck …"

"They're not going to check behind our ears!"

"Pity we can't change your clothes."

"Mum!" yelled Callum, from his end of the row. "It's about being a scarecrow. They're dirty, tatty, ragged. It's not a fashion show. The more worn and tired we look, the better. Wait, did you say *national* TV?"

Alec looked at Oliver again, the man was changing into a fresh jacket, become the image of the urbane entrepreneur he usually projected in the village.

"Contacts, Callum, my boy. Got a friend at the BBC who's a Halloween nut. If all goes well today, we might even get them onboard for a vigil on the last night."

My boy. Alec hated the man's patronising tone towards them all plus he was only a couple of years older than Alec. Jarringly, the man had a lifestyle way beyond his own. Birth. Wealth. Contacts. All handed to him on a plate. He'd never struggled. Then again, although Oliver was using them to his own ends—whatever they may be—Alec and the rest were also using him. He couldn't gripe about that or where would they be? For the first time he imagined the outcome of their little plan with a degree of satisfaction.

The mothers had retreated to some nearby hay bales, patting their hair and checking out their own appearances as they did so, obviously aiming to get their minute in the spotlight.

Another black shape appeared from the village, and for a moment, Alec felt as if some of the trees themselves had broken away from the wood and were marching up. As they came nearer, he realised it was the *whole* village. Every single soul determined to share this fleeting moment of fame.

A number of teens were already before the six, holding up their phones to take selfies, trying to do the same when the brunette from the BBC news came into view. No one could ever recall her name, but they all recognised her as 'that woman on telly'. That was enough for this celebrity-obsessed group.

Eventually, the cameraman was set up to her approval and everyone fell quiet. Even though he strained his ears, Alec could not make out a single word of her interview with Oliver, although both occasionally looked their way.

"What's she say?" he asked Andy.

"Dunno, can't make it out."

"Shut it, you two," said Vinnie. "I'm trying to listen and I can't hear a bloody thing."

Finally, the TV crew came over to the men. Oliver took centre stage, pretty much hiding Vinnie from view, much to the latter's chagrin. Again, there was question and answer, a little background on the story of the Woodcutter. And still he could not make out what was being said. He began to wonder if Callum's mum had damaged his hearing when she'd attacked him with the flannel.

Then he heard Oliver speak. "The lads didn't see much last night but *one* of them appeared to have been taken over by something."

"Possessed?" asked the reporter, moving closer to Oliver, intrigued. A good act.

"Possibly. But Callum, the one on the end here …"

Alec glanced along and saw Callum straighten up a little. Smile for the camera.

"Callum recited a different, and somewhat more disturbing, version of *The Summoning*."

"Would he care to recite it for us?" asked the reporter.

"Unfortunately, he has no recollection of the incident. His companions heard it and told me this morning. I've made a note of it here, if you'd like me to read it. Although I'm not sure I should. I mean, we might raise the Devil."

"You mock something you know nothing about!" A figure barged its way through the line of teens who'd swarmed forwards. Chadwick. Oliver looked annoyed, whatever he said to the minister hadn't worked and the man was pretty upset.

"Don't do it," he said. "If you wake him, you won't be safe. None of us'll be safe. We've still time. There's still time, a chance he'll fall asleep again."

Chadwick had reached Oliver's side, was trying to snatch the paper from his hand. It would have been almost comical if the man hadn't seemed so desperate. The cameras kept rolling, lapping up the unexpected drama.

"You make him sound like a sleeping giant," said the reporter. "A bit like the legend of King Arthur, who'll wake and return one day to rescue his kingdom in its time of need."

"He is not just a giant," said Chadwick, turning on the woman, eyes flashing, spitting out his words. "He's a demon, a bloodthirsty monster. About as far removed from Arthur as you could get."

"Like the boogeyman," said the reporter, unperturbed. "The monster under your bed, in your closet, in the woods …"

At a gesture, the cameraman panned back around and Alec knew he was going over the heads of the spectators, zooming in on that stain of bark and timber, through the rustling whispering foliage, into its black, black centre.

"If you knew," whispered Chadwick, "if you'd seen him, you wouldn't do this."

Only Alec seemed to hear the man. Something had changed in Chadwick's demeanour. Scepticism turned into belief. Why? All eyes returned to Oliver who was smoothing out the crumpled paper. He began to speak.

"This is the version of *The Summoning* as recited by Callum MacDonald last night. I'm sure you will agree it is slightly more sinister than the original version.

> *Man of the woods, we offer you*
> *Six of our blighted sons.*
> *Man of Bark, we offer you*
> *The wood of our children's bones*
> *Man of Oak, we call on you*
> *To cleave this gift apart*
> *Man of the Woods, we give to you*
> *Their guilty, blackened hearts."*

The watchers again turned towards the forest, a hush, soft, expectant, almost fearful fell over everything. The atmosphere was building exactly as they'd hoped but to Alec it no longer felt like play acting. It felt real.

Then he noticed the birds were no longer singing. Even Nature waited, holding its breath whilst the forest seemed to move, a swirling motion at its centre, lines appearing and disappearing as if something huge was walking through it. A path was being formed. Then it stopped. And it was as if the world exhaled.

The rest of the interview faded out. Alec could see people nodding and smiling, milling about, but again he could not discern their words. Not until the camera crew made their way back to the village with most of the village in tow.

"Why've they all gone with them?" asked Paul. "What about our moral support?"

"They'll be back," said Evan. "Len wants to wow them with the pub's famed cuisine, Oliver's got his usual agenda, everyone else wants their piece of the action."

"And us?"

"As I said, they'll be back. Oliver's got a bit of entertainment planned for tonight but I can't tell you or it'll spoil the surprise."

"Can't you give us a clue?" asked Callum.

"All I can tell you is that it'll warm the cockles of your poor blighted hearts."

They all laughed. All except Alec who felt his eyes drawn to the sprawling forest. A shiver ran down his spine. Tonight, was the night two of them would disappear and already he felt as if the script was being rewritten. Someone else directing the show.

CHAPTER TWELVE

Oliver had been pleased with the day's events, they'd mostly gone according to plan. Mostly, because that bloody Reverend Chadwick had reneged on his part of the deal, seemed to want to put a spanner in the works, although in truth his interventions merely ramped the tension higher. For that, he would be spared—for the moment.

Liz and the camera crew were making their way back to the field, ready to film events whilst the men slept—and the youths did sleep despite their discomfort and their denials; the country air soon knocked them out. The crew needed to be present to watch the next part of his plan, to capture the disappearing of two of the young men, an apparent selection by the Woodcutter. He hadn't told the men who he would take, nor had he yet decided. That was why he'd returned to the cottage, to rest a while and consult with Grandma and the Woodcutter, choose his blades.

The storytellers were right about this being about the apprenticeship. Except they didn't realise *he'd* been the apprentice and it was the current ongoing ritual which formally marked the end of that stage. Tonight, he would begin to etch the grains on his skin, knots and whorls for each life taken. Already he had carved a design on his arm for his offering of Fred. It was bandaged and covered at the moment as it healed. Liz had assumed it was some intricate tattoo.

He took down the small mirror and placed it on the table, picked up the scalpel waiting for him. Oliver stared at his reflection, his eyes appearing as black pools, studying the valley of his face. He raised the blade to his cheek, slid it along the skin, etching flesh with rivers of blood and gradually, vines and leaves began to appear as if on canvas. He made no sound as he mutilated himself, the cuts deep enough to ensure they scarred, textured his bark. Eventually, he finished, looked from himself in the mirror to the carving on the back of the door, nodding with satisfaction. The apprentice would soon become the master.

Oliver ignored the splatter of blood down his front, allowed it to crust and dry on his shirt. He waited quietly for his skin to heal before applying the cosmetic concealer he'd taken from Liz's special effects crew. They'd spent an afternoon teaching him the tricks of the trade, reducing themselves to hysterics as they turned him into the legendary monster, Liz into Grandma. There was even a photo somewhere. He didn't want to hide himself again but soon there would be no need for such tricks. If anybody noticed anything, they wouldn't comment, accept it as part of Oliver's production.

Then he moved to the bed and lay down, closed his eyes against the night, he would allow himself a short rest before he carried out his final trial. The silence became even more profound, a blanket stilling his thoughts and allowing his eyes to close, his mind to sleep. His breathing was steady and regular, deeply he breathed in, inhaling more of those motes disturbed by his presence, allowing them to find a new home after years of mouldering in the dark.

Gradually shadows formed around him, he sensed his visitors had arrived, Grandma and Woodcutter nudged at him to wake up. It was time to talk. Oliver swung his feet onto the floor, tried to get his bearings. His head felt groggy and the light was blurry. The shapes moved in front of him. One small and bent over, shuffling its way to the rocking chair where it sat and began to rock to and fro, the creaks a reminder of that childhood summer's soundtrack.

"Here we are again, boy," said Grandma, "although you're not a lad, full grown man at last."

"Old enough to take my place," said the Woodcutter, "if you prove yourself."

The giant was leaning against the cold, dead fireplace, his dark shadow looming over grandma. The axe was at his feet.

"Should say you've been doing a fine job so far. Couldn't have set it all up better myself."

Oliver looked at the two shapes, they still seemed slightly fuzzy but their words were sharp, like the blades glinting on the wall behind him. He could feel their approval, their pride in him.

"Will you come back ... properly?" he asked. "When I've decorated the tree, made the offering?"

"Of course, lad," said Grandma. "I've missed our little family, wanted us to be together again. It's been so long. But we always knew you would come back. We've been waiting for you. This is your home. Come here, boy. Come and sit near me, like you used to."

Oliver staggered across the room, his head reeling. A firm hand reached out and steadied him, the Woodcutter, guiding him to sit beside Grandma. He slumped onto the stool so recently occupied by Fred, shook his head to try and clear the fuzziness.

He was not allowed to rest as a fist hammered on the door.

"Open up, Oliver! We need to talk."

Reverend Chadwick. The man was becoming a hindrance. His hand twitched, reached out steel.

"No, lad," said the Woodcutter from the shadow. "Not yet. We need our man of the cloth to preach his empty words a little while longer. But soon, soon you can have him. In the meantime, we weave our web around him. Keep him on side. Let him in."

Reluctantly, Oliver made his way to the door. "How d'you know I was here?"

"Saw you march into the woods, didn't I? We all did. Must say you've got the tongues wagging, I mean no one's ever gone in these woods – or at least gone in and come out again as far as I can remember."

"Yes, well, superstition and all that," said Oliver. "You know what it's like around here."

Chadwick peered over Oliver's shoulder. "Either way, hope I'm not disturbing you. I thought I heard voices."

"Must've been the radio," said Oliver smoothly. "Come in, you can tell me what's got you so riled up that you had to come calling at this time of night."

He stood aside to let the minister into the cottage, smelt the whisky beneath the mint. His ancestor had polluted the woods with his presence but Chadwick was acceptable. His faith was a sham, although he concealed it well enough from his dwindling congregation. *Let us talk to him, said Grandma and the Woodcutter.*

The reverend sat down in the rocking chair, accepted the drink Oliver offered. Behind them in the shadows, Grandma and the Woodcutter watched.

Oliver regarded his visitor for a moment. The man did not believe in God, but he did believe in an old folk memory. "I'm curious," he said. "You really believe the stories about Grandma and the Woodcutter. I thought you would've ascribed that too, to superstitious belief."

"Many have trouble believing the Bible," said the reverend. "I will include myself in that, in all honesty. For my part I consider many of the tales as fantastical, mere morality polemics to ensure the obedience of the uneducated. However, I have never denied the existence of good and evil, especially in society today. The news is always full of reports of man's inhumanity to man. Greed, corruption, murder, all is there in black and white *and* around us in flesh and blood. I believe the couple known as Grandma and Woodcutter existed and that they truly were evil individuals with warped minds, playing on people's fears for their own ends. I believe those who came after and claimed to be them reincarnated were deluded but their delusions too, were birthed from a desire to do harm. Some places carry that influence, a feeling that seeps into your bones, into your thoughts." As he spoke, the minister shivered, cast his eyes around the small room as if sensing a presence.

"Are we really alone?" he asked.

"Can you see anyone else, besides us?" replied Oliver.

"No," said Chadwick. "But I get such a strange feeling."

"Finish your drink, Reverend," said Oliver. "It'll make you feel better, dispel the shadows and demons you're so frightened of."

"I'm not frightened of any demons," said Chadwick. "It's human devils that concern me. I've been reading my father's old papers, his diaries. He mentioned you in them. All those years ago, when that couple lived here and they sucked you into their charade. I doubt many people round here remember that, what would the effect be on them do you think, when they realise what you did? I mean once Fred opens his mouth ..."

"But Fred won't be opening his mouth," said Oliver, fixing his eyes on Chadwick.

The minister paled at Oliver's words. "Where *is* Fred? I haven't seen him lately. What have you done to him?"

"Me? I've done nothing," said Oliver. "He came to see me and then left. I dare say he's hanging around somewhere, licking his wounds."

"You trivialise his loss?"

"No, no, of course not," said Oliver. "We had a chat. He forgave me. I was a child after all."

"And are you still that child?" asked the reverend. It was his turn to lean forward and look into Oliver's eyes as if searching for something there.

"No," said Oliver. "I'm a man trying to make a living."

Reverend Chadwick leaned back, allowed the chair to rock a little. "Something that's hard to do these days," he said. "Live. I have little time left. Sometimes I wish I could have more but seeing you, what you've become, I think I'll be glad to be gone. GodBeGone if you like."

A poor joke and neither laughed.

And there it was. *We have him*, said Grandma and Woodcutter. *No need for us to do anything. Play along with the little man, he'll be gone soon enough but we can still use him.*

Oliver nodded his head. "I'm sorry to hear it," he said. "Is this one of those times when you try to do the right thing before you leave this mortal coil? I suppose I should at least be comfortable while you lecture me. Another drink?"

Chadwick accepted the refilled tumbler, his eyes too blurry to notice the cloudy quality of the liquor handed to him, the grains he swallowed down with the alcohol. Soon his eyes had closed fully.

"Let him sleep here a while," said Grandma. "When he wakes, he will finally be able to see us and having such a partner will be useful in bringing the villagers here."

CHAPTER THIRTEEN

With the excitement of the TV report over for the time being, Alec allowed his mind to wander back towards the woods. Apart from the funeral, he had never actually crossed its threshold. Vinnie told him he and Cam had gone in, when small, hovering at its edge, following its perimeter to see if they could guess the size of it, perhaps find a forester's track leading in. But there had been nothing.

Occasionally, they would spy a gap in the dense foliage at its rim and Vinnie, or Cam, would take it in turns to try diving in, only for the gap to mysteriously disappear and they would find themselves caught up in a tangle of branches and thorns.

Vinnie had recalled one particular time when, towards dusk, and way past the time to go home, the two boys found another gap. Larger this time, large enough for a man—or a giant—to get through. The two boys had approached but could not make that final step. Something stopped them.

"Why didn't you go in?" asked Alec. "There must've been something more stopping you."

Vinnie turned his head, slowly Alec knew, because of the growing stiffness they were all experiencing. He was looking at the crowd of trees. Two brothers in the present dwelling on two brothers in the past. One of them bridging the gap of years in-between.

"Just thinking about it actually," he confessed.

"D'you remember what you saw ..."

"What we *thought* we saw," corrected Vinnie. "We agreed ..."

"Yes, but what if you *really* saw what you thought you saw ..."

Alec pondered the memory, the glimpse of what lay beyond. What had his brothers seen all that time ago? An imaginary monster, the product of an overactive imagination? Or something real, a warning not to come any closer.

He'd been told Callum's dad owned the land this side of the wood, his holding curving part way round its edge. The remaining land skirting the perimeter belonged to two other farmers, one being Andy's dad.

"Who owns the woods anyway?" asked Alec. "Andy?"

"Not our family," said Andy. "And I know it doesn't belong to old Lewis. Him and Dad talked about trying to buy it some years ago. Wanted to get into the timber trade. You know, it was around the time the government said we had to diversify ..."

"Yeah," growled Callum. "Diversify or die. Bloody suits suggested llamas and ostrich, a golf course for fuck's sake. Dad said if we were paid properly for our milk and crops, we wouldn't have to do this. But no ..."

Alec felt they were going off track. Callum was merely repeating the arguments that had gone round and round in their homes, in the village and in other farming communities like theirs. The stranglehold of the supermarkets, the imposition of airy-fairy metropolitan ideals who preferred their lanes muck free, the roosters quiet, the old traditions stopped. Nature was bloody but the city folk wanted to Disneyfy their lives. Perhaps one of these had bought the woods. Perhaps some developer.

"Oliver?" suggested Alec.

Vinnie shook his head. "No, it's not him. Cam checked out his holdings. Went to the Land Registry."

"Lot of effort, mate," said Andy. "You did all that? Why?"

"Why'd you think? Cam had a feeling Oliver was one of those types who never does anything unless there's something in it for them. Even this … I know everyone wants to raise money for the village but I wanted to make sure he wasn't going to use us any more than he has done others."

"You don't want us to be scammed," said Callum, understanding.

They could all appreciate that. There'd always been a hint of something shady about the man. Made sense to check him out. If you were going to get into bed with the Devil, it made sense to take precautions. And this had all been before Alec arrived in the village, when Cam and Vinnie were first discussing the idea with Oliver and they hadn't known of his link to the tragic history of the past and to themselves.

"What about the Land Registry anyway? Did it tell you anything more about the woods?" Callum seemed curious.

"No …" said Vinnie.

"Why not? I thought all land records were held there …"

"Yes. But when I searched for GodBeGone it didn't exist. Oh, I found plans of the area, maps. The three farms around it, the village. But the wood itself did not exist. I have raised a query but they said it would take some time to investigate. If I want to fast track it, I'll have to pay."

"How much?" asked Andy.

"Too much for me," said Vinnie.

"Then that *doesn't* rule out Oliver," said Alec. "And I might be able to help you with that. Speak of the devil."

Oliver's 4x4 was bouncing over the ruts. *He'd had enough of the walk, the symbolic pilgrimage already*, thought Alec. Then he saw the trailer and another tractor following behind with a huge flatbed carrying something massive.

"Your dad's going to have to replough, Callum," said Vinnie.

"They're making a right mess of the field. Keep this up and it'll be a right quagmire.

"All we need is rain …"

As if on cue, grey clouds rolled above them darkening both the sky and their mood.

"Suppose it had to happen," said Alec. "Do you think they'll give us umbrellas?"

"Nah, forget it," said Callum. "Oliver's really getting his kicks out of this. I reckon he'll make us suffer as much as possible. This is a bloody stupid idea and parts of my body ache that I never knew existed and I'm bored out of my fucking head …"

"What did I say about language?"

Oliver stood before them, the TV reporter at his side, holding on to his arm. *Christ, he was a quick worker*, thought Alec.

"But as regards your little problem of boredom, I've taken steps to remedy that. Tonight, is going to be a night of tall tales. You'll hear some wonderful stories, guys. And of course, a bonfire to warm us up in case our tales are too chilling."

"And that thing?" asked Callum nodding his head in the direction of the flatbed. It looked like a giant woven basket.

"Thought we'd create our own version of the Wicker Man. Add a bit of 'folk ritual' to proceedings, the punters'll love it."

"Our version?" asked Alec.

A farmhand brought over a huge piece of flimsy wood at that point. He turned it round and Alec gasped.

"And this is the face he'll wear," said Oliver, grinning triumphantly.

Alec stared. It was a crude etching but the whorls and tattoos carved on the face were not only like those he'd seen in the illustrations in the book. From the sharp intake of breath beside him, he knew Vinnie recognised it too. Carved into their brother's face. They should've been prepared for this but it was still a kick in the gut. He needed to remind himself why they were doing this— to get back at Oliver. So far, he seemed to be doing everything he could to rub *their* faces in it.

"Proper little Halloween treat you've got together," said Eric. "Didn't you choose the wrong night for it though?"

"Perhaps next year," said Oliver, smoothly. "But tomorrow is about all of you and the village. I didn't want to distract from that."

Callum's mum came up to them. "The phone won't stop ringing, Oliver. We've sold a load of tickets already."

"More money for Little Hatchet's fund," said Oliver, turning to the reporter. "Shows people don't want the rural way of life to die."

"After expenses," muttered Andy.

The woman glanced at him and looked thoughtful. Oliver didn't appear to have heard.

"I think what you're doing is wonderful and unique," she said. "Has anyone told you by the way, you've got quite an online fan club?"

"What?"

"Cool."

"Hey, Oliver. Any chance you can bring your iPad nearer. Show us exactly what you lot have been posting?"

"Sorry," said Oliver. "You're not going to see it until you're down. Don't want you acting out of character."

"Out of character? What have you been posting?" He struggled against his ties then tried to force his immobilised body closer. The ropes cut into him again and their burn forced him back.

"Don't worry. You've all been presented in a very positive light."

The small group of teens responsible for filming each day's events and writing up the blog entries giggled and whispered at his words. Alec frowned.

"Hope you're right, or you're in big trouble when I get out of this," said Vinnie.

His companions laughed.

"And I don't see what you find so amusing. I mean the same applies to you as well. What *have* they written about you lot?"

Eric's stomach growled loudly. "Forget the bickering, ladies. I spy lunch."

Their mothers were back. This time they were allowed down to relieve themselves in the nearby 'facilities'—the hedge in other words, a screen thoughtfully put up for them. Nonetheless, Alec was very aware of the small handheld cameras following them. If one of them came round their side, he swore to God, he'd punch them.

He stretched as much as possible as he made his way back to his post. His limbs were becoming increasingly numb and he'd barely been able to prevent himself from falling when they'd been released. Unlike Eric who'd collapsed in an embarrassing heap, a moment very definitely caught on camera.

With hands tied, others had to feed them; yesterday, by their parents and he assumed the same would happen again today.

"Hold on, ladies," said Oliver, as the women were about to approach. "I've got a nice little treat for your sons. Here they come."

Another sleek Range Rover was making its way towards them. The windows were tinted. The TV crew were filming the vehicle, the reporter announcing its arrival, naming the occupants as each got out in their own version of rural attire.

"Fuck me, I've died and gone to heaven," said Vinnie.

The young men continued to stare as the six female 'stars' of Model Mania swayed towards them. They seemed to float over the mud, angels of perfection coming closer, closer.

"Men. These young ladies have donated their time and services to Little Hatchet's fund. They will be part of our Spooktacular storytelling session, plus they've agreed to photo calls and autographs."

They'd get through that quick, thought Alec. Only a handful of villagers and most of them so old they wouldn't recognise the stars. And then he looked up again. People. Hundreds of people swarming up the field towards them. It was all getting out of hand. How could they possibly cope?

Another turn of the head and he saw what Len'd been up to all morning. A huge marquee had become a beer tent. Even a couple of portaloos placed further down the field.

How on earth had all this happened and he hadn't even noticed? Because he kept watching the woods, he realised. It was as if it hypnotised him, taken him away for hours on end. He wanted to ask the others if they too experienced anything similar, but that would have to wait.

The models had opened up the sandwiches, were walking towards them. Nita. He recognised her straight away. His favourite of the bunch was walking straight to *him*. His mouth was suddenly dry, he couldn't speak. Instead gasped like some stupid country bumpkin rather than the cooler cosmopolitan type he always imagined himself. A month in the sticks, involved in a family revenge drama and spending three nights like some bloody scarecrow. He could not have imagined a more bizarre turn of events if he'd tried.

"Hi," said Nita. "Hope you like chicken." She held the sandwich towards him so he could take a bite. "A little at a time," she cautioned. "Do you mind if I share?"

No, he did not. Could only stare as her perfect teeth bit into a tiny sliver, her lips closing over the piece to chew slowly, carefully. He swallowed and she fed him another bite.

Then she held a straw to his lips and he drank swiftly from the can.

"Thanks," he croaked when he'd finished.

"Any time," she replied and gave him a peck on the cheek before moving over to the circle of hay bales serving as seating in front of the giant wicker effigy of the Woodcutter.

None of them spoke, continued to stare at the women who were being interviewed by the reporter. Liz, he thought her name was.

"Knew you'd like that," said Oliver. "This event is getting bigger and bigger." He was rubbing his hands.

"What about health and safety, planning and all that?"

For an off-the-cuff event this was all surprisingly well organised.

"Sort of thing I'm good at," said Oliver, smugly. "Someone comes up with a good idea and I see it through."

Alec heard Vinnie growl. The others also looked annoyed. One day somebody would come along and burst Oliver's bubble. Alec smiled. That day would be soon. The bigger the event, the bigger his downfall. *Where was Fred?* This was what he'd dreamed of.

The news reporter had rejoined them. Oliver slipped his arm round her. Alec noticed she didn't look completely comfortable at that, the look that passed between them, but nor did she shrug him off.

"What story are you going to tell tonight, Liz?"

"The one about the Woodcutter of course. The full, unexpurgated version. I mean who would pass up the chance of a captive audience."

"Come on," said Oliver. "Show me the script and I'll buy you a drink."

The two headed towards Len's marquee leaving the group alone.

The six of them seemed to have been forgotten as everyone bustled about to make things ready for the evening.

"Ever feel like you've become part of the scenery, invisible?" asked Eric.

"Thought we were the stars of the show," muttered Vinnie.

Alec felt that way, too, but fought it down as he noticed how everyone had put so much effort into the setup: the bonfire, the circles of bales for seats, the food and beer tents. If he wasn't tied up, he'd be enjoying himself.

"At least our mums haven't forgotten us," said Andy.

"Your mum, maybe," said Vinnie.

"Is it because I'm here?" asked Alec.

He received no answer which was answer enough. Occasionally he glimpsed Carol around the village and she'd glared at him before scurrying away. Vinnie didn't seem to mind her absence from the field too much. Alec sensed there were many rows at home and not all about him.

He watched the new arrivals approach with their food. Had it been that long since lunch? These lapsed moments of time were beginning to haunt Alec.

"No models for you this time, I'm afraid," said Caitlin, Callum's mum.

"Only us."

"Nah, you could give them a run for their money any day," said Vinnie.

"Get on with you," said Caitlin.

"Yeah, I mean if I were …"

"Vinnie," warned Callum. "That's my mum and I'm right here."

Alec couldn't help smiling. Vinnie was a terrible flirt, always had been apparently. His own father declaring him 'all mouth and trousers' as they'd watched him work his way through the female population of the village. Yet the comment here was intended to be harmless, something to make the women feel good about themselves and Alec appreciated that.

Another comfort break and they were back in place. Oliver coming over briefly to whisper something to Andy and Eric. Probably about the 'disappearances' to come. The others knew it was to happen although the details had been kept from them, to provoke a genuine reaction, Oliver said and refused to be drawn any further.

The light began to fade. The grey clouds remained but not gifted them rain, instead they sped up the gathering dusk so that night fell so quickly Alec felt he'd been plunged into a big black hole.

Then he heard a low rumble, the sound of a generator kicking in and a small circle of spotlights appeared. Not to break the darkness completely but enough to highlight the storyteller in the circle, hint at the shape of the giant standing behind her.

A small fire flickered in front of her and it crossed Alec's mind it would only take a random spark to jump and the bales would go up in an instant. Judging the distance, he realised Oliver had paid heed to some safety precautions at least. The audience remained in shadow.

Alec shivered. For some reason, this didn't feel like a friendly gathering despite the soft murmur of voices as they waited, the aroma of beer and cider as drinks were dished out.

Apart from Liz, only one other person was remotely visible and that was Reverend Chadwick. He'd not seen the man for some time.

A week into retirement, Chadwick remained in the village but had become something of a recluse. Now though? A man of the cloth supporting a pagan ritual?

All in a good cause, he'd said. Besides it was a mere fairy story, a morality tale of sorts from long ago and the old stories should not be lost. Then Oliver entered the ring and a hush fell.

"Ladies and Gentlemen. Welcome to the inaugural *Night of the Woodcutter!* An event borne with the purpose of supporting a cause very dear to our hearts, the village of Little Hatchet," he paused to allow a smattering of applause, "and also to revive and maintain many of our rural traditions. One feature of those long-ago days was the tradition of the travelling bard, the wandering storyteller, who would sit by the fire on nights like this and entertain folk with stories to both chill and thrill the heart. Tonight, we revive this lost feature of rural life and I ask you to put away your phones and cameras (except those of you who are recording this for our sponsors ...)"

Sponsors? Oliver mentioned nothing about sponsors.

" ... and of course our friends from the BBC."

Muffled cheers rose at this and the cameraman stationed to Andy's left with his back to the forest, gave a small wave. Not that anyone else could really see.

The forest. GodBeGone Wood rose up out of the darkness, its leaves muttered at him, drew his attention away from his companions, the branches reached towards him, splintered fingers seeking his flesh, probing his face, roots slithering beneath the ground, running up through the soil, wrapping themselves around him. Tighter than the ropes already binding him. Then they pulled him down into the soil, the clods choking him, filling his mouth, his nose, eyes, taking him away, taking him back, reclaiming him ... Alec forced the images away, tried to concentrate on what was going on around him. He heard Oliver speaking.

"Thank you, Miriam for that rather ... um ... extraordinary rendition of the Nun's Tale. Another round of applause everyone."

A drunken cheer went up.

"And without further ado, I hand you over to Liz Riverdale, a familiar face to you all, at least if you tune to the good old BBC. Liz has a story guaranteed to send a shiver down your spine, consider the very real danger these young men have put themselves in. Ladies and Gentlemen, Liz Riverdale."

Liz smiled at the hidden audience, assured and confident. The crowd leaned forward. The cameraman had swung round and was sweeping across their faces, hovering a little longer on Alec's than the others.

"People of Little Hatchet, and those of you from beyond its borders. Look around you, and tell me what you see. Darkness? Yes. The moon. The slumbering countryside. The safe glow of light from the village. All exactly what you would expect from a rural spot like this. But look again. Look behind you. Do you see something more? Something huge, lying there in the background. Although it's not so much in the background any more. It's there, on the edge, crawling closer."

Alec watched the people watching her. She held them in the palm of her hand. Their eyes were wide, bright, they were lapping it up. Obediently they turned their heads to take in the landscape as she directed, back to the village, to the fields and then—fleetingly— to the woods. For some reason, their gaze did not linger there.

"You have already heard the words of The Summoning from Oliver Hayward. These were the words used to call up the giant known as the Woodcutter from GodBeGone Wood, the forest which surrounds our village, that mass to which I directed your attention a moment ago, and which, from what I understand, you have rarely entered. This morning, you heard another version of The Summoning, its words darker, its message crueller, horrifically clearer. Will you hear something different still tomorrow? Perhaps. If you survive the night."

Liz paused again. Allowed her words to sink in.

Alec had to admit she was good at this. Captured the mood and tone perfectly.

There was more to her than an autocue reader.

"Who was the Woodcutter, you ask. I would change that slightly and ask, who is the Woodcutter? Because he does exist. He lives in those trees behind us, in GodBeGone Wood. The forest is his home. Why has no one in recent times ever gone in? Because of the ancient barrier created by the priests who walked the bounds. You should also be thankful this barrier has prevented the Woodcutter from getting out."

Alec recalled Vinnie and Cameron's apparently abortive attempts all those years ago.

"So, he stays in the woods and looks after the trees and occasionally sleeps. But the Woodcutter will always hear if someone speaks the words of The Summoning, even if it is said in a whisper, he will still hear because these words are bindweed wrapped around his blackened heart. These words break down that invisible barrier around the trees, especially when it has been weakened through neglect, and allow him to roam the countryside once more."

Another pause. Absolute silence.

"So far, not so scary you might say. But think. What does he look like? What does he do? What is he after? Let me tell you about the Woodcutter, consider that first question. What does he look like? I could describe him, his size, his rough clothing but his skin? When you see his arms and face how can I do that and show you the real horror. No words can do him justice. So I have given you a picture, I have made his face as it was drawn in this little booklet centuries ago." She held the journal up in her hand.

"This book belonged to the ancestors of our good Reverend Chadwick here. In here is the story of the Woodcutter and I will show him to you."

At her words light flooded the area behind her, illuminating in full the wicker giant but shining most brightly on his face. There was a gasp. The monster stared down at them all. Again, his face appeared to ripple and shift. Alec could not tear his gaze away until the light dimmed a little and the shapes stilled. It unnerved him completely. Reverend Chadwick obviously felt the same way, judging by the look on his face.

"Wouldn't like to run into him down a dark alleyway," muttered someone.

"Nor me," said their companion.

Even though it was nothing more than an effigy, it seemed to have the same effect on everyone watching. Not one person scoffed or joked. They could all feel there was some truth in this story and they waited for it to be told.

CHAPTER FOURTEEN

"Like all good fairy tales," said Liz, "it began *Once upon a time* ... but this is the *true* story of Grandma and the Woodcutter and the Woodcutter's Apprentice. Not one story but three, forever intertwined and retold until somehow it became the tale of *Little Red Riding Hood*. A little girl who took on the Big Bad Wolf and won. A story which became a *lie* ..."

Nobody spoke. Even the wind had dropped and the fire muffled its crackling as if it, too, wanted to hear what Liz was about to say. Then she told the story Vinnie had recounted all those weeks ago in the Axeman's Arms. And time passed without him realising. He was walking in the woods, not with his father, but a woman. She said she'd been beautiful once and would be again. If he would help her. And he loved his Grandma, didn't he? A man, when grown would do anything for the woman he loved, for his Lilith. "Who's Lilith?" he'd asked. He woke with the sound of her laughter in his ears.

When Alec finally became aware of his surroundings, the lights had dimmed, the fire died down and Liz was hidden in darkness but other lights blazed up around the edge of the audience, behind the six on their crosses and after an initial moment of quiet, everyone started to talk. Len strode through the crowd reminding people to visit his beer tents whilst roping a few youths into becoming mobile refreshment stations.

Alec didn't feel hungry. The story, despite being so obviously an old folk tale, had hooked itself into him and as the lights rose on the spectators, he noticed one or two who didn't look happy. Recent times, Liz said. Had they too witnessed something as children?

"I need to pee," muttered Andy.

"Can't they give us a break as well?"

"Not until the end of the story telling," said Alec. "We could …"

"There's been a bit of a change in plan," said a voice. Reverend Chadwick stood in front of them. The man was like a ghost, disappearing and reappearing without a sound. "We thought we'd let you have a break now rather than at the end of the session. When Liz finishes the apprentice's tale, we want to pan the lights on to the six of you. Allow a bit of a question and answer session perhaps. Get some of the old 'uns to recount the stories they heard. It'll be more effective than if we had to stop and start for a break for you. We don't want to ruin the atmosphere."

"Trying to give the punters their money's worth, eh," said Callum. "Makes sense."

The six were released from their bindings and helped over to the portaloos rather than the hedge. It was getting harder to move, the longer they remained in one position, limbs becoming uncomfortably numb. Alec wondered if this was the moment Oliver was to be denounced. Neither he nor Vinnie had been told. Doug and Chadwick insisted they be kept ignorant of when everything would actually happen. If anything went wrong, not that it would, they didn't want the younger generation to be affected in anyway. What was to happen was the burden of their fathers.

Family once again helped them eat, although this time they were allowed to sit on the bales for a little while. As the reverend had said, when the interval was announced, their greatest ordeal was yet to come and it was best they were as prepared as they could be to face it. That the preparations involved steak sandwiches and pints of beer rather than prayers, confession and absolution, was neither here nor there.

All too soon, the six found themselves led to their crosses again.

"Glad my stint is almost at an end," muttered Andy, Eric nodding agreement as they took up positions.

"Ssh, don't want anyone hearing anything," said Vinnie. "Remember we're putting on a bit of a show. If someone hears you morons talking …"

"Don't worry, no one's listening," said Andy. "They're all trying to get another five minutes of fame, look."

They all looked. The news reporter was roving amongst the audience, cameraman trailing her. Seeking reactions to her story. What did *they* believe in? Why did they think the interest in folk horror had been reborn in the media? That was part of the angle Oliver said the news item would take, all in keeping with the Halloween theme.

"Shouldn't worry. Didn't the vicar say the spotlight would be back on us after the second part?"

"Yeah … oh shit … how?" Alec didn't need to say anything more. How were they going to carry out their plan for the disappearances, darkness and shadow was supposed to have been their cover.

"We'll have to let Oliver know."

"Oh, I think he'll have worked that out already. Chadwick's talking to him. He'll cotton on."

Sure enough, Oliver came over to them as soon as the Reverend moved away.

"Seems like a little change of plan, boys," he said. "We'll put it off until a little later. Don't worry, there'll still be a lot of people here. Once the lights go down around you lot to indicate the show's over, Len's bar is staying open for a bit longer. He didn't take much persuading. The man's taken a mint today and he's more than happy to do his bit."

"Might even help keep the pub open," said Vinnie. "He's been threatening to sell up for a while. Losing money all the time he says."

Oliver grinned. "With regards to that, I've already made a little proposition so you could say the pub's future is safe."

The group gave a low cheer causing not a few heads to turn puzzled looks in their direction.

"Pep talk," said Oliver with a grin, to the nearest audience members. "Building up the spirits for their second night."

The watchers turned back to their own conversations, easily satisfied. The sort who would fall for the little subterfuge later on. A bell rang. Time for everyone to return to their places for the evening's next instalment.

Liz was sat as before and the fire banked up in front of her. Again, Chadwick sat at her side, whispering into her ear, occasionally looking in their direction. Alec shuddered. There was something in those looks of his which made his skin crawl. He recalled the recent gossip about Chadwick's ill health, uncharitably felt relieved the man would not be with them much longer, no longer propping up the bar at the Arms, putting a damper on the evening.

Another signal from Oliver and silence fell across the fields. An owl hooted and a slight breeze blew up, rustling nearby leaves and stirring the undergrowth, sending the damp smell of a hidden world up to them to mix with the cold clear tang of night. Then that too dropped back and complete and utter quiet fell. This time she told them the story of the priest, the offering of the six. "And what you see," she finished, as the light fell on Alec and his friends, "is exactly what the villagers from all those years ago would have seen then."

The light made them blink and the spotlight made him feel uncomfortable, exposed. Despite their moans and groans earlier about the attention being elsewhere, when it was turned on them in this intense manner it was distinctly unnerving.

"What happened to those youths?" asked Liz. "They were not going to accept their fate so easily. Five of them were a group who caused nothing but trouble in the village and one who was usually the butt of their mischief. This five decided that it wouldn't be them, the Woodcutter picked but the runt of the group, Luke.

"Nobody knew how the selection was to be made until one of the group noticed the ever-growing flock of birds above them. Hovering as if waiting for a signal.

"Do you think the birds choose for him?" asked one as they nervously scanned the horizon, waiting for the monster with his axe to appear.

"Almost got my hands free," said another. "I'll be out in a jiffy."

"We still need to keep the Woodcutter happy."

"We can leave a volunteer," said the one who'd freed his hands and was working to untie his nearest companion. "You'll stand in for us, won't you, Lukey Luke. I mean, someone's got to be brave enough to face him."

The boy, Luke, said nothing, merely watched as the others were unbound.

"I know," said one. "Let's make sure the birds really choose him, I mean they like to be fed, don't they?"

"How?"

"Grab that pumpkin from over there. Farmer Cutler won't mind one from his patch for a good cause."

One of the youths did as he said and the others gathered round with curiosity as their leader carved out the insides and created a face, gruesome and leering. Then he ceremoniously placed it over Luke's head. "King of the Scarecrows, Lukey."

"Hey, I've got some bread. What about the rest of you?" A youth pulled out a stale crust from his pocket, begun breaking it up and scattering it on Luke's shoulders around his feet. The rest followed suit. "That should draw them in," he said with some satisfaction.

The five stood back, it wasn't yet dusk but the sky had grown grey with the gathering flock, their cries harsh, grating across the landscape.

"A murder of crows," said one looking up.

"Let's get home," said another. "I don't want to be here when they start, when the Woodcutter comes ..."

"Home? We can't go back there. They offered us up to the Woodcutter and if they see us, they're bound to drag us back up here. When we were chosen, it wasn't through fear, it was because they wanted rid of us."

"Where we going to go?"

"Anywhere away from here."

"The group took one last look at Luke and then as the birds began to descend, ran from the field and over the hill. They were never heard from again. Perhaps they changed their names when they reached the next town, perhaps they emigrated like so many others. Perhaps the Woodcutter got them after all. Nobody knows. Not even Luke and he was the one became the keeper of all the Woodcutter's secrets. How do we know all this? As Grandma told her story to the priest, so the Woodcutter told his tale to a child he found wandering, told him how the birds attacked him on the post ..."

"Don't you mean Luke?" asked someone in the audience.

"Yes," said Liz. "But you see Luke and the Woodcutter had by then become one and the same ..."

"What ..."

"If you let me resume my story," said Liz. "All will become clear. I will say though, that the reason the child lived was because he was known to the Woodcutter. The giant had continued to observe the comings and goings, the births and deaths in the village, the lives of those in his family. The child he rescued, the child he told his tale—Luke's tale—to was the son of his brother, his nephew.

"Luke remained on the post, bound even tighter as the other youths made sure he could not escape as they had done.

"As soon as the youths left the field, the crows swooped down to attack. Initially, they pecked warily, sensing the life within him, waiting for him to lash out. But his hands were bound behind him and his feet strapped together. He could not move if his life depended on it. At first, he had cried out in fear and the birds would flap up, disturbed, but when they realised he could do nothing, they remained on their perches, ignored his cries which became lost beneath their raucous chorus. Nobody would have been able to differentiate his voice from that of the birds, nobody would have seen him beneath their black cloak and so nobody came to his aid.

"The musty smell of feathers in that first attack caused his body to cough and hack as his airways clogged up. The fluttering brushing against his skin was a light tickle. It wasn't too bad. They would dive in, bite at parts of the pumpkin, grab a bit of food and fly away. Gradually they would fight each other for what remained, stabbing with their beaks to stake their claim, darting at the little food scattered around and over him, often pecking him in the process. Where he was clothed this wasn't so bad but his exposed skin soon began to bleed and the feathers brushing over the scratches and exposed skin caused an unbearable irritation. His body felt as if it was on fire and the birds that returned, even though the food had gone, were still hungry. They saw the blood and dipped their beaks into the puncture holes and drank from him. Others saw his torn flesh and would grab a shred and tug. His death was one of so many cuts.

"His eyes which he had opened from time-to-time, he kept firmly shut. Eyelids squeezed together as tightly as possible. Something told him if he opened them, he would not be able to see for much longer. He knew birds regarded eyes as a delicacy. So dusk fell but for the boy, it had already become night. A never-ending night of continual attack. A swarm moved over him, claws and beaks pecking away as if he was so much grain in the field. Despite the heat of pain, he would occasionally shiver from the cold as another piece of clothing was ripped off and the formerly protected flesh was exposed to the night air and the birds. At this, more would come back in to dine. And as he no longer saw, so too he no longer screamed. The last time he had opened his mouth, a bird attempted to grab his tongue ..."

"Ugh," said one of the audience.

" … and it was by sheer luck," continued Liz, "the bird had been shaken off and he'd been able to close his mouth quickly. He had felt the pull in his mouth, tasted copper, spasmed against his suffering but he kept his mouth shut. Soon it would make no difference. These birds went for the soft parts, like the lips which he'd sealed. As they stabbed at him, he could taste them. Dead meat and musty corn, rot and decomposition. His stomach clenched and he wanted to gag as his mind drew images of what they had previously fed upon but he could not, would not open his mouth and so somehow, he kept the bile down. Focused the pain away from himself, perhaps the one thing all those years of torment had done for him was to prepare him for this moment. It hurt though and he cried."

"The poor thing," said one of the models. A soft light reflected over the group of beautiful women and even from this distance, Alec could see tears on their cheeks. This story had profoundly affected them and many in the audience. It wouldn't last long though. They would soon hear how Luke changed and eventually turned into the Woodcutter. There would be no sympathy for him then.

"The last thing he remembered from that night was the sound of voices, of feeling rough hands untie and lift him up, carry him as if he was no more than a feather. He knew the Woodcutter had him at last. But he wasn't afraid. He'd survived his ordeal at the beaks of the crows, had suffered torments in the village for most of his life. There was little he felt could hurt him anymore. So he resigned himself to his fate and allowed himself to be carried into the wood.

"There, Grandma tended to his wounds, used her potions and spells to restore him to health, heal his mind, build his strength. Then the Woodcutter took him and taught him how to use his axe, how to carve the flesh so that it drained as it should, how to cut out the rot from villages."

"Rot?" asked Len.

"Whilst many condemn the Woodcutter for his role in allowing Grandma to continue, he has also served to mete out justice to those who hurt and abuse others. This was something Luke identified with and allowed himself to become a willing host to the Woodcutter once the giant's earthly body neared the end of its time and he needed a new host. For you see, although the Devil decreed the Woodcutter's flesh would die, his soul would be left to drift in torment, unless he found another body to occupy.

"This was all explained to Luke as years went on. Time had mellowed the Woodcutter in a way it had not done to Grandma and he was determined his young apprentice would know everything, be allowed to refuse if he wished."

"And if he did refuse?" asked one of the spectators.

"He could live but he would have to stay in the wood. Luke would've been happy with that but he'd come to respect the Woodcutter and so eventually became the host. Time went on and Luke, now the Woodcutter, continued as had been done over the centuries until eventually the time came to choose a new apprentice. This was about a hundred years ago I reckon," said Liz.

"The Woodcutter came into the village and marked the doors with his axe. But the families refused to give up their sons. Instead of the butchery of the previous time however, the Woodcutter did not come back. And when it was clear no retribution was to be paid upon the village, they assumed he was gone, died or become a ghost haunting the forest. Still nobody went into the woods to find out. It continued to close itself off as always and the memories soon became regarded as nothing more than stories, a folk version of an urban legend, perhaps there had once been a grain of truth in the tale but it had been so embroidered it had all been lost.

"The truth is, the real truth is, the Woodcutter has merely been sleeping, as has happened from time to time in different versions of the tale. He will walk again, they say, when the village once more decides to offer up its sons."

The sons, thought Alec, as she paused. They were the answer to everything. Their blood. Their bloodline. The sins of the fathers paid for with the blood of their sons. Already, he sensed he was following their footsteps. There was a path somewhere in those woods, marked out for him, waiting. He could not take his eyes from the forest.

CHAPTER FIFTEEN

"So here we are," said Liz. "A village offering up its sons. Who d'you think the Woodcutter will choose? One? All? We'll have to wait and see."

"I lay odds on young Vinnie," called out Len. "Woodcutter's taken pity on those poor girls he's forever chasing. Reckon he wants to give the rest of the male population of these parts a chance."

Everyone laughed at that and even Vinnie chuckled, although he did look a little embarrassed. Alec knew his brother was enjoying the spotlight but this sort of attention could get personal quickly, especially after his last little escapade. In a small community, even a stranger can learn a lot in a short amount of time.

He could see Suzie's dad, glowering behind Len. The angry father. It was only because Vinnie was part of this stunt, he hadn't taken him apart. Suzie's dad was a bull compared to Vinnie, but Vinnie was quick. The master of the getaway. A slippery customer. He felt there was something about his younger brother that at times he didn't quite trust. An ugly feeling but one he was sure would go once he got to know him better. His mother's doing, he knew. A childhood of trusting no one.

"Wouldn't mind if the Woodcutter did take him," said the man. "If he used his axe to cut off a certain part of that young man's anatomy, reckon he'd do us all a favour."

More laughter. Vinnie flushed brighter.

"Let him have his moment," whispered Alec, "get it out of his system. Then he'll be calmer once we're down from here. In fact, this is probably the safest place you could be."

"Why don't we bet on it?" called another. "Len, you open a book. Winner keeps half, half goes to the village fund."

Alec could see Len grinning, rubbing his hands together, sensing yet another opportunity to make money. There was a general hubbub as the audience trotted back to the marquee with Len, who would no doubt sell them another drink or two as he took their bets.

It left a small group but one looking thoughtful, more considering of the stories Liz told, the group included Doug. He looked serious. Admitted to Alec he was having a hard time pretending to be happy about everything whilst knowing what Oliver had done, what was going to happen at some point. Alec watched as Doug turned to Liz, hoped he wouldn't give anything away.

"You said that some villagers may be aware of the Woodcutter's story," said Liz, "may have been involved or knew something of its origins, do you know who they are? Are they here?"

Alec saw Doug look directly at Reverend Chadwick, Liz following his gaze. She got up and made her way over to where he sat, both close to Andy's post, so the group were able to hear all that was said.

"Reverend Chadwick, isn't it?" Liz said comfortably. "Oliver introduced us earlier. I understand you are amongst the oldest inhabitants of Little Hatchet?"

"Pretty much. And my family, as well as the Eades and Reeves families are amongst the original settlers of the community. You can find their presence in the parish registers goes back hundreds of years," said Chadwick.

Liz smiled. "So you've probably heard this story before?"

"A long time ago. Caused trouble then and it's going to cause trouble now despite all the good intentions. I mean, this village deserves all the help it can get, but this is not the way to go about it."

Alec frowned. Chadwick had agreed to put on a front, go through with Vinnie's madcap idea. Had he had a change of heart? Finally found God? Or perhaps this was his particular script. Liz moved in closer as if scenting prey, her focus firmly on the minister.

"Reverend Chadwick, you seem to know, or indicate you know, the truth of this story. Why don't you share it with us? I mean if it's going to cause trouble then we should at least be prepared. Shouldn't we?"

Chadwick stared into his own drink for a while and then raised his face to Liz's. Alec had never seen it so grim, not even during the few Sunday sermons he'd attended recently before the minister stepped down, having already served years beyond his tenure. You didn't retire from St. Simons, they said. It let you go when it was ready. Never religious in the past, Alec had started to feel dirty, his soul stained, as the spell of the woods increased its hold on him. He'd hoped the church might help. It hadn't.

"Whether I tell it or not, it's too late," he said. "He'll come. You've woken him and he'll come. And not just him, but her as well, old Grandma. Even the Devil himself is walking."

The temperature dropped. Alec shivered. Everything else faded and then there was only him, Reverend Chadwick and Liz in a small pool of light. He couldn't even sense the others at his side.

"Strong words coming from a man of the cloth. Tell us," urged Liz. She'd turned herself slightly and given an almost imperceptible nod to her cameraman who'd taken up position to her right and started recording.

"You want to know how I know it's true? Because Luke was Fred Groves' great great uncle and the child he told the story to was Fred's great granddad, William. William was a close friend of my own great granddad and he also served as verger in the church. Even with that, he had a reputation as a bit of a lad about town, bit like young Vinnie here," said Chadwick nodding in his direction. "But he was still a god-fearing soul. His family history haunted him and even my own great granddad couldn't help him. He spent more and more time with his head in a pint pot. Telling his tales in the Arms, telling anyone who'd listen so they'd buy him a drink. Family thought the drink would kill him, seemed to want to drown himself in it. Then we thought it would be old age. But in the end, he had enough. Hung himself. From the same tree as my own forebear."

Liz nodded sympathetically. "So many lives and histories tragically intertwined," she said.

Alec listened in astonishment. This link to the Woodcutter, to Luke, was something new, something Fred never mentioned during their beery conversations. The added sense of a truth lying beneath the old fairy tale, as he still regarded it, strengthened his unease. What did that mean for them? What would come out of the trees? Where was the old bugger?

"I was a young nipper at the time and folk didn't think I paid attention so they would talk around me. From what they said of William, he was a little old man in the end, a husk. When I went out to look at the tree, I couldn't figure out how someone as frail as him got up there. But he did it—apparently. Determined, they said."

"Did anyone query that it might not be suicide?" asked Liz, moving in even closer, sensing something much more to add to her story.

"No," said Chadwick. "Nothing like that ever happens around here. Not unless it involves the Woodcutter ..."

There was a moment's silence as Liz seemed to consider something. Then. "Tell me. Have *you* ever seen the Woodcutter?"

The Reverend looked at her and then turned straight towards Alec. "I have," he said firmly.

"Christ," said Alec, his nervousness increasing.

"They're mugging for the camera," said Vinnie. "No biggie. Don't let it get to you. Remember the plan."

"Why didn't they tell us they were going to say all this?" asked Alec.

"To get a better response from us, you dope," said Vinnie. "Shock, horror. Always good for the ratings."

The lens switched to the men briefly but returned to Chadwick.

"When, when did you see the Woodcutter?"

The majority of the audience had once again taken their seats and started to pay attention to this impromptu interview. All were listening intently.

A low whoosh, as if branches were parting, reached Alec's ears. Leaves rustled and muttered. It felt as if GodBeGone itself was listening in.

"Not long after Fred's Great Uncle died," said Chadwick, "I'd gone to the tree where he'd hung himself. People tried to keep *that* from us kids at least, but me and Fred—we are the same age—followed Mum and Dad one day when they went there again, trying to make sense of it all. When they left, we remained behind. Looking up. That's when he came. We weren't aware of him at first. Then I noticed the birds stopped their usual twittering and all the other noises you usually hear, the cows in the field, the mice scuttling about, had dropped away. He stepped out of the forest and this great big shadow fell over us. It was like he'd turned off the sun. Terrified, I was, wanted to run for it, so did Fred, but we couldn't move and after a while, as he continued to stare at us and us at him, we realised he wasn't going to harm us. Even though he had that bloody great axe in his hands. Excuse my language."

"How did you know? How could you tell?" asked Liz. Her voice a whisper, an actress whipping up the tension.

"Because he was smiling at Fred. And then he spoke. Said as he was Luke's kin, he had nothing to fear from him, provided he never caused harm to anyone. I was relieved he paid no attention to me."

"What did he look like?"

"Big, he was big alright. Not quite as tall as that thing over there," said Chadwick nodding at the wicker effigy, "but not far off it. His face was scarred, as if he'd hacked at his own face with his axe and so were his arms. It made him look like wood. All knotted and ridged. And on his arms were vines and leaves. He looked like a walking tree. Told Fred he was sorry about his great grandad. That he hadn't meant to upset him when he was a child, that he hoped he wasn't scaring us … and by that time, he wasn't. Strange, but true. Said he'd come to make sure we knew he'd decided to sleep. His body you see, was wearing out and he was supposed to hunt for someone new to take over but he didn't want to do that. Not after Great Granddad had passed. He felt guilty. Centuries of guilt had piled up, worn him down, see—seems even the Devil can't completely still a being's conscience.

"But he also said if he was going to sleep, to stop the whole cycle once and for all, he had to do it now, if he left it any longer, he wouldn't be in control of himself, that Grandma would force him.

"He said she always came back when he was weak, to make sure she would get her cloak. And because he hadn't done that yet, he knew she was on her way from wherever she'd hidden herself. It wouldn't just be the lad who would become his apprentice he would be forced to take, but the offerings for the cloak. He didn't want to be part of it anymore. Something in his spirit, perhaps a remnant of Luke, was changing him."

"And he's waking up," said Liz. "What could cause that?"

"This," said Chadwick, sweeping his arm round in annoyance. "This whole ridiculous circus. By setting these men up as offerings, even if it is a charity stunt … sorry, Alec," he paused and looked slightly guilty, seemed to consider something as he looked at Oliver, and then the anger flushed over him again. "It's like pulling the trigger. Planting these lads there. You've done it now. He'll wake and he'll take one of them for his own and the others, they might be given to Grandma or he might spit them out, pick others from the village. And they will bleed slowly and die horribly, hanging alone in the darkness …"

"So you're saying the story of Grandma and her cloak is also true?" Liz's eyes were wide and her face grown pale. She was either putting on a very good act or come to believe what Chadwick was telling her.

"Must say he's doing better than I thought," whispered Vinnie. "Didn't think Chadwick'd come on side like this. Great performance!"

"You think he's making all that up?" asked Alec.

"Course, you don't think any of that is true, do you," said Vinnie. "You know he's ill, not long left apparently. Seems he's going all out to put this right for Fred before he pops his clogs."

Nobody had told him that bit, although the minister hadn't been looking too well of late. Whether it was true or not, he'd got the audience's attention, added to the atmosphere of the evening, stitched another little thread of their plan into the Woodcutter's tapestry.

He shivered in spite of himself. Found himself searching the dark landscape, homing in on GodBeGone Wood, seeing the branches moving as if something was cutting a path through its midst. Something large, something monstrous was making its way towards them.

He felt the ground shake beneath him. Again, that image of a child and his father walking in the woods came to mind. He watched the cottage door open, saw their faces. It was himself and Doug. The certainty was growing that this was no dream but one of those long-buried memories of his childhood.

"How'd Oliver manage that?" asked Andy, noticing the movement.

"Bloody good effect," said Vinnie.

Alec kept quiet. He knew this was not Oliver's doing. Chadwick's own expression told him as much.

"He's coming," said the minister, staggering to his feet and almost falling over.

"Old boy's had too much holy water," laughed Vinnie.

Another tremor. Liz too, rose, stood in front of her camera as if to speak and then a stronger pulse through the soil. The reporter stopped and looked around. Everybody else stood. A strange look flitted across Chadwick's face, he became strangely calm, appeared almost resigned. *Perhaps it was part of the act?* thought Alec.

Again. This time the vibration travelled up the posts to which they were attached. And again. The feeling buzzed through his body, jarred his teeth.

"Hey man, look at you!"

Andy was laughing at Alec, Vinnie too.

"What?"

"Your hair, mate. Stood on end, like the old Van der Graaf wotsits from school."

He looked at Andy, partially hidden in darkness and then at Vinnie. It was his turn to laugh. "Same goes for you, mate."

"What! No!" Vinnie almost howled. His hair was his pride and joy. Product was his favourite word.

He could hear the others chuckling. Callum, Paul and Eric had all been so quiet, it'd felt as if they weren't there.

"You okay?" he called to Callum.

"Until now," said Callum. "Managed to catch a few z's."

"Sleep! You managed to sleep!" He was older by far than the lads alongside him, his body protesting in ways theirs wouldn't for some years yet. He envied their ability to seemingly drop off in this manner.

"Yeah, those spotlights sort of hypnotised me and the one down this end is quite warm, made me feel all, I don't know … cosy. And what with his reverence yammering on, I nodded off."

"So did I," said Paul.

"Me too," said Eric.

"Well at least you've woken up. Looks like it might be showtime."

Oliver came over to them. Worry lines appeared across his face, made him look a tad older for once.

"Something wrong?" asked Alec.

"Huh? Um, no."

"Really like this tremor thing, like a mini earthquake," said Vinnie. "Effective eh. Fee fi fo fum and all that."

"I didn't …" Oliver began, then he stopped and seemed to reflect. "Earthquake, ah yes, that's what it is."

Alec studied Oliver. The man was not telling the truth.

"Perhaps we should cut you guys down," he said. "Safety precaution and all that."

The ground shook again, harder.

Oliver looked determined, picked up the loudspeaker. "Ladies and Gentlemen, I apologise for this announcement but due to circumstances beyond our control"—another tremor—"I'm going to cut short this evening's entertainment, and, if you don't mind, because we truly want no harm to come to these guys, I'm going to cut them down. We can recommence tomorrow if the tremors subside. You must all agree safety first …"

Already, most of the spectators had sprung up and were making their way back down the field, walking at first, and then with each successive jolt, breaking into a run. Len had roped in some of the locals and was hastily filling the back of a van with his bottles and barrels, and his takings. Soon Alec could see nothing but the red lights of the vehicle as it made its way back down the field.

Oliver's workers were rapidly taking down the spotlights and in a matter of minutes, the field was empty, except for Oliver and Chadwick—and those on the crosses.

"You said you were letting us down Oliver," said Alec, his teeth chattering in response to the vibrations buzzing more and more frequently up through his post.

"Yeah, come on mate," said Vinnie. "Get us down."

Oliver made to go towards them but Chadwick grabbed hold of his arm.

"No," he hissed. "You leave them be, they're not yours any more. You've offered them up, they belong to the wood. It was what you wanted."

"Oliver …" Alec tried to catch the man's eye but he refused to meet his look, gazed straight past him and into the darkness.

"I'm sorry, guys. This has got to be seen through. Alec," said Oliver, turning towards him. "You wanted to help this village. Well,

I can go one better than that. I can *give* it its life back. But first we have to pay the price. She'll expect it and … I promised. I have to keep my promise."

"Promise?" asked Vinnie. "What promise? What are you on about? This is all a bloody fairy tale, a pantomime. Not to be taken seriously. Not real."

"I'm sorry," repeated Oliver. "It is real. It was real back then and it's real today. Took me a while to remember. They're almost here. I promised to help them come back properly so everyone can see them."

Alec stared at Oliver. It was as if he was seeing him for the first time. Instead of the self-assured businessman, his face had taken on a manic quality, his skin glowed in the remaining light as if feverish. Was he going down with something? The man didn't look too well.

"That's what this is really all about," continued Oliver. "Bring the Woodcutter back and you'll get Grandma. Get Grandma and she will be able to do so much for us all."

Reverend Chadwick came closer. "At what price? And what about after? You can't put the genie back in the bottle. Once they're here, they're here and you can't control them."

"You weren't too worried before," sneered Oliver. "Didn't say no to a cut of the profit."

"I didn't think you meant any of this," said Chadwick. "It was all pretend, a crazy idea. The script you gave me …" He stopped for a moment, considering. "Between you and Fred … I don't know what to think anymore. I'm too old, too tired, too sick for such games. I humoured you both, thought it the easier path: give Fred some peace, help the village make some money. Oh, I believed there may be something in the old stories—but not all … this." He waved his arms around.

"Script?" asked Vinnie. "So all that stuff about you seeing the Woodcutter when you and Fred were kids was made up? I knew it! See, Alec. Fairy tales."

"Minor embellishments," said Oliver. "He did come back then. Fred saw him and was supposed to give his version tonight but as you can see, he isn't here. The Reverend kindly offered to tweak the story so we could still put on a performance."

Alec's head was reeling. He was cold, hungry and with the continuing vibrations rumbling through the field, churning up the black hole of the forest in front of them, he felt trapped. He no longer knew what to believe. The stunt could merely be a supremely sophisticated script, much like the TV programme convincing someone zombies were real, that Derren Brown thing. Or … or whatever caused Oliver to behave as he did as a child had come back.

The seed planted at the time of those long-ago murders, bursting open and triggering the madness of delusion. Or … it could all be real. He used to complain his life was boring, mundane but at least it was safe. He regretted coming back to Little Hatchet with every bone in his body.

"Get us down, Oliver," he said. "Now."

But Oliver wasn't listening and nor was the minister. Both had their eyes fixed firmly on GodBeGone Woods.

"Will you bloody idiots stop all this shit," cried Vinnie. "The cameras have gone, everyone's gone. You can forget whatever fucking script you're supposed to be reading from and bloody well get us down, NOW."

His friend's words had as little effect as Alec's. They might as well have been invisible.

"God doesn't live in my woods," said Oliver.

His woods. And his voice seemed to be different, was deeper.

"I've watched you, Reverend Chadwick, flitting round the village, poking and prying. Your father was the same and his father before him and the one before him. Right back to the one who hung himself on that tree. God has never had anything to do with the church of Little Hatchet because the vicar didn't believe in him. And you come from a long line of nonbelievers."

"Yes, well, perhaps you're right," said Chadwick.

This time, Alec felt a mask slipped, that they were hearing the truth of the man at last. Nor did the minister seem to care that they heard him. He had shown some reluctance when agreeing to help them set up Oliver.

"But the living has been a good one, especially when it only requires a weekly performance or two in the pulpit. Bit like the theatre really. I've been a damn good actor if I say so myself." He turned to the men. "I don't mind admitting this finally. It's cathartic and after all, who are you going to tell in the short time you—or I—have left?"

The man's face began to reflect the feverish quality of Oliver's. Perhaps they were both suffering from the same illness.

"Actor?" said Oliver, still using that strange rumbling tone. "Yes, we always knew you were acting the part but because you were the last of your line, we decided to let you spin out your days in the church. There'll be no more ministers in Little Hatchet after you, even though this is the time you truly need one."

"Oliver," Alec tried again, his friends echoing his own attempts. Their voices became high-pitched, shrill. Something was seriously wrong. He looked at Chadwick, noticed for the first time how the man's eyes seemed to glow against the pallor of his skin. So pale, so gaunt.

As if he hadn't eaten for a long time. *Hungry.* Where had that come from?

The ground shook harder than ever and the posts bearing the youths groaned at the movement, tilted at its force.

"Do you believe now, Reverend Chadwick?"

The old man simply stared at GodBeGone Wood, horror written across his face.

The tremors were becoming even more regular, paced out as if somebody was stepping across the landscape. A giant's strides coming closer. Oliver's expression was one of excitement, Chadwick's one of dread, fear crawled across the features of Alec's friends.

Then something seemed to bring Chadwick back to the present as he whipped round, dashed over to the bound men. He managed to cut Callum down, then Andy, Eric and Paul.

Oliver paid no attention. Only Alec and Vinnie remained.

"Shit," cried Vinnie, as the earth seemed to move beneath them. "Get us out of here. Get me out of here."

And then the shaking stopped and the few remaining lights which illuminated their corner of the field went out as a shape so large brought with it its own darkness and plunged the world into shadow.

"You woke me and you called me," said a voice so deep, it was as if another earthquake had been summoned.

"No," whispered Chadwick. "It was a mere act, a play. Not real."

The creature's face was slowly coming into focus as he moved slightly and the remaining one beam of light miraculously, scarily lit up his face. Alec heard someone let out a small scream and realised it was himself.

"I know you," he said to Chadwick. "But so long ago, when you were nothing but a boy."

"I remember," said Chadwick. "You told me and Fred your story."

So there'd been some truth to the minister's tale. Why had he claimed to be following a script? Alec was finding it hard to separate fact from fiction.

"And still I was summoned, when all I wanted to do was sleep. When you knew the danger."

"Oliver here …"

"Ah, yes. Oliver. We knew each other long ago. I've heard your voice in the woods, seen you in the cottage. I think we've talked occasionally but I am not fully awake yet. I find it hard to concentrate."

"We've brought you an offering," said Oliver, his voice determined. "They will wake you. Bring you back properly. You can take them."

The giant turned round and peered down at the man. "Take them? Why what have they done? What crimes have they committed?"

Alec wanted to look away but the giant fascinated him. And then he noticed a small red dot in the darkness behind, a small glimmer of light, the shape of movement ... as if someone were filming them. Shit. This was still part of Oliver's plan. A Halloween docudrama, and the rest of the country would see him scream on national telly. He cringed, wanted to say something to the others then thought better of it. No. He would let them make fools of themselves then his scream might be forgotten. Perhaps he could tell Vinnie. Whilst he pondered his dilemma, he relaxed, paid closer attention to the performance in front of him, marvelled at the effects used to create the appearance of the Woodcutter, began to appreciate Oliver's qualities as an actor. He really was good. That confused expression on his face was perfect.

"I have made you an offering ..." said Oliver.

"But an offering of no purpose," replied the Woodcutter.

"No purpose?"

"Those who I must take, those in whom I will live, must be those with a blackened heart, someone whose taking will bring light back to the village. Remember the words of the Offering. When I take them, I carve the darkness out of them. That is what these ridges and chasms on my skin are: the pits of guilt and sin. The two men you have left are not enough for me."

"Woodcutter, what of Grandma?" asked Chadwick. The reverend was conveying the right mix of terror and curiosity, asking questions the audience would want answered.

The monster let out a deep rumbling sigh. "She is on her way."

"Then she will bring prosperity to me ... us," said Chadwick.

"Who has filled your head with such tales, *little* man? You think you can summon such as I or Grandma and command us to do your bidding? You have no power over us. I should take *you* ..."

The minister paled, his certainty disappearing. "The stories said you would be so grateful you would grant the person who made the offering a wish."

"The old bastard's after something," muttered Vinnie, struggling against his bonds.

"Vinnie," hissed Alec. "Don't say anything more. Remember, it's pretend, an act. Look behind the shadow, there's a camera filming."

"What? Shit. They're making us look like fucking numpties." Vinnie struggled harder. No longer through fear but anger. Alec knew if he got free, the first thing he would do would be to lay one on Oliver as hard as he could.

The businessman paid no attention to the struggling Vinnie, the mutterings behind him. Shock seemed to have immobilised him completely.

"I am not some genie in the bottle," said the Woodcutter. "You're a simpleton who knows nothing. Tonight, I still have some control over myself so I am choosing to leave you all alone, a last promise to the remains of my family. But do not return. If anyone comes back tomorrow, then I will no longer be what I am tonight. It will be too late."

Then the giant turned and strode off into darkness.

Oliver and Chadwick immediately grabbed the posts with Alec and Vinnie and cut them free. The two fell to the ground, groaning loudly. Then Vinnie lunged at the vicar.

"You prick. You fucking …"

Alec pulled him back. "No, leave him. He's not worth it. And if the Woodcutter's really returned—I mean he didn't say he was going back to sleep, did he?—then he'll be going through the village like a dose of salts and who do you think he'll take?"

They all looked at Chadwick. His face pale, shining in the dark.

"Come on," said Oliver. "My Range Rover's over there. I can give you a lift."

"Let's hope he doesn't come back," said Vinnie, reluctantly accepting the offer.

"He only gave us one night," said Alec. The red light in the gloom vanished. Filming had apparently stopped. The first Act was over.

CHAPTER SIXTEEN

Chadwick watched the receding red lights of Oliver's Range Rover bounce away over the field. He'd recited lies and half-truths, tried to keep to the script they'd given him, not wanting to frighten the audience, trying to use the pretence as protection. It was a drama, a production after all. Entertainment. Except it wasn't.

They would meet again soon, for the last time, until then, he wanted to breathe make his own peace—speak to the woods.

Slowly, he walked towards the waiting forest. The tremors had stopped, the trees settled. One thing Chadwick knew, he was no Daniel going into the lion's den. He was a man of no faith, paying lip service to both religion and tradition and believing in neither.

One, the one whose uniform he wore, had proven to be of no comfort. There'd been no voice or moment of revelation. Nothing to justify his preaching of the words in the book which lay closed to him in his study. The presence, or spirit, it described continued in its absence. If it had ever been there, it had abandoned him. The merciful God who forgave all sinners obviously thought him unworthy. The assumption angered Chadwick. He regarded himself a decent man, one who valued life. But what was the value of life?

Beside the path entering the wood loomed his tree. He stared up at the strong bough already searching for him. His fingers stroked the rough bark of the trunk, felt the ridges and whorls, the imprint of age like the lines on his palm. Man and tree spoke to each other through touch, each recognising the other as kin, renewing acquaintance. He leant his forehead against its bulk as a child to their mother, then he stepped back and looked up at the empty bough. If the noose had already been prepared, he would've slipped it over his head then and there. But the play wasn't over yet.

Amongst the mess and the chaos of lies and revenge, greed and hypocrisy, he needed to try to put things right. Persuade those who believed this to be a mere act, a reality TV phenomenon that beneath it lay real danger. It wouldn't be easy. Oliver's money and connections had dazzled them.

"Why choose Alec as the apprentice?" He had looked straight at Doug when Oliver originally mooted his 'reenactment'.

"Because of Cameron," hissed Carol at his side. "At least Alec will get to walk away. Cameron didn't."

"But that wasn't anything to do with the man," said Chadwick. "The inquest said it was natural causes, an accident."

"He said he asked Cameron to leave. If he hadn't, Cam would still be alive. He deserves to be punished." Carol refused to budge and Doug agreed with her.

How could a man, whose son had been taken away from him as a five-year-old, treat his returned child son this way? When he thought of Doug and Carol, one word always rose to mind. Guilt. This was all Carol demanding proof his love for her and their children overrode any remnant of feeling for Mary and Alec. And Doug agreed to it. Not because he loved her more but because he loved her less. His guilt kept her content, maintained the illusion of their happy family. Neither considered the man at the centre of Oliver's scheming. The lead actor, the starring role was being given to an innocent man. He had done nothing to any of them, yet he was to be offered up. The lamb to the slaughter. The thought made Chadwick pause. Here at least was a parallel to the Holy Book.

It had all backfired so badly. Oliver, delusional and completely wrapped up in the myth of the apprentice was turning fantasy into reality whilst still cloaking it in the aura of make-believe. People will believe what they want to believe. Poor Alec. The one bright spot in all this had been persuading Mary to leave and take Alec. Doug and Fred had spent many days taking the boy walking in the woods, showing him the cottage which would one day be his own—when he would become the Woodcutter. Chadwick tried to get them to stop, told them the Woodcutter was a myth and to fill the boy's head with such nonsense was to condemn him to a life of madness. They'd refused to listen and so he'd intervened. It appeared Chadwick hadn't stopped his recruitment, hadn't saved him, merely postponed the inevitable. Doug never forgave him.

The minister continued to walk the path Oliver had cleared and widened, passed the cottage and entered the camouflaged track to the Old One.

He welcomed the touch of the cold night air, the sight of his breath misting before him. Such sensations were stark reminders he was alive. The hidden companion he'd seen in the trees when he'd walked with Fred, which had taken more solid form when he offered up Cameron, still hanging from Old One, was nearby. All those years he'd denied the existence of the Woodcutter, sought to consign the folk memory to oblivion had done nothing except allow his resurgence. He had not believed because he could not comprehend. Now he'd opened up his mind and the truth was nearby.

The giant was not flesh—yet. He needed his host for that. Chadwick sat on the trunk next to the woodman, much as he had done with Fred a few days ago. He found his acceptance of the present, of his coming death had removed his fear.

"So, man of God," said the Woodcutter. "You believe in me at last."

Chadwick laughed. "I don't have much choice, do I. Not when you're sat next to me with that bloody big axe."

It was the Woodcutter's turn to laugh. "What use is a woodsman without his axe."

They were quiet for a moment.

"Listen," said the Woodcutter.

Chadwick listened. He could hear the hoot of an owl, the cry of a fox, the groan of wood.

"Nature speaks to us in so many languages. Humans however refuse to listen unless it is in their tongue. So much is lost in translation."

"And that's where you come in," said Chadwick, beginning to understand.

"I bridge the gap, together with Grandma. Although she often appears in your stories as an ancient crone, believe me there are other ages of woman."

"Yes," said Chadwick. "But the image of an old witch makes for a better legend, increases the fear of the wise woman." His eyes returned to Old One. "Yet she is born in blood."

"Aren't you all?" asked the Woodcutter.

Blood dripping into the vat. Blood coursing through his veins. Soon they would merge and his blood would be given too.

CHAPTER SEVENTEEN

"I must say," said Liz as she joined Alec and the others in Doug's kitchen the next morning, "you really got me going last night. I mean Chadwick, and then those ground tremors and the shapes across the landscape. Quite a theatrical production. And how you coached the audience to respond like that, fantastic acting. Even Oliver. Seriously, I didn't think he had it in him. If I hadn't been told otherwise, I'd have thought it real. And that giant, I mean, wow, just, wow."

Alec stared at her. His mind was still groggy from lack of sleep and last night's events. His mind hadn't allowed him to shut down and rest. Instead he'd gone over and over everything he'd seen, tossing and turning which added to his agony as the numbness of his limbs, the deadweight of their burning ache, added their own noise to the chatter of his brain.

"You got it all on film then?"

"Spotted us, did you? Yeah, we had a couple of cameramen in the field. We're hoping to do some initial editing today. You're not allowed to see it until we're done."

"I can't believe we fell for it," said Vinnie, shaking his head. "That fucking ... *thing* seemed so real."

Liz continued to smile and nod happily. "It was terrific wasn't it? Can you imagine the drama, the tension, when you go back up there?"

Vinnie choked. "We're going back?"

"Of course," said Liz. "You should see the edits we've done so far on this. It's going to be great viewing. Certainly give *Most Haunted* a run for their money."

"But the Woodcutter said we weren't what he wanted," protested Alec. "That'll be on film. How do you explain us going back?"

"Didn't you hear her," said Vinnie. "Editing. They'll twist the video until it shows what they want it to show, cut out the bits that went a bit off script—and I think the bloke playing the Woodcutter did wander occasionally."

Alec began to feel claustrophobic; the small kitchen was crowded with friends and family and even though he couldn't see it, he felt the presence of the forest, closer than before.

"Will Chadwick be joining us?" he asked Doug.

"I rang him an hour ago, no answer," said Liz. "Expect he's gone up there already. Marvellous man. A real find. Didn't he remind you of Vincent Price in those Hammer Horrors?"

Alec felt the way Liz was speaking change the mood in the room. She was turning the events of the previous night from their initial uncertain horror and shades of embarrassment into an amazing display of make-believe. Scripted or not, he wished they'd been told. He didn't want to appear an idiot on the screen. That bloody scream of his.

"We'll see if Fred's in on our way back," said Doug. "He really should be up there, being a descendant and all."

Fred. Where had he been hiding? He hadn't been seen in the village for days and his empty seat in the pub made the place feel strangely deserted. A horrible feeling that something had happened to the man began to take hold. He'd ask Oliver later, after all he was supposed to have been the last to have seen him. The last thing Fred had said was that he was going to pay the man a call.

On cue, Oliver walked into the room. That was a drawback to living in the country and leaving your doors unlocked. Anybody could wander in, and usually did.

"Time to get you guys back up at the field." He was smiling and rubbing his hands together but Alec noticed faint smudges of black beneath his eyes.

"Are you nuts!" said Vinnie, still annoyed at having been duped so well. "After last night! You had us screaming like girls. Not to mention what you did to our hair!"

Everyone laughed at that. They had looked like idiots. But did it matter? Soon it would be Oliver's turn.

"Last night's *performance* was perfect," said Oliver, "but we do need you back up there to see this through."

"You're having a laugh," said Callum. He'd been griping about his aches and pains all morning.

"Oh guys, guys," said Oliver. "This is the last day. One more day of playacting and it'll be over and the village gets the investment it needs."

Still Alec felt an element of doubt. It had crept in during the early hours when he awoke to the noise of silence, remembered the atmosphere of the night, the giant. Pretend. Really? Had to be. What else could it be? Hallucination brought on by the cold, by the lack of movement, the woods. Those bloody woods.

"Remember it wasn't real," said Oliver. "But the deals I've done and the contracts I've signed to get this show up and running are. They need to be honoured. If we don't see through today, I won't be able to follow through with any of the investments I'd planned in the village." The threat did not need to be voiced further.

"The Axeman's Arms," said Vinnie, understanding at once. The one bright spot in the village for them all, it would kill the community stone dead if it closed. In a way it was the one place that anchored them.

Still there was something about Oliver's denial that got to Alec. The look on his face last night, that confusion had *not* been faked. Was something else at play?

"You were as shit-scared as the rest of us," he said, the earlier doubt turning into an itch demanding to be scratched.

"It was pretend. I swear," said Oliver. "Look, let's give this another day, one more night and should there be the slightest tremor, I promise you, I'll have you down like a shot."

Alec watched his father silently ponder his words, his acceptance. Still performing for Oliver, deceiving the man. He couldn't wait for this all to end, when Oliver would be exposed for the monster he was and Fred would be satisfied. Or would he? Why had he begun to feel there was something else going on behind the scenes.

"Look, son. The business really needs the investment and we'll be with you the whole time. Any shenanigans from Mr Hayward here, and I promise you I'll be the first to deck him," said his dad.

"Hang on a minute," said Oliver. "I'm doing all this for you ..."

Doug laughed. "We're not naïve. We're perfectly aware you *never* do something for nothing but believe me that's ok. All we ask is that you're honest with us."

"Of course, of course," said Oliver, grinning. "We're all grown men ... and women ... of the world here."

Still, Alec couldn't help but notice the strange look of relief passing across his face.

And so that was how Vinnie, Callum and Alec found themselves heading out again.

"Think you men should walk," said Doug. "Exercise those muscles of yours."

They groaned but all obeyed. It made sense to move as much as they could before they found themselves tied up again.

"We'll pop in to Fred's on the way," he continued as they walked.

No one answered at Fred's cottage.

"I know where he hides his door key," said Doug, rooting around under a plant pot. He opened the door but a few minutes later came out looking worried. "Fred's not there. Bed's not been slept in."

"I'm sure he's fine," said Oliver, jumping in. "Probably walking off a hangover."

The group stared at Oliver for a moment before reluctantly moving on.

"We *will* call on Reverend Chadwick, however," said Doug.

"Fine," said Oliver, sighing.

A car beeped and passed them. Liz and her cameraman in their own truck. Then the rumble of another van. Len making his way back up to the field. The lure of money too much to ignore in these straitened times. Word had got round that yesterday's events had been choreographed.

"Hope this won't take long," said Oliver as they knocked on the minister's door.

He was right. It took no time at all. The minister wasn't home either.

"Probably leaping around the edge of the wood, trying to summon the Woodcutter," said Callum. "Practising hamming it up for the cameras again."

"Is that in the script too?" asked Alec.

"Eh?" Oliver looked distracted, not quite sure of himself but he recovered. "Come on, let's get this show on the road. Get it over and done with. I swear the grief these few days have given me haven't been worth it."

"Will the girls be back?" Vinnie cut in.

Alec grinned. His brother could always be relied on to find a bright side. He'd learned he was a glass half full type of guy.

The walk seemed long although it was only a mile down the lane and then straight up to the field. Six posts stood there, hammered in anew. He could not see Eric, Paul or Andy. "How'd *they* get out of it?" he asked Oliver.

"What d'you mean?"

"Eric, Paul, Andy. They're not there."

"Should be," said Oliver. "Liz is expecting them. We have an extra little touch to add to the story."

"Such as?" queried Callum.

"Their doors were marked," said Doug. "Everyone was talking about it when I went to get the paper. Surprised because ours wasn't, nor Vinnie's or Callum's from what I can gather."

"Black hearts, eh?" chuckled Vinnie. "Wonder what those dirty little sods have been up to."

Nothing, thought Alec. From what he'd been told in his short time in the village, they'd rarely ever put a foot wrong. Vinnie called them the conscience of the group. Unless it had all been a show and they did have some guilty secret. After all, didn't they say you could never totally know those around you, even those closest to you? And then they were in the field and Alec found his thoughts interrupted.

It was not as full as yesterday but there was a hard core of villagers. He recognised them as mainly belonging to Chadwick's God Squad, the group that used to attend his midweek sermons. Sometimes those meetings had been outside, in Chadwick's garden which backed onto GodBeGone Woods. Occasionally, Alec wondered if the Church had been built in its current position as a deliberate challenge to that brooding mass, or had the trees simply marched forward, showing how inconsequential man truly was, that it would be such an easy matter for Nature to reach over and swallow him up. The Woodcutter had shown the humans no respect.

Their three missing friends had also attended those meetings. On the insistence of their parents, they said. They had to, didn't they? *Honour thy father and thy mother.* And it was just Chadwick droning on. A bit more hellfire and damnation than they'd heard previously in the church, made it a bit more interesting, but if they were honest, they said, they tended to zone out when he really got going. Alec wouldn't be interested in any of it. Nor would he have been, except perhaps they knew something of Chadwick's obsession with local history and had been quite pushy with regard to the publicity stunt, now he actually thought about it.

"You know something," said Vinnie, serious again. "It feels as if somebody, somewhere, is playing a great big joke and we're the punchline. I don't know about you but I seriously don't like the vibes I'm getting."

"Don't worry, lads," said Oliver. "Nothing's going to happen to you. I mean we're filming everything …"

"Yeah, like *Blair Witch*," said Callum, still refusing to let go of the idea of it all being a film.

"And that is fiction," said Oliver, "like all this."

There was a general chatter as the small group made their way past them. People smiled and waved but Alec, too, felt there was an undercurrent and it was nothing to do with their own intentions. He stared at the ground as they trod through the ruts, searching for any sign of their visitor from the previous night or evidence of the rumblings of the ground but there was nothing.

Liz was up by the posts already speaking to camera as they filed reluctantly back to their positions.

"And after last night's bizarre, and I must admit, scary events on this very spot, we welcome back Callum, Vinnie and Alec. They have agreed to see their ordeal through to the bitter end and I can tell you, the money has already started pouring in to the Little Hatchet GoFundMe page. It's truly heart-warming to see how much people want our rural communities to survive. As the day progresses, remember to check back at the fund page, the address is shown at the bottom of your screen and consider donating. And why stop at the target shown? Why not make it more? Considering what these young men experienced last night, I'd say they're worth sponsoring for that bit longer. And in all honesty, I didn't expect them to return. When you see the full video tomorrow, you'll understand why. Today, we get to the truth of the matter. So here I am, with everyone else to await the return of the Woodcutter. In the meantime, and whilst everyone is getting ready, here are a few teaser clips from last night. Remember to tune in tomorrow night to see the full, unexpurgated version. I can guarantee you some real scares. So, sit back and enjoy …"

"Do we get to see?" asked Alec.

Liz smiled. "Why bother? You were here, weren't you?"

"I'd like to see how you made us look," he said.

"I can assure you, you were all fine."

Alec wasn't so certain.

Nor was Callum. "If you've made us out to be a bunch of cry-babies. I'll ..."

"You'll what, Callum?" asked Oliver. "Think you'll find you're a little tied up at the moment."

"Ha, ha, very funny," growled Callum.

"Don't worry guys," said Liz. "I promise you, you've come across great."

Alec tuned her out. He wasn't going to get anywhere. It was almost as if they'd never been away. Except the story-telling circle was gone and all the bales circled them so they were in the midst of things and then rising up, right in their field of view was the bonfire. It appeared not to have been disturbed by last night's events, tell a lie.

It had changed. In fact, seemed much bigger, the mask more monstrous. Although that could be because of the perspective and he hadn't seen it properly the previous evening, its completion happening as darkness fell. He tried to look away but those huge empty eyes followed him.

"One hour down."

"Huh?"

"We've done an hour. If it keeps up like this, we'll die of boredom," said Callum.

Better that than like last night, thought Alec.

"Really wish those models were back here. It would beat looking at that ugly thing."

The three of them stared at the bonfire.

"You seen *The Wicker Man?*" asked Callum, slightly more cheerfully.

"Don't even want to think about that," said Vinnie. "Wouldn't put it past old Chadwick to offer us up."

"He's keeping out of the way, isn't he? I mean his flock's here, but he's not."

"Probably hiding with those three little rats," said Vinnie. "Ready to pull some other stupid stunt. Like last night."

The thought kept Alec on edge for the rest of the day and he sensed it in his friends too. Their bindings chafed, rubbing their spirits the wrong way.

Occasionally, Liz would return to them, bringing another local to recount some old bit of lore and then they'd wander off. Both reporter and cameraman were beginning to look as bored as the youths felt. They perked up when Len declared it was time to light the bonfire and send the Woodcutter back into the darkness.

As four locals set light to the base, Oliver stood in front and recited the verses from the previous day before standing back and allowing the effigy to be viewed without impediment.

It was just like that bloody film, thought Alec and for one awful moment he could've sworn he heard someone scream amongst the flames before dismissing it. The heat was intense and he could feel it even after the construction collapsed in on itself and died down, slowly turning the field black. Tonight, it seemed they'd skimped on the spotlights, unnerving him further. And then even that went out. So too did the voices die away. With a start, he opened his eyes. He'd fallen asleep again, as it seemed, had Vinnie, now stirring next to him.

"What the fuck," said Vinnie. "Hey, where is everyone? Is this another bloody stupid trick? Another little scheme to make us look like wallies on camera? Oliver! OLIVER!"

There was no answer.

Alec tried. "Doug! Dad!"

It sounded embarrassing, pathetic, but he'd promised to stay with him. Why hadn't he told them about this bit? He scanned around, trying to see the telltale red dot indicating the ever-present camera, see if they were still filming.

Nothing.

"They're gone," said Callum. "Every single bloody one of them. Even Len. They must've drugged us, put something in our food so we didn't see them go."

"We've been stitched up," growled Vinnie, furious. "This was supposed to be some simple cheesy stunt … plus a bit of payback for Oliver."

"Well, I don't know about you," said Callum, "but if we're being abandoned like this, I've no bleedin' intention of hanging around. And what's this about Oliver?"

"We'll explain later," said Alec. "In case you hadn't noticed, we're not exactly free to move here, are we?"

"Not yet," said Callum, "but after last night, I made sure I brought along a little insurance policy. I'll have us out in a jiffy."

"Bro," said Vinnie, "I take back everything I ever said about you. You're a bloody legend!"

"What?" Alec craned to see.

"He's got a knife. Lucky they tied our hands behind the post and not in the scarecrow style of last time."

A weight lifted from Alec's chest. They would be free soon and then they would track down the whole bloody village if they had to. Anger at their abandonment kept the fear at bay, the sense something else lurked in the darkness, watching them. Even so, the minutes stretched as Callum hacked at the ropes. The binds burned into Alec's wrists as Callum pulled at one side to allow the blade space to cut, the heat added to by the sting of the knife itself when it slipped and nicked his skin. Alec swore quietly, kept from yelling at Callum. The man was doing his best. You couldn't shout at someone for that, especially when they could walk away and leave you more alone than you'd ever felt before in your life.

Eventually, they were free.

The three stood rubbing sore wrists, stretching out aching limbs. Alec looked down the hill, beyond the village. The forest had drawn closer. The illusion of swallowing the settlement, stronger. Part of him wanted to run in the opposite direction, like that earlier five. But they never made it, did they, a voice murmured in his head. They thought they were running *away* but instead found themselves running *to*. Whichever way they went, the forest had risen up and stopped them—as if it was trying to stop them.

"Come on," he said. "Let's get back down to the village, find everyone. It's going to be something straightforward like Len's put on a special offer."

"Would that get everyone?" asked Callum. "There's a few on the field who don't drink. Why would they have gone?"

"Because like everybody else in this poxy little place, they can't resist the chance of a good laugh," said Vinnie.

The thought cheered Alec. They tripped and stumbled their way across the ruts but were soon back out on Copse Lane. The road took them straight into the village, an arrow darting at its heart. Crossing the settlement boundary, it seemed as if the air shifted around them.

"I don't like this," said Callum.

"What?" asked Alec.

"This," he swept his arm in front of them. The cottages lining the lane were buried in darkness.

"Probably gone to bed—or down the pub," said Vinnie. "There's lights on down there."

A golden glow shone from the hub of the village. The Axeman's Arms had become an oasis in the dark.

"It still doesn't feel right," said Callum, as they neared. "I mean, where's the noise, the smokers outside?"

"Surprise party," said Vinnie, marching up to the door, preparing to push it open. "Reckon they're getting ready to shout BOO!" He burst inside with Alec and Callum close behind him. They cannoned hard into him, nearly sent him flying when he abruptly stopped.

"What the …"

Alec's eyes swept the room. Not a soul was in sight. Nor did it look as if anyone had been in. No empty pint pots littered the tables. No bottles or half-eaten meals.

"I seriously don't like this," said Callum.

Alec could only agree.

Vinnie frowned for a moment and then slipped over behind the bar. "Right, gents. What'll it be?"

"Vinnie," said Callum, "I don't think you should be doing that."

Vinnie looked at them. "We've been set up to look like cretins. We have been abandoned during something which was supposed to be a fun *whole* village affair, and everyone still appears to be playing silly beggars. Well, pardon me but before I do any more prowling around out there, I am going to have a stiff drink or two. You are welcome to join me."

"What about Len?" Alec expected the landlord to pop up at any minute. Rant about thieving little toe-rags.

"He won't mind," said Vinnie. "He's made a fortune from us the past few days. But I can write him a note if you want."

Vinnie pulled them all a pint and then a shot of whiskey each. They drank in silence.

Alec felt the warmth return to his body. He finally began to feel human again, the air of displacement which followed him from the field receded a little.

"So," he said, "what now?"

The other two considered carefully. Reluctant to speak. He didn't blame them. They were all safe, warm, inside. Any suggestions would involve going back out there. He just wanted to sit and relax.

"Well, your home is next door, Vinnie," said Callum. "We try there first."

It made sense but the early feeling of foreboding came back as he stood at the front of his home. Like the rest of the houses around them, it was bathed in darkness.

"Come on," said Vinnie. "It's getting a bit nippy out here in case you hadn't noticed."

And it was. The temperature had dropped and their breath misted the air. Vinnie's fingers trembled as he inserted the key in the lock, turned it. The door swung back noiselessly. The three made their way cautiously along the hallway before heading upstairs.

Alec was about to call out but Vinnie stopped him. "No. If they're asleep, they'll have my guts for garters for waking them."

"Waking them?" said Callum. "Don't you remember that bit this morning where Doug promised to stick with you in the field, make sure you were okay."

He remembered alright and that's why he was more disturbed than he wanted to admit.

Vinnie knocked softly on his parent's bedroom door. There was no answer. He knocked again, slightly louder and then Alec reached past him and pushed the door wide.

"Hey," said Vinnie but stopped as he found himself looking at an empty bed.

"Shit," he said. "I don't like this, not one little bit."

Callum had already turned and was running back down the stairs, sprinting up the lane to his own house.

"We should go after him," he said to Vinnie.

"No, let's check out Eric and Andy's houses, they're only over from you. We'll check there and *then* go after him."

"I don't think we should split up," said Alec.

"It'll take a minute and we *know* where he's gone," said Vinnie, picking up Doug's car keys from the hall table.

"What if he vanishes," said Alec, "like everyone else."

"He won't," said Vinnie, but Alec heard the doubt in his voice.

They quickly ran over to their friends' houses and found them deserted, exactly like Alec's.

"They can't have gone far," said Vinnie. "Come on, we'll drive up to Callum's."

They returned to Doug's car. As Alec got into the vehicle, he looked down the street. "None of them can have gone far," he said. "They've all left their cars behind."

"There you go then," said Vinnie. "They've got to be nearby. Let's get Callum."

They found him sat at the end of the drive to his house.

"They're not there," he said as he slid into the back of the car. "What now? Call the police?"

"And say what? A whole village has upped and vanished. They'll think we're having a laugh."

Alec slapped his forehead. "You know we've been bloody stupid. Missed the obvious."

The other two looked blank.

"Phones, you pillocks. Phones."

Silence fell as the three texted their way through their contacts. Then they looked at each other. *No one* had responded.

They looked at each other, their faces pale in the glow of the overhead light.

"I have one final suggestion," said Alec, "before I declare the situation officially screwed up."

Vinnie put his hand on the ignition. Eager to get going, be doing something. "Well, where to?"

"Oliver's," said Alec. "Think about it. He's got a bloody big mansion and he has been known to throw a party. Plus, it might be where Doug and Chadwick stick the knife in."

The engine started before Alec even fastened his seatbelt.

Vinnie looked furious. "If I find that bastard is throwing a party and has not bothered to invite us, I swear I'll make him sorry."

All of them were out of sorts. Alec assumed they shared the same underlying fear none wanted to give full expression to, the feeling of abandonment, and also that vague, nagging feeling that perhaps they'd been set up for some awful candid camera experiment currently being live-streamed on YouTube.

"Will you tell me what you mean?" said Callum. "What's going on with Oliver and you? I'm not stupid. I've felt there's something you've been keeping from me and the others."

At a nod from Vinnie, Alec explained exactly who Oliver Hayward was and why they'd gone ahead with this very public event.

"Bloody hell," said Callum, when Alec finally finished and the car was almost at Oliver's door. "He's come back here, pulled this stunt and has *no* recollection of what he did. I don't know how you could all even bear to be in the same room as him, let alone go along with this event."

"It's not what we wanted," admitted Alec, "but it's what Doug and Fred asked of us. Although obviously they haven't filled us in with all the details otherwise we wouldn't be running around like blue-arsed flies tonight."

They met no traffic, saw no lights.

"Nothing here," said Callum, studying the silent house. "Let's go over to my place. Try and think things through. Think what to do next."

But Vinnie was already out of the car, running up to the front door, the gravel crunching under his feet breaking across the night.

"Come on," he shouted. "If no one's home, we might find something inside telling us what's going on. I mean this is his bloody headquarters. He does all his planning here, doesn't he?"

Vinnie was right. And then the clincher.

"Hey, the door's unlocked. Means we're not breaking and entering."

Vinnie's grin was caught in the beam of the car's lights. Alec reached across and turned off the ignition. He didn't want to risk a flat battery. They followed Vinnie into the house.

CHAPTER EIGHTEEN

When Oliver had outlined his additional plans for the village in terms of investment, a number had jumped at the chance. A once-in-a-lifetime opportunity to get rid of debt, let someone else carry the worry. They knew his record, the millions he'd raked in, his reputation as King Midas.

It reassured them they were securing the future of the village. The mutterings about his character, the hints of a dark past, all vanished at the sight of the numbers written on their cheques. You don't worry about what's gone before when the present is crowding you with insecurity and killing hope.

There were still some secrets they didn't know. The hidden millions which actually put him in the billionaire class, the profits from shady deals in a shark-infested stock market where he was the biggest shark of all. The buried development in the woods where, if all went to plan, the ground would yield an even greater return. It would be interesting to see their reaction to that little experiment. The census taken when he'd first looked at the property revealed roughly one hundred souls. An easy number to manage.

Nor did they connect him to Rosie. A couple, Reverend Chadwick and Doug Reeves still seemed somewhat suspicious but he'd dealt with Chadwick, could work on Doug. The newcomer, Alec, caused him some unease. He felt as if he'd met him before but couldn't place him. It would come to him eventually, he was sure. In the meantime, he was nothing to worry about. Always concentrate on the events you can control, was his motto. Everything else would follow.

And they had followed him. Every single man, woman and child. He'd bought them all—well, almost all. Lulled by his generosity in the field that evening—the free bar, the plentiful food— he'd generated a bond between them, one of a reborn camaraderie, one of hope for the future. By giving them this, and those earlier financial inducements, he held them in the palm of his hand.

The group paused at the edge of GodBeGone Woods, peering into its darkness, no doubt remembering all the old stories.

"We're going in there?"

"Where else," said Oliver. "It's perfectly safe. I've been going in and out for weeks and come to no harm. I can assure you everything you've heard is mere fairy tale. I've got a special place for us to wait. You'll have everything you need, I promise."

"In there?" came the same doubting voice from the back of the crowd.

"In there," confirmed Oliver. "Follow me and you won't get lost. And remember, no torches, apart from mine. We can't have the lads spotting lots of lights dancing through the trees. It'll bring them here immediately. And I don't want that yet."

"But we'll never be able to find our way!"

Oliver fought down his irritation, kept his voice friendly. "As I said, follow me, keep close together and you'll be fine. The track is quite obvious and I'll have my torch."

There was a slight grumbling as Oliver flicked on his light but they fell in behind him and followed him into the trees. Curiosity, excitement, a day out of the ordinary. This, as well as the money, drove them on. It was human nature. It didn't stop them muttering behind him.

Vinnie's parents were at his heels.

"You sure you told them?" Carol, Vinnie's mother.

"Course he told them," said her husband. "Stop fussing."

"I still don't see why we had to hide out here. Thought he would at least let us stay in that big mansion of his."

"Don't be daft, woman. That's one of the first places they'd look. We can't be picked up by the cameras out here."

Oliver listened to them all bickering. The price he'd paid had given him the village. He owned them all and so did the woods. Oliver thought back to the TV stunt which originally inspired him, given him the idea, the perfect cover to carry out Grandma's wishes. A hypnotist convinced someone the world had undergone a zombie apocalypse. It had made for incredible viewing. Oliver might not be giving the world zombies but he would be giving them Grandma and the Woodcutter. He ran a hand over his cheek, sensing the carvings beneath his cosmetic camouflage. Liz and her team had taught him so many tricks. That had been one of her last.

"A little further," said Oliver guiding them along the narrow forest track. The dense trees muffled the voices of those behind him and gradually they fell quiet. The stories of the woods were no doubt playing on their minds, few admitted to going in, some had never come out.

It was so dark, you could barely see the person in front of you. A number were already pulling out their phones to use as torches despite his earlier order, little glimmers of light bobbing along, giving them some reassurance. They were far enough in he doubted they could be seen by anyone outside. Besides, they wouldn't need them soon. A few more steps.

The darkness ended abruptly as he led them out of the canopied tunnel into an area awash with light. Spotlights beamed across the workspace lighting up rigging and machinery, vehicles and portacabins. He made his way over to the largest portacabin, the one the workers used as a canteen, and threw open the door.

"There you go," he said. "Food, drink, enough for you all. The other cabins are also at your disposal. You'll find camp beds, wash facilities, everything you need."

He had paid off his workers, given them a surprise holiday. A reward he said for all their hard work. There'd been no argument from them and they were almost done anyway.

"What is this place?" asked Carol, her concern for her son temporarily forgotten by the sight in front of her.

"The reason he's bought us all out," said Len. "That's a drill rig over there. Reckon that's what's been responsible for the tremors we've had recently. He's been fracking."

All eyes turned on Oliver. He shrugged his shoulders. "Just a small test rig."

"I don't remember anything come up about this at the parish council," said Len.

"Because it didn't," said Doug.

"No need is there," said Oliver. "I own the land, we're miles away from anywhere. It's a little experimentation. Who's to know?"

"You can't do this. It's not right." Reverend Chadwick spoke up.

The villagers thought he was talking about the fracking. Oliver knew he meant something else entirely.

"Will you listen to me?" Carol's shrill voice rose above the hubbub of their latest discovery. "I don't care about all this"—she waved her arm to take in the development—"for the moment. That can be sorted later. What I do care about is my son. You still haven't said whether you told them or not. Will Vinnie be okay? Will they all be okay?"

Pointless questions. Oliver looked at her curiously. "Why so worried about Alec all of a sudden? You weren't worried before because of who he was. Didn't want anything to do with him."

Her face hardened, her voice was cold. "I don't care about him, but the others are our sons. I don't want them to come to any harm."

He saw Doug flinch at her words, she didn't notice her husband's reaction. Doug's conflicting emotions were clear. He hadn't really wanted Alec to be the scapegoat. Carol had forced him and he'd given in. A weak man. He pondered Alec. How would he react to this betrayal by family and supposed friends, the people he thought had welcomed him into their midst, accepted him?

Oliver stood in the middle of the crowd. They'd gathered around him, made him the eye of the storm. "I … um … I do have a little admission," he said.

"I knew it, I knew it …"

"Ssh woman," interrupted Doug as his wife looked ready to erupt. "Let's hear him out."

Oliver smiled his thanks at Doug. "I was going to tell them, believe me, but after some discussion with the film crew, we felt it better to keep them in the dark so to speak. It would make their reactions much more genuine. And from the likes the live-streaming has been getting, I would say it's been well worth it. The results have been phenomenal. Look, all you have to do is go in the cabins, grab a bite to eat and enjoy the show. It'll all be over before you know it and we'll have made a pretty penny for the village. Now I've got a bit of business to take care of, so Len, I'll let you take charge of things here. I'm relying on you to keep everyone happy. As per our agreement."

It didn't hurt to drop in these reminders of ownership. It kept people obedient, malleable. His lies were coming easier and easier. The script he'd explained to the villagers hiding another story, other actions. Only after it reached its conclusion would they realise ignorance was truly bliss.

"Where are you going?" asked Len.

"Back to the village. The lads won't see me but I'll be keeping an eye on them. Make sure they don't do anything silly. I hope that's of some reassurance?" Oliver looked at Carol and she gave a somewhat dissatisfied nod. It was as much as he could, or wanted, to give.

The crowd dispersed into the cabins, forgetting about the fracking, minds focussed on the 'missing' young men, curious as to their next steps.

Oliver, Reverend Chadwick and Eric remained.

"You know what you have to do?" Oliver asked Eric.

"Yeah, though I don't know why it has to be me," he grumbled, eyes fixed on the cabins, hearing the laughter, obviously feeling he was missing out.

"You didn't complain at the extra money, did you?" said Oliver. "I could always offer it to one of the others."

"No, no," said Eric hastily, the cash refocusing him as Oliver knew it would.

"Good," said Oliver. "Tell me again what you have to do."

Eric recited it all, including the paths he would take, the stories he would tell them. He had it nailed. Chadwick always said the young man had a phenomenal memory. It was why he'd been chosen.

"Excellent," said Oliver, tapping his iPad and noting where his targets were. Eric needed to move.

"Get yourself out to Shrewsbury Road, stop them leaving, get them back to the wood. Here."

He pulled out a phone, a map and small dot appeared on its screen. The dot was Alec.

"It's a tracker," he said. "Make sure you turn it off when you find them. Don't want them getting suspicious."

Eric looked at him. "You went to all this trouble, really? Why didn't you fire up What's App, use their maps?"

God the man was irritating. Did he really think he hadn't thought of that? "Because I've blocked mobile signals round here, stopped our friends from using their phones. Stopped pretty much everyone actually." He couldn't help grinning at the frustration on Eric's face as he tried to get service on his own phone.

"Go and do what I've paid you to do," he said as Eric showed no sign of moving.

The man returned his useless phone to his pocket and took Oliver's, offering a sarcastic salute as he did so, and disappeared. It left Chadwick and Oliver in the beam of the spotlight. Oliver felt exposed.

"Walk with me, Reverend?"

It looked as though it was the last thing the minister wanted to do but Oliver knew Chadwick would come. He knew the man had a speech prepared, was champing at the bit to lecture him again on the folly of the path he had chosen.

"Don't you think the re-enactment has gone far enough?" he asked.

"Not by any means," said Oliver. "I intend to see it through to the end. I never start anything I don't finish."

"But this, this is meddling with things you don't understand."

They entered another tunnel of trees, as dark and narrow as the previous one which had taken them to the clearing. He doubted Chadwick would notice any difference.

"On the contrary," said Oliver. "I understand everything. And you will too. Once you've spoken to Grandma."

Chadwick grabbed his arm, fingers digging in, pinching his skin. Oliver winced, shook himself free. They had stopped and the trees circled themselves around the pair, trapping them. No, not them. Chadwick.

"She is a witch of legend," said Chadwick. "Nothing more. That couple all those years ago. That was drugs."

"Do you seriously believe that?"

Chadwick's silence was answer enough.

"I must thank you by the way for not reminding people of that time."

"Don't thank me. I recognised you when you visited the village before you bought the old estate. I wasn't completely sure, and there's not that many of an age still here to remember. But I told Fred. He deserved to know, be prepared. I would like to know where Fred is," said Chadwick. "You said he'd come round, realised it was for the good of the village, although how *you* ever convinced him of that I don't know."

"I'm taking you to him," said Oliver, as the trees opened up the path ahead of them. They bypassed Old One. Oliver could hear the creak and groan of its ancient boughs, hear their whispering leaves, feel its hunger.

Reverend Chadwick fell quiet but Oliver could sense his anxiety—and his fear. Despite his protestations, the man believed more than he let on. He had his own family history to guide him after all, and didn't they say history had a habit of repeating itself? Oliver could hear his heavy breathing, could almost feel the rapid beating of the man's heart vibrating through the air.

"Nearly there, Reverend," he said, knowing this would be no reassurance.

The path started to widen a little, the trees gradually pulling back to reveal the night sky, clouds obscuring the stars, maintaining the gloomy curtain. It was enough to allow them to see the outlines of the cottage, the fence, clearing.

"I wish this place had been destroyed," said Chadwick, as they stood at the garden gate.

"That was intended, apparently," said Oliver. "When I found the papers relating to this place, there was an order for demolition. A local firm hired to carry it out."

"Why didn't they?"

"Seems the firm, no more than a father and son, went under. A fire, unexplained, at their yard, whatever. Don't you remember? The place was left to be reclaimed by Nature and then I rediscovered it."

"How did you … how did you feel when you saw it again?"

He'd expected Chadwick's question, his curiosity about the human condition was what drove him on. Led him into tight corners from which he had to extricate himself. For the reverend, the cottage would not be a corner. It would be his dead end.

"Relieved," said Oliver. "It was like a weight lifted. To know I hadn't imagined the place, those glimpses I had which my parents said were all in my mind, were simply nightmares. You've no idea how it felt to finally realise I hadn't been going mad all these years. And then when I got to work on the cottage, it felt like I'd finally come home, that I was whole again.

"But the memory of Rosie. I mean, to have to cope with that, to come to terms with your part in it."

"My part? I was a child remember. That was all. I'd merely done as I was told."

"You felt no guilt? I mean surely … Rosie had been like a mother to you." There was no disguising the incredulity in either Chadwick's tone or expression.

"I remember," said Oliver. "But Grandma needed her …"

"Grandma didn't, doesn't, exist," insisted Chadwick. "It's a fairy tale. We all *know* that."

No they didn't, thought Oliver but he didn't answer. There was no point. Sometimes people would only believe the evidence of their own eyes.

"Come on in," said Oliver. "I think it's time you two finally met."

They had entered the garden. The gate swung shut behind them. Neither man touched it.

"Is Fred inside?" asked Chadwick, as they reached the door.

Oliver noted how he ignored his reference to Grandma. Dismissed it as madness. Continued to move forward as he sought the truth behind Fred's disappearance.

Oliver pushed open the door and stood back for the Reverend to enter first. He could see the tug of war going on behind the man's eyes as he glanced back at the path and then into the cottage. It was his last chance. Did he know that? How many people turned their back on the one chance they had to save themselves, knowing they condemned themselves in the process? For Chadwick, the question of Fred had hooked him, reeled him in.

Reverend Chadwick stepped across the threshold, ducking his head in a slight bow, and into the light.

Oliver closed the door behind him, running his fingers over the grains and whorls of the carved face, knowing he carried the same visage, that they were one. It was time to show himself. He could not deny the Woodcutter any longer. The apprentice was ready to summon his master.

"Go and talk to Grandma," he said, nudging Chadwick forward, towards her chair.

"She's waiting for you." She wanted him, this preacher man. Made that clear in his dreams. His cloth, she said, would not do for her cloak, but she wouldn't mind wiping her feet on it.

Chadwick reached towards the rocking chair. Oliver had moved it from the side so it faced the fire, giving Grandma the full benefit of its warmth although obscuring any view of her except her back.

"Go on," he urged. "She's not quite herself yet. It'll be a different matter once she's got her proper cloak."

"Proper cloak?" Chadwick's face paled, his hand clamped firmly over his mouth.

"You'd best sit down," said Oliver. "I need to wash up. Go on, she won't mind sharing her hearth."

Oliver turned away from Chadwick and grabbed a rag, rubbing it vigorously over his face, scraping away the fakery to reveal the true. A quick glance in the mirror and he let out a deep sigh of relief. He could finally be himself, be who Grandma and the Woodcutter wanted him to be. He turned back as Chadwick finally stepped round in front of Grandma, watched him stagger back and steady himself against the stone mantel.

"No, Oliver. No. What have you done?" Chadwick started to make his way back across the cottage floor, back to the door, a slow, stumbling movement.

Shock always slowed a person down, mused Oliver. Liz had been the same. It gave him time to pick up his axe, get to the door before Chadwick.

"Oliver! What have you done to yourself? To Liz? What is this madness?"

Oliver stared at the Reverend who clasped his hands together in front of him. Begging or praying? He couldn't be sure. Both considerations were pleasing. He smiled at Chadwick.

"I've done what Grandma asked me to do. What Grandma needed."

"But ... but ... that's Liz, not Grandma! Oliver, for God's sake!"

"God? God doesn't walk in these woods, Chadwick. He certainly didn't come in with you, did he?" Oliver stood over the minister, felt himself grow tall, become a giant, towering over the insignificant priest. "And my apprenticeship will be at an end. I will be the Woodcutter. As I was always meant to be."

"Apprenticeship?"

"You know the story. You know what has to be done."

"Done? I don't …"

"The sacrifices. The cloak for Grandma. Once I get them and Old One has them, she'll come back, properly."

"Those are stories, man. Fairy tales and you've got one thing wrong. In the stories they took only young girls."

"No, not stories," said Oliver, feeling the axe tingle in his hand, the blade expectant. "And it doesn't matter whether male or female. Any will do. The old legend merely dwelt on the girl victims as they made a better story. A spookier tale to tell around the fire on a cold winter's night."

It was true. Grandma had said. Provided they were fresh, with years ahead of them, they were all the same to her. This was why Chadwick was spared contributing—to her cloak at least.

Chadwick swallowed hard. Oliver was getting used to seeing fear in a person's eyes, smell it on them. It excited him, knowing the power he wielded.

"Then what use am I?"

Did Chadwick expect this to be reason enough for a lifeline?

"She wants you, don't doubt that." Oliver watched as his arm swung up, the axe blade glinting in the dying fire. It was as if light was also vanishing with the life now carved by his blade. The arc so swift, so sudden, the minister had barely been aware of it.

"A quick death," he said, as he bent to pick up the body. "You should be grateful for small mercies."

"More than the priests showed to me over the years," said Grandma. "They could be so cruel. Go and hang him up. You know where."

The Preacher's Tree. The one from which his ancestor had hung. It would be fitting.

He looked down at Grandma. She'd been pleased with the host he'd given her, made her young and beautiful once more. Wearing Liz's face would allow her so much more freedom in the days to come. Woodcutter and Grandma, young again, like those early days. A wonderful, wondrous rebirth. He stooped down and kissed her lightly on the lips, so cold beneath his touch, despite the warmth of the fire. Soon she would be back, warmth and passion coursing through her.

Oliver adjusted the weight of the minister over his shoulder and left the cottage. He needed no light to guide his path, the trees knew which way he was to go and opened up before him. Occasionally, he would hear a shout and a laugh from the direction of the fracking site. There was plenty there to keep them amused and he doubted any would be wandering back to the village any time soon.

He'd made it clear any monies agreed would be forfeit should anyone leave the site in the next twenty-four hours. Nobody argued. After all, what was one day to create one of the greatest Halloween stunts of the year. Plus, he'd taken a few precautions in terms of food and drink. They would all sleep well.

Oliver arrived at the wood's boundary and placed the reverend on the ground. He rummaged in the undergrowth and pulled out a rope he'd prepared earlier. He swung the end carrying the noose up and over the bough and then tethered the loose end around the trunk. The noose was slipped over Chadwick's bloodied head and then Oliver unravelled the rope to pull the body high up into the boughs before tying the rope off properly this time.

The minister swung there like a giant crow. The branch creaked beneath the weight but held. There were still hours to go before dawn. Oliver breathed in the night air, felt it cool the sweat of his exertions, washed him with its calmness. Across from the wood he could see the fields rolling into the distance, his mansion high up on the hill. He doubted he would live there again. His home was in the woods. Around him night's creatures got on with their own work, hunting, dying. Like him. Ghosts flew across the sky, night owls, keeping him company as his own ghosts resurfaced.

Then he heard a scream, the cry Eric promised to let rip as he stumbled out of the woods and ran towards Callum's house. His was to be the howl of a madman, of someone who had seen something terrible, needed their help. Had he left anything to chance? He didn't think so. Once they were following Eric, they would, no doubt, hear the villagers partying at the fracking site, get a brief reassurance from their friend so they would continue to follow him. Then Eric would keep his side of the bargain.

With a last smile up at the moon, Oliver turned and headed back into the woods. He had one last job to do at the cottage before he turned his attention to the making of the cloak. He hadn't lied when he told Chadwick Fred had been at the cottage. The man's body was hidden round the side, buried beneath an old cloth. Grandma permitted him to hang from Old One for one night. A concession born of his request to hang where Rosie had been found. He felt it right to give the man his family back. Oliver picked up a shovel and began to dig.

Father and son were to be reunited at last.

It did not take long to dig the grave. The soil in the garden had been turned relatively recently and not compacted down. Oliver rolled the body into the hole and then laid the bundle of tiny bones on top of him before covering them with soil. Despite digging up the garden when Rosie's body had been discovered, the police never found her child. Grandma had kept him hidden.

The exercise rejuvenated him. Oliver felt his nerves tingling, his body had never felt as alive as it did at this moment. He grinned as he returned inside the cottage to select the extra shrouds he would need.

"It's nearly time," he whispered to Grandma, as he added more logs to the fire. "Nearly time for us to all be together again."

The woman didn't answer but her face too, was set in a grin. Her smile following him as he left the cottage, went deeper into the woods.

CHAPTER NINETEEN

Ablaze of light shone from the door as they neared the entrance. Vinnie was busy lighting up the house like a funfair. Only a short while ago, Alec would've been panicking at entering this way, dreading a furious Oliver storming in after them. Now, he would rather that than nothing. If it drew him out of the woodwork, then so be it. The relief would be worth it.

Vinnie was already in the lounge, picking up a few letters and files lying on the coffee table. Throwing them down again.

"His office is down the hall a way," said Callum. "I came here a few times with Dad when they wanted to talk business. Although I don't think it was business they discussed."

"What makes you think that?" asked Alec.

"Because nothing ever came of it. No new deals. Nothing. Once or twice I thought maybe Dad was considering selling his land to Oliver but when I asked him about it, he laughed and said no, they were *looking to the future.*

"How long ago was that?" Alec was curious.

What had the two men got planned? It seemed like an unlikely pairing.

"Six months or so ago. When he first moved here."

"One of those fly-by-night deals Oliver was always coming up with," said Vinnie, dismissively. "Come on, show us the office."

Callum led them down a corridor leading off the hall. The walls were lined with pictures of Oliver and various celebrities, businessmen and politicians. His face smiled out from the paparazzi photos, the framed newspaper clippings. This was the CV he wished to display to anyone intending to do business with him. His message was clear. He mixed with the great and the good. He had influence. He was successful. If you entered his domain, you too could share in that.

Vinnie opened the door on a sleek, but stark, modern office. Surfaces were clear of any papers. Everything was shut away. Alec's heart sank.

He made his way over to the desk and sat in Oliver's chair. Allowed himself to briefly enjoy its comfort before leaning forward and tapping the desk's surface in annoyance.

"Thought he might have left us something to look at," said Alec.

"Tried the drawers?" asked Callum.

Alec reached down, expecting to meet locked resistance. Vinnie did the same to the filing cabinet. The drawers opened. He obviously didn't expect anybody to get this far. Soon the room was littered with files and papers as the men worked their way through the mound of information. They discovered nothing and the drawers were empty. Except. Alec found his eye drawn to the small sofa running alongside the window. The area was well lit and Alec could see there was something underneath the chair. He got up and made his way over, reaching down to pull it out. Another old journal, similar to the one he found with the Woodcutter's story in it.

"Why's it under the sofa? And there wasn't just a book but a thin file pushed further back. Accidental?"

"Breadcrumbs," said Alec.

"Huh?"

"Like Hansel and Gretel, a trail of breadcrumbs to lead us out of the woods."

"Or into them," said Callum.

They could all feel the presence of the forest, a pressure continuing to build, unavoidable, demanding.

A blinking light attracted Alec's attention. "Look. We're being filmed."

"Security," said Vinnie.

"No," said Alec, completely convinced they'd been set up again, although how Doug had agreed to put him through this was beyond him. "They're still filming us. Probably going out on the internet …"

"The blogs!" said Callum. "We haven't viewed those, haven't seen the edits or the comments."

"Good call," said Vinnie, approvingly. "At least one of us is thinking straight."

Alec ignored the dig. He wanted this all to be done and over with.

A laptop sat on Oliver's desk. The password proved easy. In no time, Alec fired it up and was online.

"Nothing," he said, hitting the table in frustration.

"Nothing? What the fuck do you mean?" asked Vinnie, pulling the laptop towards him.

"Exactly what I said. No Facebook posts, no twitter feeds. Those hashtags they threw at us don't exist. Nothing on YouTube either."

"That's crap," said Callum. "We were being filmed. We saw it. And not just that bloody woman and her cameraman. I mean the others in the village, taking selfies, all that stuff."

"Yeah," said Vinnie. "Well, Alec's right. There's nothing here. I've checked everyone's posts."

Alec moved to the window, found himself staring in the direction of the woods. The sound of his two companions muttering drew him back to the present.

"Didn't think Oliver would manage that bit," whispered Callum to Vinnie. "Seems I was wrong. Knows his tech! This is going great! He hasn't got a clue!"

"Ssh!" hissed Vinnie.

"What are you two talking about?" asked Alec, turning to face them.

"Huh? Nothing, nothing. Just saying about Oliver's set up on the field."

From the way they looked at each other, Alec sensed there was more to it than that. Then he dismissed it as a thought struck him. "Could this be Doug and Chadwick. Making it look as though we were all being filmed, feeding into Oliver's ego, making it all look authentic. I mean if there's no film, then there's no evidence of any of us being involved if it all goes pear-shaped. And the whole point of this *was* to set Oliver up for the final night, flip it round so he became the focus and not us. Public humiliation, justice of sorts for Fred."

"Could explain it," said Callum. "Sounds reasonable enough, although I still would've expected one of the kids to come up with a sneaky post or something if that was the case. You know what they're like."

"And it still doesn't explain where they've all gone and why they haven't told us," said Vinnie. "Makes you wonder if they're still filming."

"Course they are," said Alec. "Even if we can't find posts online, we know remote cameras were put up to film us for the TV crew. We watched them setting them up, didn't we? He dotted them everywhere. Like bloody confetti. Those are the ones which'll still catch us."

Callum shrugged. "Perhaps they forgot about us—either that or alien abduction." He grinned at Vinnie.

Alec noticed his brother's uncomfortable response, the shake of his head.

Any further contemplation was interrupted as something rumbled below their feet, a gentle tremor compared to the previous night, but a tremor nonetheless.

"There's one place we haven't looked yet," said Alec.

"I'm not bloody well going in there in the middle of the night," said Vinnie, knowing exactly where he was referring to.

Alec thought of the forest. It felt as if tonight was to be the night the village was finally swallowed up.

Chapter Twenty

"What now?" Callum looked pale, curious and not a little scared.

Alec knew he must look the same to the others. They had every right to be scared. Nothing made sense any more. Oliver's mansion breathed slowly around them, sent dark shadows shifting along the office walls. Alec felt as if they were being enveloped in a bubble, lifted into another world. Nobody spoke for a while.

"I need to get out of here," said Vinnie, abruptly standing up. "I can't breathe."

He headed off without waiting for the others.

"Vinnie!" Alec and Callum ran after him. Alec convinced if they split up, one of them would disappear. They found him leaning against the car, breathing heavily.

"You okay, mate?" asked Alec. A stupid question.

Vinnie merely groaned and buried his face in his hands. "This is so fucked up."

The other two slumped beside him.

"We're not going to find anything out," said Alec, feeling the last of his energy drain away from him. "We've looked everywhere and we're knackered, spooked. I suggest we go home—well to one of our homes—and try and get some kip. It'll be different in the daylight—hopefully."

"Yeah, go home, have a few drinks and sleep. Pretend this never happened. Sounds good to me," said Callum.

They decided on Andy's house. It was in the village but didn't have the wood brooding over it as obviously as it claimed the view in both Alec's and Callum's homes. It also had the advantage of Andy's dad's supply of booze. Although neither of the other two houses lacked in that respect. They figured Andy wouldn't mind in light of what they were being put through.

Vinnie had talked to Alec about this, the dependency village folk appeared to have on alcohol—even though they didn't appear to buy much in the pub. Said he'd never considered the whys or wherefores before. Accepted it as part of village life, and helped himself as often as the opportunity arose. Alec had a glimmer of understanding. There was a history to this place which was seriously messed up and even worse, hidden from view.

They drove back along the silent lanes, lights on full beam, never having to dip because no other traffic shared their route.

They did not talk, nor did they listen to the radio which, it turned out, emitted only white static. Like the villagers, the radio stations had also vanished off the face of the earth. They sat oblivious to each other and each occupied by their own individual thoughts.

"Christ, Vinnie!" Alec found himself jolted forward, his seatbelt rigid, digging hard into him. His head jerked back, his neck protested. He didn't turn to look at his brother. The car's lights picked out a shape, small but human, at the edge of its field of illumination. It stood still and he knew whoever it was, was watching, waiting.

He shot a look at Vinnie. The man's knuckles were white, gripping the steering wheel as if it was a safety anchor. His eyes were huge, shock carved its name across his face. Beads of sweat appeared on his brow. Alec heard a click behind him as Callum undid his safety belt and opened the door.

"Callum, I don't think you should—" He didn't have time to finish his sentence as Callum sprang out of the car.

"It's a person," he cried, "they might know what's been going on."

Alec looked ahead again. The shape remained there. It felt … predatory. He quickly unclipped himself and bounded after Callum. Vinnie remained immobile in the car. Eyes still fixed in horror.

"Callum!" He almost had him. Reached out and grabbed him, pulled him back. Just as the shape stepped towards them, allowed the light to illuminate her features. It was *her*. Grandma. Alec stepped back, pulling Callum with him but with each step, so too did she approach. He didn't want to look at her, even as his eyes locked with hers and started to pull them towards her. The sound of a revving engine broke the hold, not completely but enough to be aware of Vinnie nudging the car towards them. With a final effort he tore his gaze away and dashed back to the car, a short distance but it felt like miles, as if his legs were running through treacle. He pushed Callum into the backseat and jumped into the passenger side. He heard a clunk as Vinnie applied the central locking. Then he revved the engine harder, slammed on the accelerator and drove straight at her.

Alec could only watch. He dreaded what was about to happen, was terrified but already knew this creature was not someone who would allow themselves to be killed so easily. And sure enough, as they got closer, the body seemed to become transparent, started to fade so that at what should have been the moment of impact when her face, so aged and wicked, loomed over them, she vanished.

Vinnie did not stop until they reached Andy's house.

"This is not real," muttered Callum in the back. "This can't be bloody real."

"We all saw it," said Vinnie, finally letting go of the wheel and collapsing back against the chair, Alec noticing the tension visibly draining away from him now they were safe. "We all saw *her*."

"But she wasn't there in the end," said Callum. "Was she? So what? We all saw a ghost?"

"Or perhaps a hologram," said Alec, remembering Oliver's boast that he'd a box of tricks guaranteed to put the wind up anyone. "Oliver said he had a few surprises to deliver an 'authentic' experience."

"Well, he certainly succeeded there," said Callum. "I feel like an idiot. An idiot who could do with a drink."

"Come on then," said Vinnie, pulling the keys from the ignition. "Let's get inside and get pissed."

They followed Vinnie up the garden path but Alec couldn't resist taking another look at the nearby houses. They all still lay in darkness, nobody's dog barked, nobody's door slammed and beyond all that lay GodBeGone Wood. He shuddered and followed the others inside.

Andy's house was unlocked. No surprise there. It was familiar to them all but neither he nor Callum mocked Vinnie when he pulled the bolts across and set the chain on the door and then did the same in the kitchen.

"Even if it's his old man, he can bloody well explain what's been going on around here before I let him in."

They went round the house closing every window, every curtain. Turning on every light. If a stranger drove through the village at that time, they would have wondered at this one dwelling ablaze with light in the small hours. No one drove through however, and no one else in the village came knocking to ask if everything was alright because at that particular time, as the men had discovered, there was nobody else in the village—apart from themselves.

They'd settled down in the front room, Vinnie pulling bottle after bottle out of Andy's dad's well-stocked drinks cabinet, dumping it down in front of them.

"I'll take anything and everything tonight," said Vinnie, pouring himself a scotch.

"Go on, help yourselves."

They drank glass after glass, drowning their fear and memory of their recent experiences. Not wanting to talk at that moment, simply wanting to forget. Alec wondered at himself. He'd been practically teetotal all his life. How things had changed.

"In the morning," slurred Vinnie, swaying as he stood. "In the morning …"

Alec heard him stumble up the stairs and crash into Andy's bedroom door.

"Reckon we should turn in too," he said to Callum, helping his friend to his feet. Despite the amount he'd drunk, Alec still felt surprisingly—and unwillingly—clear-headed. He hoped sleep would still his thoughts. They found their way to the spare room. Passed Vinnie's whose door was still open, showing him lying face down on top of the bed, already snoring heavily.

Alec dropped Callum onto one bed and then sank onto the other. Unlike his friends, he pulled the blankets over him, felt that if he buried himself beneath their layers he would be safe, unseen. As he sank into sleep, he didn't know the wood didn't need eyes, instead *felt* their presence, was able to stretch its ancient consciousness out across the village and through chained and bolted doors, up the stairs and through bedding. So it watched and guarded them, not as a protector but more a gaoler over his prisoners, preventing escape.

The three slept deeply, even Alec, and none were visited by the nightmares they'd expected. *There was no need for that*, thought the wood, *when the daylight would come soon enough.*

They slept through the remaining dark hours, the grey of approaching dawn, the first rays of the sun. They slept as the herd of cattle on Callum's farm vocalised their distress at not being milked. They slept through the morning news being transmitted across the country. They slept through Liz Riverdale's pre-recorded breathless report of the village time forgot, where ancient and terrible customs had been revived, bringing with them the threat of something monstrous. *Stay tuned, viewers were told, for one of the scariest Halloween's ever.*

The three finally emerged from their rooms at midday, staggering down to the kitchen where every sound was amplified and normal daylight streamed in. They kept their voices to a whisper and their eyes half-closed. None of them noticed the lights they turned on last night were switched off, or that curtains opened and blinds lifted. If they thought about it at all, it was to assume one of the others had done it at some point.

"Ugh," said Callum, burying his head in his arms.

Vinnie pushed a packet of aspirin towards them and Alec took two gratefully. His head throbbed but he did not feel as bad as Callum and Vinnie looked. Part of him had held back a little last night and he was grateful for that small mercy.

"So, talk?" he asked.

The other two shook their heads.

"Not yet," said Vinnie. "More coffee. Fresh air."

Alec nodded and went to the back door, unbolted it and opened it wide. Andy's garden faced the side of the church. It was normally a tranquil scene. The lawn was well-tended with jasmine climbing the fences and small shrubs forming a border, interspersed by occasional, although bare, rose bushes. Beyond that was the ancient stone of St. Simon and the small stained-glass window showing a miniature version of its larger brother above the altar. Beyond *that* and you would then notice the omnipresent wood, that great dark line drawn against the sky that would run round the village and remind you there were some invisible barriers you couldn't cross.

Alec tried to push those thoughts to the back of his mind and breathed in deeply. The air was clear and sharp, it carried that autumnal tang which cleared the head and refreshed the spirits. He closed his eyes and allowed the small breeze to gently play over him. For that one moment he felt normal, could almost pretend nothing had happened. Then Vinnie and Callum came out and sat down on the bench by the door, clutching their coffee whilst trying to light cigarettes.

"So, talk," he said.

"I still can't believe anything that happened last night was real," said Callum.

"I think it's a great big hoax," said Vinnie.

"And yet," said Alec.

"And yet," echoed the others.

"So, plan?" asked Alec.

Vinnie finished his coffee and stubbed out his cigarette. "Shower and change for me. I stink. Then we go over to Alec's. Then up to Callum's. We'll feel better."

He hopes, thought Alec.

They left Andy's house without even leaving a note.

"Reckon they can do with a few nasty surprises," snarked Vinnie. "They ran out on us. Look at it as a payback."

Alec hadn't objected. After all, what had they done? Drunk their booze, slept in their beds. Nothing more than an adult version of *Goldilocks and the Three Bears*. They walked quickly to Doug's, the idea of a shower sloughing off both dirt and bad mood pulling them all on. Alec found himself again looking at the family photo on the fridge door when Vinnie returned, towelling his hair dry.

"You know it's been over a month," said Alec. "And I still haven't met Carol."

Vinnie looked guilty. "I suppose we should have told you sooner, but Dad didn't want to upset you. We thought in time, she would come round."

"Come round to what?"

"To you being here. I mean you heard Dad talk about your mum, how much he loved her. Well, my mum's always had a bit of a thing about being a replacement, always felt second best if you like. Then Cam died going to see you and you came back. I know it's stupid but she blames you for his death, has made it clear she doesn't want to see you."

Alec thought back to the funeral. "Bloody hell, Vinnie. Why didn't Doug tell me? I'd've stayed away, let her see her son buried."

Vinnie shook his head. "No, no. That bit was true enough. She was too upset to attend. Had to be sedated. Doc's got her on anti-depressants at the moment. Dad's working on her, trying to get her to come round but it'll take time. Until then …"

Coming to Little Hatchet, Alec had only ever considered how he was gaining a new family. He had not considered he might be damaging one in this process.

"Look," said Vinnie. "Don't blame yourself. None of this is your fault. It's our parents' problems. Let them deal with it, we've got more pressing matters on our hands today."

In that moment Alec felt very much like the younger brother. The idea of a shower, and clean clothes was already boosting his spirits and thankfully Vinnie didn't take too long with his. They all stood, ready to leave, taking a moment's pause at the door.

"What if everyone's still gone?" asked Callum.

"We have to find out one way or another," said Vinnie and he opened the door. Like before, the houses lay quietly around them. An occasional dog barked. Len's cat strolled across from the pub. The village seemed to be asleep.

"Perhaps everyone had a late night at that party we weren't invited to," said Vinnie.

Alec doubted it but it was a reassuring thought.

Slightly more cheerful, they crossed the street and made their way to Alec's flat, entering the book shop via a side entrance. It was still quiet, the grandfather clock which claimed pride of place behind the shop desk ticked noisily in the silence.

"Give me a minute," he told the others and grabbed clean clothes, blasted himself beneath the shower. He even shaved. It was as if he was trying to scrape off every sense of contamination from recent events. Before he returned to his friends, he grabbed a rucksack, shoved a load of clothes and his laptop inside, made sure his wallet held his bank card and driving licence and then summoned his friends.

"Callum's next," he said. A thought occurred to him. "Hold on."

He went back to his flat's spare room. There was a safe in there which his dad used for the shop's takings, only making the long arduous journey to the nearest bank—twenty miles away—when it was worth it. A lot of business was done online so there wasn't normally much money in the shop but his dad *had* gone to the bank three days ago. He wasn't expecting much.

"Bloody hell," said Callum, peering over Alec's shoulder as he opened the safe door.

Alec was as shocked as his friends. The safe was full, packed with bundles of notes.

"There must be thousands," whispered Vinnie, awed at the sight.

Alec swallowed, stunned. Then after a moment's pause, he grabbed it all and shoved it to the bottom of his bag.

"I need to check something before we go to Callum's," said Vinnie. "And I'll get some of my gear while I'm at it."

They went back to Vinnie's house and watched as he prised up a loose floorboard in his dad's empty bedroom.

"The old bugger usually keeps a stash of spare cash here," said Vinnie, yanking it free. "Thinks I don't know." He shoved his hand in the gap. "The old sod has been holding out on me," he said, pulling a wad of banknotes out. He rooted around a bit more and before long had a pile of money to rival Alec's.

"Bastard! Where'd he get all this money? Where'd *your* folks get theirs?"

Alec was completely confused. From what he knew of the business, Doug didn't have the ability to get that amount of money together. Unless some sort of deal had been done. But what?

"My place," said Callum, sounding firm, decided. "Let's see if we can make it a hat trick?"

They piled back into the car. This time Vinnie drove slowly, allowing Alec and Callum time to scan the village for signs of life. Nothing. Yet again, Fred wasn't in his usual position at this time of the day, leaning over the garden gate, watching the world go by.

"Same as before," said Alec.

"Let's hope that 'vision' doesn't appear again," said Vinnie. "I could do without that."

"I think we'll be safe," said Alec. "Light's all wrong in daytime for those sorts of special effects." Hopefully.

The first thing they heard when they arrived at the farm was the sound of the distressed cows.

"Shit," said Callum. "Look, we'll have to see to them, you two give me a hand."

"Are you serious?" asked Vinnie.

"Yeah, look at 'em. We can't leave them like this. Help me herd them into the shed. You won't have to touch anything."

It took some time and much shouting and swearing from Vinnie before they got the cattle into place. Whilst raised in the country, Vinnie had long had an aversion to farm animals.

"We'll leave you to it," said Vinnie, as Callum secured the teats into place. "Clean up … again. Good job I've got a change of clothes *and* you've got a washing machine."

Alec laughed. Even under these trying circumstances, he was still the same appearance-obsessed man he'd always been. He said it was one of the secrets of his success with the girls.

The farmhouse was as quiet as their own had been, which in a way was even more worrying as the three dogs, so ever present, were missing.

"Perhaps they went with his old man," said Vinnie, heading upstairs to shower yet again.

It wasn't just vanity that compelled this obsession with cleanliness. In part it was down to that incident so many years ago when he'd got shut in the barn. Callum's dad always asserted it was an accident, something spooked the animals locked in there with him. He'd hated cows ever since.

Alec put the kettle on, rooted through the cupboards for something quick and easy to fix for them all. His stomach growled as he opened tins of beans, put bread on to toast. It would do. He was perfectly capable of cooking a meal but he felt they didn't have time for that. They'd slept through most of the day and the afternoon was advancing. He grated a mound of cheese, nibbling at the block as he did so to quieten the protests of his body. His headache had completely gone, fading away as their distractions came to the fore.

As he piled the food on the plates, Vinnie reappeared and Callum entered the kitchen.

"Better open the windows if we're going to eat all that lot," said Callum, grinning. "Keep mine warm."

It was his turn for the ritual cleansing.

"Found anything?" asked Alec, looking up from his food. Callum had returned, drying his wet hair with an old towel.

"Not looked yet," said Callum. "I need to eat."

Their plates were cleared in no time but they continued to tear at the loaf of bread in front of them. They were still hungry. Callum sighed and went to the freezer, pulled out a bag of oven chips and a pizza.

"Twenty minutes," he said. "I reckon we've got time for that."

Alec shrugged. Twenty minutes. Not long in the great scheme of things. As the oven timer counted down, Callum went over to the old hearth, containing a range which looked as though it hadn't been used for years. He knelt down and slid open the door at the bottom, drawing out an old tray. It was filled with money, as much as Vinnie's and Alec's.

"Well this shit got weird," said Vinnie.

"As if it wasn't already weird in the first place," said Alec. "The village has disappeared and not only that, they've left behind huge sums of cash we'd have expected them to take with them."

"I don't understand," said Callum. "I seriously don't understand."

Alec looked at them. "I think," he said, "we should go over to Axehampton to speak to the police."

"No," said Callum, "that's no good. Station closed last year. Don't you remember? Nearest one is Shrewsbury. And you know if we turn up there with a load of money and a wild story, they won't believe us. Will probably keep the cash and send us back."

"We need to get them over here, show them what's going on," said Alec.

Callum yawned. "Look, I dunno about you, but I can't think straight at the minute and I don't want to deal with the Bill in this state." He yawned again. "Sleep," he said. "Another hour's kip, *please.*"

An hour's escape was more the truth of the matter. Experience told him those amounts of money, hidden as they were, were usually the result of something dodgy. The idea of just leaving the village and its inhabitants behind began to appeal to him—and then he remembered Cameron, his plea to help Vinnie. No, he would stay until he'd reunited his brother with the rest of the village, found the answers to their questions, and then he would go.

Oliver had thrown his money around and the village grabbed at it. How could they take it knowing he had blood on his hands? Or was that *why* they'd taken it? As part of their perceived settlement, the righting of wrongs.

Blood money.

CHAPTER TWENTY-ONE

The screams and shouts startled Alec from his sleep. He was angry he'd dozed off when they should've been scouring the countryside for their missing families, neighbours and friends. He stumbled down the stairs to Callum's kitchen, crashing across to the door to the yard.

"Shit, Alec. Make enough noise to wake the dead, why don't you," said Callum, following him down.

"Didn't you hear that?" he asked. "Someone's in trouble out there."

"Screech owl," said Callum peering over his shoulder into the sleeping farmyard.

"Get them all the time round here."

"That wasn't no screech owl," snapped Alec, rubbing his eyes. He was exhausted but the noise carried terror with it, a fear of something primal.

"What's going on?" Vinnie joined them at the kitchen door, looking none too happily into the blackness before them. "Christ, it's one o'clock. Alec?"

Alec frowned. Callum had only wanted an hour's respite, now he wanted to simply go back to bed as if everything was normal.

It didn't feel right.

"He heard an owl," said Callum, "that's all. Come on, let's all go back to bed. God knows we need to sleep."

There'd been no other noise and Alec reluctantly allowed Callum to turn him round and guide him back to the stairs. Vinnie remained by the door for a moment and then as he moved to close it, the cry came again.

Alec shot back across to the door and swung it open. "See, we *all* heard that and that ain't no screech owl."

He glared at Callum as he spoke.

"Yeah," sighed Callum. "That's no screech owl. So, what do we do?"

Alec stared at him. "You're seriously asking that question. The village has disappeared and we hear someone in trouble and you ask us what we do? We go out there of course. Find whoever it is and help them."

"I dunno," said Vinnie. "I think we need to get the police in."

"Our phones aren't working and the landlines are down," said Callum.

"Now you want to get the police?" snapped Alec. "Sure you don't just want to go back to bed?"

"Then we get in the car and drive there."

"And what happens to whoever it is in the meantime?" asked Alec

Vinnie shrugged.

"I vote we get in the car, find them and then go over to Shrewsbury," said Callum.

"I'm okay with that," said Alec. "If we have someone needing help with us, they're more likely to take us seriously. Vinnie?"

"Yeah," he said. "Not that I'm too happy going to see the boys in blue."

And still they remained. Until the scream came again. Nearer this time. Alec grabbed the car keys off the table and headed out. Vinnie and Callum following. Vinnie protesting it was his car and he should drive.

"Sounds like the top of the lane," said Callum. "They're really close."

Alec turned the ignition and pulled out onto Shrewsbury Road. Right took them to the town. Left took them away and back towards the village, and the person in distress. He turned left. He drove slowly, cautiously. The lights were on full beam, picking out details in the hedgerows, reflecting the eyes of a rabbit, a fox, as they passed, settling on a shape slumped over a gate.

"There," said Callum, grabbing Alec's arm and almost causing him to drive into a ditch. "There. Someone's at the gate. They don't look in a good way."

Alec brought the car to a stop, turning it so its lights fell in full on the figure. "Shit, it's Eric!"

Vinnie and Callum scrambled out of the car and Alec swiftly followed them.

"Eric, what the fuck happened to you?"

Callum had his arm round Eric's shoulders was turning him round, holding him up. Their friend's face was white with shock, his eyes huge. There was blood down his front.

"Get him in the car," said Alec. "Quick, we need to get him to a doctor."

But as they started to guide him towards the car, Eric resisted and tried to turn away.

"No, no," said Eric. "I'm okay, it's a scratch but … but we need to go into the woods … the others are there, they need our help."

"Others?"

"Yeah, Paul and Andy. Oliver took them, said it was all part of the show but I dunno, there's something about him that's a bit off. I think he's got a screw loose if you ask me."

"He may be nuts," said Vinnie, "but he's got a bloody good business head. We're all going to make a mint from tonight. You know that don't you?"

"Not as much as he's going to make," said Eric. "Not to mention what he's done to you three. Set you all up to look like right village oiks."

Alec felt his skin grow cold. The horrible feeling in the pit of his stomach which refused to go away as the idea they'd been had kept nudging at his mind, solidified. "What d'you mean?"

"He's fixed up a big reality TV con," said Eric, gasping for breath. "Cameras everywhere following you around the countryside. You're okay here. That's why I stopped here. Made sure we didn't get picked up by anything."

"But I don't understand," said Callum. "We knew this was all staged, a setup for the story of the Woodcutter."

"Yeah," said Eric. "That and more. I guess you've noticed the village has disappeared. He's set *you* up. Building it into a big return for the Woodcutter and Grandma. You were going to be shown as gibbering wrecks and then he'd throw off the costume and ... well, you get it."

"So everyone's okay? Really?" asked Alec.

"Yeah, they're in the woods."

"But you said they needed our help," said Alec. "How can they if they're alright. I don't understand."

"The villagers are fine but I'm not so sure about Andy and Paul. We need to get to them quick before Oliver does something stupid. I told you he was nuts."

Eric pulled away from them and slipped into the field. Alec went to follow but Vinnie grabbed his arm. "Wait, how do we know we're not being set up again, that the cameras aren't on us now?"

"You'll have to take my word for it and I can show you where the others are though I really think we need to get to Paul and Andy first."

The three looked at each other.

"I don't think we have any choice," said Callum. "I think whatever's happening we need to go with Eric. Get to the bottom of everything once and for all."

"But it might be fake. Like everything else," said Alec.

"Then we find that out too and deal with it," said Vinnie. "And I know exactly how I intend to go about that. I wouldn't reckon Oliver's chances much if he's really made us into prize fools."

"Are you sure you're alright to go on," said Alec, "I mean the blood."

Eric glanced down at his front. "It's nothing, a few scratches from the branches that's all. Took a few wrong turns trying to get out."

"You went in and you came out," said Callum, staring at him.

"Yes," said Eric. "So have others. Come on."

As they trudged across the field, cresting the brow of the hill and then heading down towards the dark mass of the woods, Alec couldn't help but dwell on Eric's explanation, his appearance. It still didn't hold true.

"You were screaming blue murder back there," he said, after they'd walked on in silence for some time. "Why? You seem calm enough now."

Eric shrugged. "I was spooked. I'd listened to those stories back at the field, felt the ground rumble—although that's down to his little fracking experiment apparently— and then seen what he'd arranged in the woods for the three of us. I managed to get away and ran, got myself snagged on the branches, got lost. Frightened myself shitless, you could say. And I don't care telling you. You would've felt the same in there."

"Don't you think that whatever he was organising for you three— and you still haven't told us yet—is just another piece of theatre for the bloody cameras?" Callum continued to be the voice of reason.

"I can't tell you," said Eric. "It's … I'd rather you see for yourselves."

Their pace had grown slower, the nearer they got to the woods.

"See those little red dots in the branches?" Eric pointed up at the lights. "They're cameras. They'll be filming our every move as we go in, sending it back to those watching. They can't reach us here but in a little while, everything we do and say will be captured on screen."

"Then we go along with Oliver's little plan," said Alec. "We go in and pretend we don't know anything. That we're still unaware of everything that's been going on. Just following you to rescue Andy and Paul. And it'll give Vinnie a chance to mug for the cameras, redeem his shattered ego somewhat."

A quiet ripple of laughter ran through the group at Alec's words. They could go into full-blown hero mode instead of prize pillocks. As they closed in on the woods, Alec noticed how they all stood taller, pulled their shoulders back. Vinnie was even managing to swagger a little although the effect was ruined when he tripped over the ruts at the edge of the field.

The entrance stood before them, a long cold black tunnel.

"Right," said Vinnie. "Let's go in."

But Alec didn't answer, barely heard him as a low creaking noise caught his attention. He turned his head towards the sound, trying to pick out where it was coming from. Somewhere along the boundary he was certain.

"Alec, come on."

Still he didn't move, instead continued to peer into the dark, straining his eyes, finally resting on something swinging from a tree further down.

"Alec."

He didn't hear them, turned away towards the swinging shape, pulling out his phone to get what light he could, nearing the creaking, groaning sound, raising his torch. He found himself staring into Chadwick's sightless eye. The other socket didn't exist, half his face didn't actually exist, the head split in two exposing brain and bone. The noose fastened around the neck in such a way the body did not slip from its grasp. Bile rose in his throat and he could do nothing but retch heavily into the grass at the reverend's swinging feet.

"Alec! Alec?"

The sound of the others running towards him did nothing to stop him. He continued to heave until his stomach was empty. And when he finally straightened, wiping his mouth with his sleeve, he could not look back at the reverend's corpse.

"Oh my God!"

"Eric, did you know about this?"

It took a while for Eric to answer as he too responded as Alec had done.

"You think I would know about this and not tell you?" he asked. "Chadwick was alive and talking last time I saw him."

"And when did you see him?" asked Alec.

"With Oliver, before I left to get you lot," he said.

"Do you think Oliver could've had something to do with this?" asked Alec.

They all reluctantly looked up at the hanging minister again.

"Possibly, I don't know," said Eric.

"Do you think we should cut him down?" asked Callum. "It doesn't seem right to leave him hanging there."

"Leave it," said Vinnie. "The less we touch anything round here, the better. Don't want the police thinking we were involved in this in any way."

Whilst Alec didn't feel comfortable leaving the dead vicar there, he was more than happy not to have to touch him. He was even happier to leave him behind as they made their way to the entrance to the woods. Nevertheless, the image of Chadwick's face was lodged firmly in his mind and he was unable to shake it as they walked on.

"Andy and Paul," said Vinnie, finally breaking the silence. "Why're you so worried about them?"

"You saw Chadwick," said Eric.

"If that was Oliver," said Alec.

"Yeah, well. It's the whole Woodcutter business. The stories. He said he wanted it *all* re-enacted."

"What do you mean *all*?" asked Alec.

"Not just the selection of the Woodcutter's apprentice, although that seems to have gone by the board. He didn't mention anything about that to me, the last time I saw him. Apart from that it was taken care of. It's Grandma's cloak. He's got an obsession about it."

They had all pulled their phones out, were using them as torches.

"Are you sure you know which way to go?" Alec was looking around. Could see nothing apart from the bank of trees and scrub.

"There's no other way except on," said Eric. "Have you seen any other turn offs? We'll come to a fork in the paths up ahead. One'll take us on to Oliver's little fracking development, the other to Paul and Andy. We'd been told to wait at the cottage. Creepy place. Oliver had had us waiting there until he summoned me to meet him and Chadwick. The reason I wasn't too worried was Oliver's girlfriend, that Liz whatsername was there as well. She seemed perfectly happy."

Grandma's cottage. The one from the old stories, the fairy tale which turned into the story of *Little Red Riding Hood*. The ground trembled beneath his feet and immediately he thought of the Woodcutter roaming the land again. They had summoned him after all. The monster of legend recalled. Another rumble.

"Remember Oliver's been testing for shale gas with that bloody fracking rig of his," said Eric. "Don't let it spook you."

Alec pushed his thoughts down, berated himself for being stupid. He said nothing to his friends. None of them spoke. He knew Vinnie and Callum were trying to imagine what they would find, as was he. What was going through Eric's head, he had no idea. He was part of Chadwick's God squad though, he could be trusted to a certain extent because of that—couldn't he? He must be suffering at his mentor's death.

The path led them into a small glade. In its centre stood a cottage, surrounded by a low picket fence. It looked ancient but well-tended. There was a light reflected in the fire, dancing as if from a flame.

"Someone's home," said Vinnie.

It was a strange place, it felt cold, cruel. An odd choice of word to describe a building, he considered. As they approached the door however, he decided it was completely apt. The carving in the door. The horrific mutilated face of the Woodcutter stared out at them as it had done in the pamphlet, as it had done from its place on the bonfire.

"Abandon hope all ye who enter here," laughed Vinnie.

Alec noted the lack of humour in his laugh, the underlying unease. Eric stepped forward and knocked at the door.

"Knocking? Why don't you just go in?" Alec asked.

"I … don't know. Felt like the right thing to do," said Eric.

For someone who had rushed to get help, Eric seemed very slow in moving forward. Vinnie stepped in front of Eric and pushed the door open. No doubt thinking of the cameras which might be trained on them. He wanted to be the hero of the day. Unfortunately, he ruined that initial impression by running straight back out, dry heaving in the garden.

Alec reluctantly entered the cottage, almost falling over on the slick of blood on the floor, following it to find another even more horrific sight seated in the chair by the fire. Liz.

The young woman they had all seen and admired on Oliver's arm, sat rigid and unmoving. Her skin was grey and her face was set in a terrified grimace, a look which could even be described as a smile. A blanket was wrapped around her shoulders and her body huddled over. As Alec moved slowly back, you could almost imagine the figure was Grandma. A little old lady hunched in the rocking chair by the fire.

He could barely breathe. The air was metallic and cloying, oppressive. As he moved backwards, he forced himself to scan the remainder of the room, noticing the small bed in the corner, the workbench and tools. And that face again. Carved into the back of the door, the Woodcutter's cruel stare bore into him. It was too much and Alec raced outside to join Vinnie.

Callum and Eric stood on the threshold but didn't go in. They could see the blood on the floor, their friends' reaction. That was enough to send them staggering back, unwilling to get any closer to what Alec and Vinnie had seen.

"Liz," said Vinnie. "It's fucking Liz. What sort of a monster would do that?"

"And I think this is where Chadwick died as well," said Callum, pointing to a crucifix lying in the blood near the door.

The minister always wore it.

"We better find Andy and Paul and then get the hell out of here," said Vinnie.

"With you on that," said Alec, scanning round for another path. "Which way?"

"Over there," said Eric. "It's the only other way out of here. I shouldn't have left them."

His voice choked on a sob. Alec squeezed his shoulder. "You did the right thing, mate. You thought something was wrong and came to get help."

"No," said Eric, "you don't understand. It was pretend. It was all fucking pretend. Oliver was paying me. Gave me a bit of extra money to come and get you, lead you in here." He was crying and then suddenly he was on the floor as Vinnie leapt between them and punched him in the face.

"Vinnie," said Alec. "For Christ's sake, leave it."

"The toe-rag set us up," said Vinnie. "He bloody well set us up. How do we know he didn't kill Liz, and Chadwick? Always was a bit touched, wasn't he?"

Eric was curled up in a ball on the floor, crying. Vinnie looked ready to launch himself at the man again but Callum grabbed his arms and held him back whilst Alec attempted to pull Eric to his feet. As he did so, he noticed the disturbed earth, in the shape of a grave. He let go of Eric and headed back to the cottage.

"Where are you going?" called Callum, struggling to hold onto Vinnie.

"I think we need to get something to protect ourselves," said Alec. "There're tools inside, something we might be able to use."

Vinnie shook Callum off and followed him, he said nothing to Eric who trailed after them.

As Alec moved along the workbench, inspecting the small selection of hatchets and knives, he detected a strange, musty smell. It reminded him of the smell in his mum's garden shed. She used it as a storage area for all sorts of odds and ends when she'd gone through a 'crafty' phase. She had even used it to store some sacks of wheat for the rustic crafts she sometimes made to sell at local fairs. That particular idea had soon fallen beside the wayside and the wheat remained forgotten in the corner of the shed for some time. Only when Alec fell sick with dizzy spells and hallucinations did they rediscover the wheat and the doctor was able to confirm the cause of his illness. He sensed its presence again, breathed it in, ignoring the coppery tang of blood, detected the familiar rotten fishy smell. Immediately the room began to spin.

"Out," he said to the others, pushing them back to the door. "Now."

"But the tools."

"I've got some, although I think the ones used to cause the damage we've seen are still with the person who wielded them." He continued to push them back until they were outside again.

"Alec, what the fuck was that for?" demanded Vinnie.

"The air in there. There's something bad. It's the same sort of smell we had back home in our shed some years ago. I used to do odd DIY projects in there but I started to feel funny. Even began to see things. Had to see the doctor and we eventually tied it to some old sacks of wheat in the shed. We had to strip everything out, air the place thoroughly. Fumigate. Doc said it was ergot poisoning."

They were outside, looking back at the cottage.

"Oliver said he spent a lot of time here, doing it up," said Eric. "If it's the same stuff, then he's been exposed to it for ages. Do you think …?"

The thought lodged itself in Alec's mind. "If he's done all this, it could explain everything."

"I think," said Callum, "we need to find Andy and Paul. Now."

They were all gathered at the entrance to the one tunnel through the trees which they had not yet explored.

"We could go back," said Eric, his reluctance to go any further a stark contrast to his pushing them on before.

"We could," said Alec, "but Paul and Andy might be in trouble and from what we've seen, I wouldn't want to risk their chances."

"What about our chances?" blubbed Eric. "What about us?"

"Hamming it up for the cameras?" sneered Vinnie. "This part of the script."

"Forget the fucking script," said Eric. "And there aren't any cameras here. Can't you see? We're on our own and I am not staying here a minute longer. I did not agree to this, any of this. I'm getting out of here."

Alec stared at Eric. If he came with them, he'd be a liability. He'd turned into a complete wreck. "Look, why don't you go back," he said to Eric. "Take the car and go get help."

Eric snatched the offered keys from Alec's hand and sprinted back the way they'd come.

"What'd you do that for?" demanded Vinnie.

"He'd be a liability, wouldn't he," said Callum. "This way we can hedge our bets. Get someone from the outside here, get help and we can go on knowing someone'll come soon."

"Makes sense," said Callum.

"Here," said Alec, handing out the tools he'd grabbed as they left. A knife, and two small axes.

Vinnie took an axe, swung it a couple of times. His face was grim. Alec knew he'd use it if it was needed. Callum took the knife, leaving Alec with the other hatchet.

"Ready?" asked Vinnie.

Alec and Callum nodded. Alec tightening his grip on the handle, feeling it there made him feel stronger, safer. They walked into the unknown tunnel. Alec wanted to shout his friends' names but there was something about the wood which told him it was best not to. Who knew who might be listening? His ears strained to pick up every snap of a twig, every rustle in the undergrowth. His eyes, adjusted to night vision, pushed against the black but only succeeded in creating twisted shapes and deformed monsters from which more than once he prepared to run. His companions were the same and he knew their pale faces and wide eyes, anxious and fearful were a reflection of his own.

"How far do you reckon?" he whispered.

"Don't know," said Vinnie, also keeping his voice low.

"Ssh," hissed Callum. "We need to stay quiet. Don't want anyone hearing us."

The track narrowed and roots rutted the path. Alec tripped over one and put his hand out to steady himself. His fingers curled round a thick vine and as he shone his torchlight over the area, he saw many such tendrils wrapping themselves around the trunks, weaving in and out to create the impression of a wattled fence. Between the trunks, this living palisade intertwined with dark-stained forms, occasional flashes of dull white. As he straightened up, his hand unconsciously tightened around his support. Beneath the vine, he touched something cold, something dead.

He directed his beam, illuminating other things buried further back, the light picking out one which they all saw and retreated from, its empty sockets following them.

"How many do you reckon?" asked Callum.

Alec swept his torch over the adjacent area, saw more bones buried in amongst the wood.

"Could be animal," said Vinnie.

Alec retrained his light on a skull in answer. It was answer enough. No one said anything else but they found themselves moving faster. The sound of a heavy thud up ahead brought them to a sudden stop. Vinnie turned his torch off and they all followed suit, creeping forward as quietly as they could. What they saw was beyond any horror film Alec had ever seen.

The path ended in another small glade dominated by a huge oak tree. Alec stared up into its all-encompassing canopy. Its reach was far, its boughs huge. And there were shapes hanging there, shapes a little like the one of the Reverend they'd left behind them at the edge of the wood. Two shapes, thankfully wrapped in some sort of shroud, so they did not have to look at their faces. They hung there, not swaying and occasionally, something dripped down.

Down into a wooden vat placed below the body.

A couple of lanterns hung from nearby trees to illuminate the area so they could clearly see what was being collected in the vats, see the man currently moving another vat into place. Three more vats. Alec looked up. There was nothing up there. But there were ropes hanging empty, waiting. He knew who they were waiting for.

"Come on in, lads," said the man.

He had Oliver's voice but when he turned, he no longer wore the same face. Instead Alec stared at the lines and curves carved into his mutilated skin. He looked exactly like the Woodcutter.

"Watch what you say," muttered Alec to the others. This was going to need careful handling.

"Glad you could make it," continued Oliver. "Although I see I am one short. Never mind. I dare say I'll catch up with him later. Five is still enough for Grandma."

"Oliver," said Callum. "Oliver. Where are Andy and Paul?"

"Eh? Oh, those two. Where they're supposed to be of course."

Oliver was leaning on the largest axe Alec had ever seen. Its blade appeared dull, covered, he realised with the blood of his friends. He'd experienced so many shocks in such a small space of time, he felt numb to this one. Hopefully Eric would fetch help soon, family and friends would come looking for them. This madness would stop.

"Oliver," said Alec. "I think you're sick."

"Too right he is," muttered Vinnie.

"Shut it," hissed Callum.

"Sick? Oh, I'm not sick. I thought I was, all those dreams I used to have. The memories of the cottage my family told me didn't exist. But I found out the truth. It was real and I wasn't sick."

"I think the air in your cottage is poisoned. You spent a lot of time in there and it's made you behave this way," said Alec.

"Poisoned? No, no," said Oliver, laughing. "There's nothing poisonous in there."

"Ergot," insisted Alec. "My mum had some growing in her shed, back home. I know because it made me ill. I think it still affects me after all this time."

Callum and Vinnie both looked at him.

"The woods," he said, shrugging. "I hallucinate from time to time; the trees seem to come towards me."

"That's no hallucination, boy," said Oliver. "The trees walk you know. They've been walking for centuries."

"If you've been poisoned," persisted Alec, "I'm sure the courts will understand."

"I don't want the courts to understand," growled Vinnie at his side. "I want them to throw the book at him. Andy and Paul, remember?"

"I know," hissed Alec. "But we need to get out in one piece. Keep on his good side."

"Good side? He's got no good side," said Vinnie. "And there's one of him, three of us."

"But he's got a bloody big axe," said Callum.

The three friends continued to stare at Oliver as he tended to his vats, apparently dismissing his visitors from his thoughts for the moment. Alec looked at him, tried to work out how they could take him but as he studied the man's body, he seemed to grow.

Alec stepped back.

"Alec? What's wrong?" Callum held his arm, was following his gaze, trying to work out what Alec was looking at.

"Don't you see?" he said, making no attempt to keep his voice down. "He's a giant. He's huge. We can't take him."

"Don't be bloody daft," said Callum. "You're seeing things. Reckon you've been inhaling whatever it is that you say has affected Oliver. He's ..."

"Callum! Look!" Vinnie's voice cut through, urged them both to look at Oliver again.

The shadow he was throwing.

Alec knew they were seeing what he saw. This was not hallucination. Not toxin induced. This was real. The Woodcutter had returned and he was stood right behind Oliver.

"I've been telling you he's back," said Oliver. "I knew he would come when he saw me. I've been his apprentice, just like he wanted."

The shadow moved closer, tamped out the light from the lanterns.

"I think now would be a good time for us to get the hell out of here," said Callum.

"While he's occupied."

"With you there, mate," said Vinnie.

The three moved carefully backwards towards the entrance to the glade. Oliver's attention was still fixed on the strange shadow which formed in front of the giant oak. Then they found the path and turned and ran. Along the tunnel with its vines and skulls, past the cottage with its dead and its buried, back out of the woods and over the fields. Never letting up until they were out in the open and gasping their way onto the road. They continued to run until they reached Callum's house and shut themselves inside.

Alec went to the phone. It was still dead. Callum opened up his laptop. The internet was down.

"Crap. What do we do?"

"Tell everyone else what's been going on?"

"Well, they're buried on the other side of the wood."

"Not the best choice of words," said Alec. "But I don't want to be going through those trees again."

"And I doubt that even Oliver could wipe out a whole village," said Vinnie. "I reckon they're safe. I vote we stay here until Eric turns up with the Bill."

"You reckon he got out okay?" asked Alec.

"Well, the car wasn't there, was it? And you saw his reaction to Chadwick, and Liz. I don't think he's in on this."

"Hope you're right," said Alec. He would have to take Vinnie's word for it, he seemed earnest in Eric's defence, maybe a little too earnest.

The three huddled together in the kitchen. None of them let go of the axes in their hands. None slept. They jumped at every sound as night gave way to day. Even the sound of the cows lowing, the call for milking went ignored. They were not going outside again until they were sure it was safe.

Then Alec heard the wail of a siren, saw blue lights cresting the top of the road. Callum jumped up, and without waiting for the others, dashed outside. Alec and Vinnie saw his body slump to the ground. The blue lights went speeding past the farm, heading towards the wood. Oliver stood in the doorway; his shirt soaked with blood.

CHAPTER TWENTY-TWO

A cheer went up from somewhere. Startled, Alec turned round and noticed the laptop had sprung to life. The screen showed the two of them in the kitchen, filthy, dirty, terrified.

Words were scrolling beneath the scene.

"Don't you want to read what they're saying guys?" asked Oliver. "You're stars. The local site's been going crazy all night. It's only been streamed to your families at the minute but when ITV broadcasts it, it's going to be major."

Callum groaned on the other side of the door. "You didn't need to hit me so hard," he said.

Hit him? What the hell were they playing at? Utterly at a loss, Alec stared at them. This was not what we planned. The intention was to set up Oliver, hadn't it? When was that going to happen—or was it?

"You little shit," snarled Vinnie, hurling himself past Oliver to get to Callum, then stopping and helped Callum to his feet.

"Vinnie, Callum? What the fuck?"

When they planned it, all those weeks ago, it was for Fred. Their anger at Oliver clear, their desire for revenge evident. Fred however, had vanished. Something had changed. What?

"Oh, you should see your face, Alec," hooted Callum. "Priceless."

Vinnie was grinning behind him. "Reckon we got you good and proper."

"Got me? All of you did this to 'get me'? What the fuck for?" Alec was totally disoriented. Why had they picked on him to be the butt of the joke? "What have I ever done to you?"

A look of shame drifted across Vinnie's face. "Nothing," he said. "But Oliver needed to be able to pull this off and we needed somebody gullible. We had to go through with it if we wanted *our* plan to work." His eyes fixed on Alec as he spoke.

The look told him the intention was still there, they just hadn't got to it yet. His own humiliation was the price. It angered him to be thought of as someone whose feelings were expendable. Doug. All that talk about rebuilding their relationship. Was that all pretend too, a ploy to keep him onside as a useful patsy?

"Mum suggested you," muttered Vinnie.

Course she did. Vinnie said she blamed him for Cam's death. What better way of getting her own back?

"Shit, Alec. I feel bad you were kept in the dark about all this but you've got to admit, it's been fucking epic. Stunt of the century. The bodies were bloody brilliant special effects dummies. I tell you something—"

"Yes?" said Alec. His voice stopped Callum short. He didn't want to hear how amazing it was, wanted to remind them not everyone had had a laugh, that someone had been hurt in the midst of all this.

There was a sound of clapping on the laptop behind him, distracting him from Callum. The screenshot had changed to show all the villagers watching. Laughing and cheering. *Mocking him.* Even his dad. After everything he'd done for them since he'd come back, even taking on Cam's role in the business whilst he was there, increasing web orders in the short space of time he'd been back. Yet Doug too, had been in on it. Put Carol's misplaced hate and jealousy above his own son's feelings. He could see Doug's face; he was there at the front. Unlike the others, he wasn't smiling, even appeared to be mouthing an apology.

So long ago, those early walks in the forest, holding his father's hand. The oath made by the village, the promise broken, their memories buried. Remembrance would come for them, as it had for him. As would Grandma and the Woodcutter.

His body tensed and he felt the weight of the axe still in his hand. Its heft was comforting, sent strength coursing through him. The ground rumbled beneath his feet and the voices of those watching quietened. The ground trembled again and he heard someone cry out, "What's that?" Then the screen went blank.

"Another trick, eh, Oliver? Still playing it out. Is it real, is it make believe?"

Alec looked over Oliver's shoulder, past Callum and Vinnie standing behind him, across the fields lit by day, and saw the woods. *She was waiting for him, ready to tell another story. The momentum of her rocking chair gathered. Grandma. She had another name. One he would speak soon.*

"Their guilty, blackened hearts," he said, looking at Oliver and advancing on him.

"What? Look here, Alec. This was all a joke. Yes, I know it was unfortunate you were the only one not in on it but we had to have someone completely unaware and I promised your father I would pay you double what the others got."

"Double!" snapped Vinnie, behind him. "You said we would all get the same."

"I lied," said Oliver. "Deal with it."

Alec moved closer. The axe still firmly in his hand. He was pleased to see Oliver back away. "Now you know what it feels like," he said. "But I also think you have another question you need to ask yourself. Am I acting—or not?" He raised the axe up and then let it fall, its blade landing in the wood of the kitchen table. He laughed. It felt good.

"Oh, your face, Oliver. Priceless. And you and Vinnie. You really thought I was gonna do it." He pulled the axe out of the table as the uncomfortable laughter of the three filled the room. "I must admit you've been very clever."

"We're forgiven?" There was a hesitant note in Callum's voice.

"Course you are, mate. I can take a joke as well as the next man. And think of the dosh we've got to spend. Holiday in the Bahamas coming up, eh, Olly boy!" He slapped Oliver on the back. Grinned at Callum. They were all back in the room. He had them all.

Callum opened a cupboard and pulled out a whisky bottle, poured a round of drinks. "Here," he said, handing out the tumblers. "Here's to Alec. He's been a bloody good sport."

They all knocked their drinks back, relief evident at Alec's unselfish response.

Alec continued to smile and nod at those he'd thought his friends. Inside he was furious. Angrier than he'd ever felt before at being made such a fool of, by his new friends, his new family. People he thought had accepted him. It was a huge betrayal. *She was rocking faster, and his pulse responded, matching her rhythm. Soon, he would call her name.*

"Your Dad said you'd take it in good part. That you would understand why he did it," said Oliver. "I'm glad you're able to see the funny side."

The funny side. Yes, he could see it, but it wasn't the joke they expected. He wondered how they would feel if they'd been made such a fool as he. Bad enough it was in front of the whole village, soon Oliver would broadcast his production to the world. He looked at the woods. His answer lay in there. Oliver noticed him looking and reached over to close the laptop lid, the screen had come back and the villagers were watching intently. Alec stopped him. He didn't care when everyone else planned on exposing Oliver. He was going to do it now. It was time. Those who knew might come on side, they might not. He didn't care. He'd already been shown he was on his own. Except for *her* and she had begun to call his name.

"What gave you the idea?" Alec asked. "I mean it meant digging up your own past. Televising *that.*"

"His past?" Vinnie had caught the conversation, realised where Alec was going.

"Forgotten it, have you?" asked Alec. "Oliver's guilty secret. Being involved in the death of Fred's wife, Rosie. She was murdered out in the cottage. And their baby. My aunt, my cousin. I mean, how did you lot feel about being involved in that?"

There was a murmur of shocked voices from the laptop. His friends, former friends as he considered them, stared him. It was obvious many knew nothing of this. At least Callum and Vinnie had the courtesy to look shame-faced. All were complicit, they needed to be told the true cost of their blood money.

"What are you talking about?" asked Eric. "You making crap up to get your own back?"

"All you need to do is google it," said Alec. "You won't find his name mentioned, I mean he was a minor but you can put it all together. And there was a photo. Find Fred Grove's name and you'll get the whole story."

"Is that how you found out?" asked Oliver, moving closer to Alec who kept his hand firmly on the hatchet. "You never said."

"No," said Alec. "Mum had some newspaper clippings. I didn't need to say anything though. You needed me for this; someone nobody would get too upset over. I didn't matter. But you needed a reason to get me to agree and that's why Fred told me about Oliver, wasn't it, Vinnie? A subtle call to family, making me feel I was part of something. You used him and you used me. And now? Well, you got what you wanted. Your event. Your money. But where's Fred? Chadwick? Why isn't Doug here for this big public exposure? What about that part of it? The main event so to speak. This was never supposed to be merely a re-enactment, was it? Or have you forgotten?"

The crowd on the laptop had gone quiet.

Oliver smiled at Alec. He didn't seem at all put out. "Oh, I see. This was to set *me* up. Expose me as some childhood monster. Well, you can see how that's worked out! Whatever you intended doesn't matter. This has been a fantastic success!"

He waved his hand at the screen. "They understand. The courts said I wasn't responsible. I'd been acting under duress. My therapist said I'd been brainwashed. They all accepted it, even Fred."

"Very convenient," said Alec, irritated by the way nothing seemed to affect the man.

Every blow dealt him seemed to roll off his shoulders with ease. "And where *is* Fred?"

"I repeat," said Oliver, looking at Vinnie and his companions, "I was a child. I was *not* responsible. No matter what Alec continues to believe. The people responsible for those deaths were caught and locked up."

"Shit. But … shit …" Andy could barely get his words out. "You used the cottage; we used the cottage. You took us there, never told us … I mean how could you return knowing someone had died there, a death *you* apparently were involved in. I mean … Vinnie … you must be as fucked up as him. The rest of us thought we were going to have a bloody good laugh, get a bit of cash. But you, Doug, Fred. With what happened to your family. I don't get it …"

Alec was pleased to see Vinnie squirm. The focus on his brother.

"Fred can clear this all up," said Oliver. "As Alec said. And there's no mystery about where the man is. He's out at the cottage."

Alec stared at him. Seriously? Fred would never go back there, despite his role in this revenge play of his. And he was certain, regardless of the motives of anyone else, that for Fred, this was a genuine attempt for revenge. He looked at his companions. Their earlier euphoria at carrying out *the* hoax of the decade gone.

"You don't think he wouldn't pass up a chance to confront his demons?" asked Oliver. "The man was stronger than you realise."

Another draught, the sound of rustling through the still open door. Old leaves drifted in, castoffs from the trees in the woods. How had they got there? The kitchen felt too small, claustrophobic. Alec pushed past them all to stand out in the yard, felt the inky blackness settle around him, its shading showing him the landscape.

It was moving, slashes of charcoal zig-zagging through the upper canopy as if giants—a giant—walked. Deep beneath his feet came those vibrations again. The Woodcutter was coming to him.

"Faster," whispered Grandma.

"Your bloody fracking operation," said Eric, behind him to Oliver. "These tremors have been happening on and off ever since the other night. Thought you said it was safe. This has become a right royal fuck-up."

Oliver's voice started to mutter a reply but Alec tuned it out. He had no interest in the drilling site. It had never been a serious option. A front to hide the summoning, disguise the walking giant, act out the man's delusions.

"What do you think, Alec?" Vinnie joined him, was following his gaze across to the woods, contrition laced his words.

"I say we go to the cottage, get Fred and then join the others. Time things went back to normal."

"But what exactly is normal, Alec?" The question was whispered in his ear but he couldn't have said who spoke. When he turned, there was nobody there.

"Nice to see we're on the same page again," said Oliver, smiling at him as they regrouped.

No. They weren't on the same page. Never had been. There was so much more going on, so much Oliver had hidden.

"We'll retrace our steps," said Oliver. "Starting with Reverend Chadwick."

"Do we have to?" asked Callum. "I know it was a mock-up but it was still pretty gross."

"Yes," said Alec. They all needed to see everything as it really was. Confusion and misunderstandings needed to be washed away. For himself? He was nearly there.

"And it'll have been taken down, won't it, Oliver?" said Eric, eyes hopeful.

"You'll've had all those people running round behind the scenes filming, clearing up?"

Neither Alec nor Oliver answered him.

CHAPTER TWENTY-THREE

Oliver stared at the men in front of him. He no longer cared what they thought and they'd outlived their usefulness. It would be amusing to see their reactions as they realised exactly what they'd done and how he manipulated them. Such moments, the public acknowledgement of personal triumph, were one of his few pleasures.

"You want to know the truth, see with your own eyes? Well, come on then. I've nothing to hide."

He grabbed a whisky bottle from the table, poured some into his hip flask. "Helps keep the cold out," he grinned. He flicked the remaining poisonous grains clinging to his fingertips away. Those inside the bottle had already dissolved: unnoticed, like so many of his recent actions. "Bring that with you," he indicated the remainder of the bottle, "might need to keep your spirits up."

He turned and stepped out into the yard. It was so quiet, clouds swept across the sky allowing the moon to play hide and seek with the landscape. Not even the hoot of an owl broke the stillness but he sensed it coming, the change. A minute or two more of peace and then the rumbling deep beneath his feet began again. GodBeGone Woods stirred in the pitch, an organism coming to life. The Woodcutter was waking, would judge the handiwork of his apprentice, *his* work.

"Come on, Alec."

He could hear Eric's voice, malicious, excited behind him. It'd been so easy to get Eric to play along. One of Nature's natural outsiders he was accepted in the village simply because of the dynamics of the small community. Whispered rumours had brought him on side and Oliver's listening ear had brought him round completely. Revenge drove him. *"Want a starring role, see someone else be the butt of a joke for a change?"* Oliver had murmured. *"Want to outdo Vinnie?"*

Jealousy and money were a potent impetus, bought so much when combined. Occasionally, he felt sorry for Alec. The man had done nothing wrong, returned simply to reunite with his father. As to the villagers, he shouldn't have been surprised at the ease with which he'd hooked each participant and reeled them in. A rural backwater, hungry for something different, was ripe for the plucking. Something as gruesome as a long-ago murder could easily be buried at the back of many a conscience.

Grandma and the Woodcutter would be pleased with him, the woods would be pleased with him. The movement across the fields was growing, the land waking up again.

The giant's breath swept against his cheek, a murmured command.

"Come on, lads," he said, rousing himself as they continued to mutter behind him. We haven't got all night."

Time to force the issue. Oliver started to walk along the lane knowing he would soon hear footsteps behind him. He was right.

"Glad you could join me," he said, barely glancing round.

"Not much choice," grumbled Vinnie. "Can't have Alec thinking we're a bunch of mad, axe-wielding murderers, can we?"

"And I'll be more than happy to open your eyes," growled Alec.

The miserable dissent amongst the group was tangible. Divide and conquer. They continued to trudge along the lane, turning off into the field where they'd initially posed as scarecrows, offerings to the Woodcutter. It was time to strip the pretence away. Blocking things out, suppressing memories, could cause untold damage. Oliver's own parents had sought to protect him and broken him in the process. Now he knew the truth, he was whole again.

"Wish we'd never agreed to it," said Callum, as they passed the fallen posts.

"You were quite amenable at the time," responded Oliver. "More than happy to take my money."

"Because I thought it'd be a laugh," said Callum. "We all did."

"And as I recall, you seemed to be enjoying it," said Oliver. "No objections then."

"Didn't it ever occur to you how sick this actually was?" asked Alec, looking at his companions.

"Yeah," said Vinnie. "Sorry, mate. Didn't realise how dark it was gonna get until old Olly here started rolling out the script and by then …"

By then, they'd all taken his money and couldn't back out. Not unless they wanted to forfeit the cash and their greed hadn't been able to give that up.

"We tried to get him to tone it down a bit. I mean the Chadwick episode was a bit gross." The group fell silent again at Vinnie's words. The thought of the perceived mutilated body swinging from the tree enough to still anyone's tongue.

It would be interesting, Oliver considered, to see their response to the reverend when they came upon him again; to realise his special effects were fully rooted in reality. They reached the edge of the field, arrived at the boundary to the woods. He turned on the narrow path leading around the perimeter to the Preacher's Tree. It was hard to make anything out at first, until the moon peered out for a moment and allowed a glimpse at the body. Even if it hadn't revealed itself at that point, the smell alone was enough to alert them to its nearness.

"Fake, Eric?" asked Alec. "How can you fake that smell?"

"It's a carcass," said Eric. "An old sheep. I put it in the hedge near here."

"Where?" demanded Alec.

Eric walked over to the place where he dumped the rotting body of the animal—and from where Oliver later removed it.

"I say again. Where?" asked Alec.

Eric shone his torch at the empty space, a look of horror growing on his face as he did so. He reached out and grabbed the bottle from Vinnie and took a long pull. Handing the bottle back, he took a deep breath and marched up to the body still swinging above him.

"Fake," he muttered. "Fake, fake, fake." He snatched the hatchet from Alec and attacked the rope looped around the trunk.

"Hey, let me," said Vinnie. "I'm stronger."

Eric shrugged him off. "No, I can manage."

Vinnie moved away and let him continue hacking at the rope.

"Get ready to catch him," said Oliver, with a laugh.

They withdrew sharply as the body began to swing, the branch creaking with its weight. Then there was a snap and it fell to the ground.

"Shit."

"Fuck."

"Oh, Jesus Christ."

They jumped back, practically falling over each other as they scrabbled away from the sight.

Eric had his hand over his mouth and Oliver could see his stomach going into spasm but he controlled himself enough to shakily cast his torch over the body. The sight drew even stronger curses and Eric dropped his light. Out of the four, only Alec seemed composed. It was as if he expected it.

The vicar's clothes were little more than rags. The birds of the fields had done a lot of damage in one day. They had feasted on eyes, tongue and lips, gorged themselves on his flesh so little remained of the man's features—the exposed brain, a mere shred in its casing.

"I told you," said Alec, there was no triumph in his voice.

Oliver observed him take his axe back, Eric's fingers unresisting, his body already swaying.

"Eric?" Callum was watching him with some concern.

Eric's face was blank, his mouth slack, open. He tried to take a step but his strength failed him and he sank to his knees. Alec and Vinnie remained stationary but Callum was at the fallen man's side in an instant.

"His pulse, I can't find his fucking pulse."

Alec pushed Callum aside and picked up a limp hand.

"There is no pulse," he said quietly.

"No, no," said Callum. "He can't be ... Oliver?"

Oliver shrugged. "Man had a weak heart," he said. "A pity."

"Come on," said Alec, rising to his feet and heading towards the woods again.

"Alec? What the fuck? We can't leave him!"

No. They couldn't leave him. He was needed as one of the offerings for Grandma. He could be compassionate. "Bring him with you," said Oliver. "We can keep him in the cottage, until needed."

Vinnie and Callum were too preoccupied to pay attention to his words but he saw Alec looking at him. Not curious. Understanding. A puzzle.

Callum took the whisky from Vinnie, almost emptied it before offering the dregs to Vinnie.

"Pass," he said.

Callum tossed the bottle into the bushes and pulled Eric's arm over his shoulder. Vinnie took the other. He'd last until at least the cottage, thought Oliver as he walked by Alec's side. There was enough poison in the bottle to get him that far.

They didn't talk. The trees around them groaned at a slight tremor and then settled. "Should've gone back," said Callum. "Got in a car and ..."

"No," said Alec. "What about Paul and Andy? Fred? Besides the rest of the villagers aren't far, are they? Out at the drill rig. They'll help us. We're perfectly safe. We go on."

Oliver looked at Alec. He must know they weren't safe. They were near the cottage, behind him he heard Callum stumble, Vinnie swear as he took on more of the body's weight.

At the door, his face its mirror if they but knew it. Hand on handle, opening into darkness. Behind him, cursing at the smell. Everything disjointed, unreal, as if swimming through treacle.

"Put him down. Hey! Carefully." The men dropping Eric to the ground.

"Smells like something died here as well," muttered Vinnie behind him, pushing past Oliver so he fell against the door jamb. A dot of light moved about as Vinnie pulled out his torch. Then the beam shot past him as Vinnie escaped into the garden, sank to his knees on the loose soil, the earth not yet settled, its occupant not buried deep enough. Vinnie scrabbling away from the cold blue hand he'd disturbed. "Fuck, fuck, fuck. I don't believe this. Alec, Callum."

Callum groaned, stumbled, fell lifeless to the ground.

"Callum, Callum!"

Oliver surveyed it all as if underwater, a mere spectator to the death around him. The ground rumbled again and he felt its vibrations through the walls as the cottage shook; the rafters too, groaning in protest.

"How did we not see this?" moaned Vinnie, looking around.

"Because you allowed Oliver to show you what you wanted to see. You hid behind his smokescreen words, self-denial is easy when paid for," said Alec.

"Grandma," whispered Oliver to the figure, whose chair had been set rocking by the minor quake. "Soon, soon, Grandma."

Vinnie's horrified gaze swung back to Oliver.

"Grandma? Grandma? What the fuck, Oliver? That's Liz in there. Dead. Eric's here, dead. Callum, dead. I reckon Fred's the one you buried here. Dead. You're a fucking nutter. Alec. Alec, mate. We gotta get help here. Alec. Alec?"

Oliver pushed himself upright, steadied himself. He shook his head to clear his vision, try to focus on his surroundings. Alec's stillness surprised him. He had not reacted to Vinnie's plea. If anything, was ignoring him, was contemplating Oliver himself. The look on his face unnerved him.

"Want to show us, Oliver? Show us it all?" asked Alec.

Vinnie was still bending over Callum, his head in his hands. "If you want to see," said Oliver. "You'll have to bring them."

Alec nodded but Vinnie looked up, confused.

"Alec, what's he on about? For God's sake … look if you're not gonna do anything, I'll go. I'm out of here." Vinnie remained on his knees, tears trickling down his face. Nothing more than a scared little boy. His little brother.

"You can't go anywhere. Can he, Alec?"

"Huh?"

Oliver's words pulled Alec back from whatever place he had gone to.

"Bring them," ordered Oliver.

Alec went over to Vinnie. "Listen, mate. I know this is hard, not to mention fucking weird but we've got to bring them with us. You take Callum, I'll take Eric."

Vinnie's mouth dropped. He looked even more bewildered.

"We need to see where he's put Paul and Andy," said Alec. "I don't want to leave these two behind and I want to see, really see what all this is about. Once we've done that, then we can get help."

Alec's calmness surprised Oliver, as did his desire to take his dead friends with him.

"Promise?" asked Vinnie.

"Promise," said Alec. "I don't think too much more is going to happen tonight."

His words appeared to reassure Vinnie who simply nodded. Obedient, too overwhelmed by circumstances to query anything anymore; resigned to doing what he was told. Oliver recognised that blank look born of witnessing horrors, the mind protecting the body to survive.

"Which way then, Oliver?" asked Alec, hauling Eric up so he had the dead man's arm across his neck, supported the weight of the body with his own.

Oliver turned and walked into the trees, entering a small tunnel previously invisible to the naked eye. They had to walk in single file as the passage was too narrow for two abreast. The men behind him made slow progress, hampered by the bodies they carried. There was a steady rustle and thud, the occasional curse, heavy breathing from Alec and Vinnie. Another tremor, this time strong enough for the two behind to collapse into the embrace of the branches and thorns weaving their guiding wall. He paused as they extricated themselves.

"How much further?" asked Alec.

"Not far," said Oliver.

"Why can't we leave these two here. Come back for them," said Vinnie.

"No," said Oliver, Alec echoing him.

Eventually they were free and they continued on their way. As he walked, he mulled over Alec's attitude. Something was going on in the man's mind. He was up to something and would need watching. Especially when they got to Old One but there, he would be on home ground. The Woodcutter would reveal himself and the problem of Alec and Vinnie would be solved. With them all strung up, it wouldn't be long before Grandma had her cloak and came back as well. The axe was waiting, his future was waiting, just as it always had done.

CHAPTER TWENTY-FOUR

The swirl of air, the murmur of trees, their whispering branches, all pushed Alec on. He could almost see Nature's breath drift past, leaving a trail of molecules for him to follow.

His own personal trail of breadcrumbs. These past few weeks the woods had continually pulled him back. The hours he'd lost in his bedroom or back garden staring trance-like at its glowering body. It was all coming together and leading him to this meeting with Grandma in the woods. Oliver was mistaken thinking he'd been chosen. Mistaken thinking the cottage left untouched, for him to discover.

It was Fred, who'd gone into the woods, cared for it, whilst all the time making sure it stayed hidden from view. He'd kept it ready for Alec's return, that much he'd gradually discovered. Oliver had been useful, provided four of the offerings. Two were outstanding.

"How much further?" asked Vinnie, struggling behind him.

A very slight rumble deep beneath him reassured him. They were watching, they were waiting. Once he'd delivered what they wanted, his family, the village, everyone would be looked after again. The village would be brought back to life. Ahead of him, Oliver appeared to disappear, a trick of the light as Alec followed through the gap in the undergrowth, the hidden gateway to the old place.

Once through, he dropped Eric's body to the ground.

"Shit, Alec. A bit more respect. That's our …"

"Friend?" queried Alec, as Vinnie laid Callum down with care. "I don't think so, not really. Do you?"

"Ok, he could be a pain but I'd still call him a mate."

"Because you had to," said Alec. "Small communities don't leave you much choice as to who you associate with. The real village is hidden beneath the surface."

Vinnie continued to stare at him, appeared almost to have forgotten Oliver. "Alec. Have you gone soft in the head? We've got two dead bodies here and you want to talk about village life?"

"Well, that's what it's all about, isn't it," said Alec. "When it comes right down to it, it's the survival of our community. Of so many communities like ours."

Vinnie's faced showed growing incomprehension. He looked from Alec to Oliver and then, finally, to their surroundings. Alec watched him take it in, the wooden vats beneath the branches of the central tree. The oak itself, its broad girth denoting its ancient origins. His eyes going up, up, widening in horror as he took in the shapes hanging there, each body dangling over the container below.

"Jesus Christ," he moaned. "I can't … I'm not … I don't know about you, Alec, but I'm going to get help! Oliver's a fucking nutter, a murderer. I don't even understand why you're standing here so calm. Unless, shit Alec. You were in on this too, weren't you? You're a fucking lunatic, you're both mad."

Vinnie was backing away from them. His hand feeling behind him for the gap they came through, an unsuccessful fumbling which sent him scrabbling around the wild barricade.

Oliver was advancing on Vinnie, the small hatchet held in a determined grip, closing in on the terrified man, raising it. Vinnie ducked and Oliver's blow missed.

"Alec! For fuck's sake. Help me!" Vinnie was grappling with Oliver, barely keeping the blade away from his throat.

Alec turned away and walked over to the oak, hearing Vinnie screaming behind him. Begging him not to leave him. The axe was still there, leaning against the trunk, waiting. He picked it up.

"Alec!"

Alec strode back to the fighting men. Oliver had his back to him and he was able to look Vinnie directly in the eye. He saw the look of relief, of gratitude and hope. He raised the axe. Oliver stepped back as if to let Alec finish the job. He was surprised to see the blade go over his shoulder and land in the wood, missing Vinnie.

Alec looked down at his brother. Sensed the Woodcutter close by, ready to claim him.

Almost one.

"You can leave," he said. "Go to Doug. Tell him where I am and who's with me. He'll understand."

Vinnie looked confused. "What? What are you talking about, Alec?"

"Coming back. I understand. This was why. He'll know."

"I don't—"

"You need to go," said Alec. "What is to happen here—you don't need to see." He pulled the axe out of the trunk. Vinnie's eyes followed the blade, it propelled his body into motion. Without another word, he backed away, disappeared into the trees.

Alec thought of the bodies hanging behind him. Five. One more was needed. And who better to fill the gap than the pretender?

It was Oliver's turn to look at Alec with confusion. He was breathing heavily, bathed in sweat. His eyes bright, pupils large.

"What do you think you are doing?" he hissed. There was anger there, as Alec knew there would be. It wouldn't last.

"What's expected of me," he said, the ground continuing to rumble beneath him.

"Expected of you? By who?" Oliver stepped closer to him. Alec could see the madness in the man's eyes. It was time to bring him back to reality.

"The Woodcutter, Grandma. Who else?" He enjoyed the look of shock on the man's face.

"You can't ... no. They chose me."

"No," said Alec. It was his turn to move towards Oliver. The bloody axe still in his hand. "They never spoke to you. You imagined it. All that time in the cottage without ventilating it properly, fumigating it. Poison, that's all. Addled your mind, made you believe you'd been chosen. Understandable, I suppose considering your childhood."

Oliver was regarding him with a bewildered look which was gradually replaced by a smile, superior, more self-assured.

"Sorry, old boy. You've got it wrong. Think it's you who's addled. You know you really should see a doctor—or perhaps I have a more effective treatment?"

A rustle stirred the branches, something dripped onto Alec's cheek. He flicked his tongue out to lick it away, tasted its copper. It was a reminder from Grandma of what he had to do. Leaving it any longer would be to waste the blood. He lunged at Oliver with his axe raised, his sudden movement catching the man off guard but he was quick, leaping back so the axe only nicked his arm.

Then it was Oliver's turn to go for him, the smaller hatchet in his hand allowing him to manoeuvre more easily, get in close.

Alec barred him with the shaft of his own axe, its strength a barrier allowing him to consider his next move whilst holding Oliver off. The man's breath, rancid and foul, fogged his thoughts briefly until Alec remembered the Woodcutter. He'd been given his strength as his apprentice. He could do this. There was no need to struggle, to grapple with this pretender. He pushed Oliver away and then stood straight, ready for the man's renewed onslaught.

"You can't win, Oliver," he said. "You never could. They don't want you. Not as you are, anyway." So many strange memories were coming back to him. Lilith. Her eyes, her voice. "Lilith wanted me," he said. "She's been waiting for me all this time, not you."

At these words, Oliver charged. "No," he shouted. "I gave her Charlie. I gave her Rosie and the baby. I've given her all ... all these."

"All the wrong ones, Oliver," said Alec. "Charlie was marked for this role and then you killed him. And you took from our family, from our bloodline. She was angry at that. So was the Woodcutter. They can't stand your cruelty. And you have been cruel in so many ways."

It was as if time slowed. He could hear every individual snap of the twigs beneath his feet, the long, drawn-out breath, the throb of his pulse. Rocking beneath his feet, the creak of wood, faster. His heart racing.

His axe was already above his head. It too was waiting for that moment when … crack! It swung down in a dazzling rush, cleaved Oliver's skull in two as the man charged towards him. Oliver didn't even register the blow, actually continued to move forward with the momentum he'd gained. After a couple of steps however, his body caught up with the fact its central control had failed and Oliver slumped to the floor.

Alec surveyed the bodies around, above him. He was satisfied. There was enough material for him to work with. Time to get on with it.

A pile of shrouds was stacked by the tree. Whilst Oliver had been misguided about being the chosen one, it meant he at least had done a lot of the preparation.

"Thanks, Olly," he muttered as he pulled the man's body onto the cloth, proceeded to wrap it round him before fixing him to the pulley attached to the tree. He swung him up quickly in order to allow the body to continue draining itself over the vat. There was no need to make any additional nicks to the flesh to facilitate this. The damage his blade had done was sufficient.

Then it was the turn of his three former friends. Friends! He'd been trying to explain that earlier to Vinnie but the man hadn't wanted to listen, to realise the truth of their relationships in Little Hatchet. It was all show, all surface. Everything true, everything of any real meaning lay hidden beneath the surface. Like the woods which had hidden its own truth for so long. As a consequence, the only emotion he felt as he dealt with the bodies was freedom. Yes, there was a pang of regret over the deaths of the young men but they would live again, albeit not in their current form. They would live in Grandma and she would thank them, look after their families.

A faint glimmer appeared above. Dawn was breaking. Alec looked up, blood and sweat slicked his body but he was satisfied. The offerings hung there like enormous cocoons, orbs swinging gently from their supports. As he surveyed his handiwork, he realised how tired he was. Waves of exhaustion rushed through him almost sending him to his knees. He left his axe behind and stumbled back along the path to the cottage. Ignoring the body decaying in the rocking chair, he tumbled onto the bed and closed his eyes. Sleep claimed him immediately.

Rumbling came from somewhere distant. Alec opened his eyes, groggy, and tried to sit up. His muscles protested, kept him prone for minutes more before they allowed him to attempt the manoeuvre again, this time with more success. The rumbling continued was growing nearer. This wasn't something from below the earth's crust, this was something alive and walking the earth's surface. Pounding, a steady rhythm. Almost locomotive in sound, a nearing engine of energy. The Woodcutter was coming for him! He needed to make himself presentable. With a groan, he rose to his feet and stumbled to the bowl on the sill. The jug at its side still held water. Cold and clean, its surface rippled in the basin before he broke its pure surface and proceeded to muddy the waters as he scrubbed dirt and dried blood from his face and hands. With the aid of a nailbrush, he scrubbed until his skin shone red, raw in its cleanliness. An old T-shirt of Oliver's, slightly grubby, hung from a nail and he swapped it for his own.

Occasionally, he would catch sight of the cloaked body in the rocking chair, but he would not look at her yet. Not until she was ready to come back. The smell did not affect him.

Louder, louder. Not one continuous sound but many. A buzzing angry sound swarming around the cottage, shouts and yells occasionally breaking free of the horde. Not the Woodcutter. He made his way to the door, and pulled it open, finding Len with his fist raised as if to break down the door. Behind him the rest of the village gathered, some scrabbling in the dirt to expose the pallid corpse of Fred, others stood in small groups talking with excited anxiety, some came from the path leading to Old One, faces pale and drawn.

Their voices fell silent, shock etched into them.

"Who you got in there?" He didn't wait for an answer, pushed Alec aside like he was nothing.

Then a blow from behind sent Alec sprawling into the garden. Len stood towering over him as he struggled to get up, his sore muscles continuing to impede his movement.

"You bastard," snarled Len. "You miserable …"

"What?" Alec stared at the man. "You think I did that? What do you take me for? It was Oliver."

"Looks like you slept in there," said Len. "How could you do that with her there, unless you helped."

"I didn't sleep. I passed out," said Alec. "Oliver went mad up by that tree. I got away, hid in here. Can't remember after that."

Others had entered the cottage, escaped its fetid atmosphere quickly.

"If it was nothing to do with you, why'd you clean yourself up?"

They were all staring at him. Accusing.

"We've seen the water, your shirt."

Doug came up behind Len. "We all do strange things when we're in shock."

He reached down to help Alec to his feet. Their eyes locked on each other. Alec could see he understood, knew. Vinnie had got the message to him.

"Time to put things right," Doug whispered in his ear. "I'll get the woman," he said straightening up.

"Doug!" Carol grabbed at his arm but he pushed her away.

"We need to leave her for the police," said Len, making to block him.

"Yeah?" said Doug. "And can you see how that's all going to go? We were all part of this 'event'. We helped set it up, played along. They'll lock us *all* away."

"Come on, Doug," said Fiona. "We didn't know Oliver'd do anything like this."

"No? I think you'll find they assume the opposite. And your families will be split up. Do you want to see your children, grandchildren taken into care?"

"So what do we do?" asked Len. "We've got bodies galore. Our own children, some of them. How the fuck do we cover that up? And the lads, Andy, Eric, all of 'em—what of their parents? And you, Doug? Shit, it's one of your sons standing there."

Alec scanned the angry crowd. Not everybody had made it this far. The dead men's families weren't here yet.

"Round everyone up," said Doug. "Get them out of the woods. There's a fracking operation going on. Tell them it's not safe, an accident waiting to happen you could say—especially as Oliver hadn't exactly been above board with the authorities about his operation."

"I don't know how we can live with this," said Len, in a low voice.

"No?" said Doug. "What about when Rosie was killed and my nephew? And they almost got Alec too back then. He was supposed to stay but Mary got him away. I lost Charlie and I lost *him, my baby*. The village said *I'd* have to learn to live with it."

"Well you did, didn't you?" snapped Len.

"Yes," said Doug. "And it's your turn. You've paid lip service for too long. Time to get your hands dirty. Consider it payback. Explain *that* to everyone while me and Alec sort this."

The small crowd had gone quiet as Doug spoke. No one moved.

"Unless of course you want to call the police? And there's a hell of a lot more dirt to be dug up round here than this few handful of bodies. We took Oliver's money for our own reasons. I'll admit to no pride in what I put Alec through. That was a mistake I wish I could take back but our aim in the end, despite how it ended was to get our revenge—mine, Fred's, Vinnie's and Alec's—on the man and that has happened, although not in the way we planned. Because we closed our ears to the woods, we forgot it had chosen Alec, all those years ago. We allowed Oliver's involvement in those murders to cloud our thinking, to drown out GodBeGone. It's time for us to start listening again."

The villagers' mood remained sullen, angry but they moved away. They'd been exposed as a backward-looking community, believing in bizarre superstition all those years ago. It had not been a pleasant experience. Better they grieve privately. After all, justice had been served after a fashion. Oliver was dead.

Once they had gone and the woods fallen silent, Alec returned to the cottage and picked up Liz's body. He felt no revulsion when he looked at the corpse. He'd been trained to this all those years ago and it was all coming back to him.

"What about all the cameras and stuff?" he asked Doug as they walked.

"Len'll sort it," said Doug, keeping his eyes firmly ahead. "Tell me, is Cameron there?" His voice wavered slightly.

"Yes," said Alec. "I had to. He was asked for."

"Like you," said Doug. "My sons. I never thought they'd ask so much of me."

"I'm sorry," said Alec. And he was.

They continued to walk through the tunnel of trees. As they entered the enclosure,

Doug let out a small groan at the sight of Cameron.

Alec allowed him a moment before, together, placing Liz's body in the circular space beneath the boughs of the huge oak. Then it was Eric and Callum's turn to be covered and finally, Oliver's. The six, the required tribute, hung from Old One's branches, unseen, though known to all who lived in Little Hatchet. A guilty secret devouring their souls.

The explosions from the fracking site barely registered as they contemplated their grief and guilt in equal measure.

"Come on," said Doug. "I think they'll spare us the time to take Fred to the churchyard. Let him rest alongside his Rosie."

Alec and Doug left the massive oak behind them, the path they walked closing in on itself as they passed.

Grandma was reborn that night as the six continued to decay above Liz's corpse. The path leading to the cottage cleared and she was able to make her way unimpeded to her old home. She would return to the Old One to finish bathing in the collected blood but she had enough energy to make her presence known. The villagers needed to see her and remember.

Gazing into a mirror, she stroked her new skin, admired her slim body, wondered at the form her Woodcutter would take. Alec had been a little boy the last time she'd seen him.

He would be here soon and then together they would return to the village, remind the people of the ties which bound them together.

Whichever way they looked at it, the woods would claim them, already the boundaries blurring a little more. Would they notice when its darkness finally embraced them? There was a knock at the door.

"Come in," she called.

The door opened and Alec stood there. She had one more task before their rebirth was complete.

"Here," she said, and Alec moved forward to stand in front of her. Slowly she carved the mark of the wood into his face and at last brought the Woodcutter back to life.

Together they left the cottage and headed for the village, their shadows stretching before them, embracing those who waited. Grandma and the Woodcutter were no fairy tale, never had been, but once upon a time …

ABOUT THE AUTHOR

Stephanie Ellis writes dark speculative prose and poetry and has been published in a variety of magazines and anthologies. Her longer work includes the novels, *The Five Turns of the Wheel* and *Reborn*, and the novellas, *Bottled* and *Paused*. Her dark poetry has been published in her collections *Foundlings* (co-authored with Cindy O'Quinn), *Lilith Rising* (co-authored with Shane Douglas Keene) and *Metallurgy*, as well as the *HWA Poetry Showcase Volumes VI, VII, VIII and IX*, and Black Spot Books *Under Her Skin*. She can be found supporting indie authors at HorrorTree.com via the weekly Indie Bookshelf Releases. She is an active member of the HWA and can be found at https://stephanieellis.org, on Twitter at @el_stevie, Instagram stephanieellis7963 and also somewhere on Facebook.

ABOUT THE ILLUSTRATOR

Elizabeth Leggett is a Hugo award-winning illustrator whose work focuses on soulful, human moments-in-time that combine ambiguous interpretation and curiosity with realism.

Much to her mother's dismay, she viewed her mother's white washed walls as perfectly good canvasses so she believes it is safe to say that she has been an artist her whole life! Her first published work was in the Halifax County Arts Council poetry and illustration collection. If she remembers correctly, she was not yet in double digits yet, but she might be wrong about that. Her first paying gig was painting other students' tennis shoes in high school.

In 2012, she ended a long fallow period by creating a full seventy-eight card tarot in a single year. From there, she transitioned into freelance illustration. Her clients represent a broad range of outlets, from multiple Hugo award winning Lightspeed Magazine to multiple Lambda Literary winner, Lethe Press. She was honored to be chosen to art direct both Women Destroy Fantasy and Queers Destroy Science Fiction, both under the Lightspeed banner.

Elizabeth, her husband, and their typically atypical cats, live in New Mexico. She suggests if you ever visit the state, look up. The skies are absolutely spectacular.

ACKNOWLEDGEMENTS

The Woodcutter is my first folk horror novel written outside the Five Turns world I created in my other books. With this story, I wanted to play with unreliable narrators, to blend the supernatural with the psychological, and keep the reader guessing as to who had really done what. The result was that this needed a careful beta read before I sent it anywhere, and I have to thank the wonderful Alyson Faye for casting her eyes over it and helping me keep on track.

I would also like to thank Steve and Heather at Brigids Gate Press for their ongoing belief in my work. I hope the feedback from readers will do their faith justice.

Thanks too to Carrie Allison-Rolling for her editorial eye and Elizabeth Leggett for her amazing cover.

And as always, I would to thank my husband, Geraint, and our three children, Bethan, Dylan, and Rhonwen, for their continual support—and much-needed mugs of tea! I love you all.

CONTENT WARNINGS

child death, violence, murder

MORE FROM BRIGIDS GATE PRESS

The settlement of Grey's Bluffs a prosperous town. An independent community dwelling in the shadows of the mountains known only as The Hungers.

Esther Foxman and Siobhan O'Clery have grown up in Grey's Bluffs, thriving out on the western territories in the aftermath of the Civil War. Devoted to one another and their home, the two set out to complete a regular pact at the Hungers to ensure that Grey's Bluffs continues to prosper.

Cyril Redstone is a man who knows death well. Becoming a mercenary after the Civil War, Cyril leads the marauding Blackhawks from one slaughter to the next. Hired to destroy Grey's Bluffs, Cyril cares little for morality, nor that he owes its founder his life.

Esther and Siobhan are left to defend the only home they have ever known from the Blackhawks, their confrontation driving them deep into the mountains.

Where the darkest secrets of the Hungers await them.

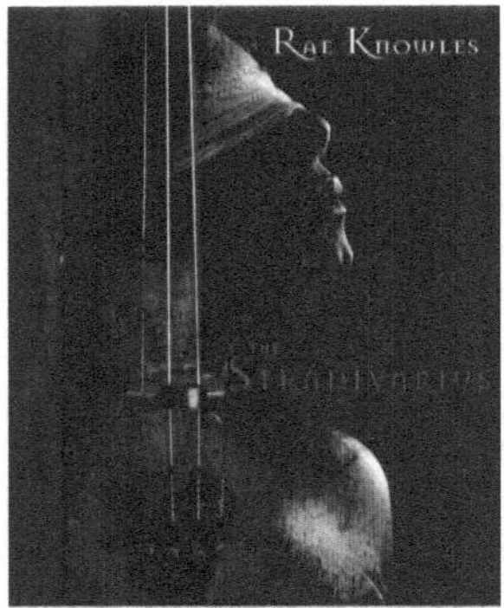

When a surprise inheritance and whirlwind romance offer Mae a chance to escape her repressive aunt, she's all too eager to elope and start life anew in her childhood home. But when she and her new husband arrive, the towering Victorian sits in disrepair, and Mae learns that her father's decade-old, unsolved murder is still a source of rumor and speculation in town.

Leading the charge to unravel the mystery surrounding her father's death is Ollie, a vibrant genderqueer and an outsider in their hometown. Sure that solving the cold case will land them a coveted job in the police department, Ollie gains access to the Victorian by agreeing to do maintenance work on the property.

Inside, Mae is taunted by a feminine specter, soft voices from empty rooms, and distinct melodies of Lady Paola: the priceless, Stradivarius violin stolen the night of her father's murder.

Forte, mezzo-forte, the measured, andante cadence.

Her hiss, her pull, her scream.

Mae fears the house is haunted by her father's spirit, her husband believes she's going the way of her mother—slipping into madness, but Ollie suspects something more sinister is at play. If Ollie and Mae can't work together to uncover the Victorian's secrets, Mae will join her mother in an institution or her father in the grave.

According to Dante, a sin is the misdirection of love—the human will, or essentially, the direction of our beings. Love the Sinner is an examination of just how those sins can kaleidoscope into horrific consequences creating a distorted and deadly landscape. These stories stand stark before you in full glaring misstep and macabre to show the human psyche in all its twisted reality.

From grief and its rage to medical meddling to ensure a new world order to bloody revenge within a quantum leap, these stories seek to solidify one absolute truth: man is the scariest monster.

Who are we if not for the monsters that we keep?

They Hide: Short Stories to Tell in the Dark collects thirteen chilling tales that weave through the shadows, exploring the nature of fear, powerlessness, and control.

A series of murders in a New England colony
An untamed beast in pre-revolutionary France
A mysterious stranger who invades 18th century Ireland
A traveling circus that takes more than the price of admission
A gathering of the Dark, telling tales on the longest night of the year, and more.

Come play with vampires, werewolves, ghosts, zombies, ghouls and the devil himself. Make sure you check under the bed and don't turn out the lights.

Visit our website at: www.brigidsgatepress.com